THE HUNGRY GHOSTS

THE HUNGRY GHOSTS

COMMENTARY ON A TALKING CAT AND A TROUBLESOME GIRL

Miguel Flores

VIKING

VIKING
An imprint of Penguin Random House LLC, New York

First published in the United States of America by Viking,
an imprint of Penguin Random House LLC, 2021

Visit us online at penguinrandomhouse.com.

Library of Congress Cataloging-in-Publication Data is available.

Book manufactured in Canada

ISBN 9780451479785

10 9 8 7 6 5 4 3 2 1

FRI

Design by Lucia Baez • Text set in Horley Old Style

Three short letters from the secretary:

Dear Childhood,
You were weird.

Dear Ghosts,
I am grateful.

Dear Troublemakers,
It's okay to be small.

this is a story told in parts . . .

CHAPTER ONE, PART ONE
the house on a hill by the edge of a cliff

THERE ONCE LIVED a wily young world that did not like to be told what to do.

Their name was Arrett.

Wild magicks pulsed through all living things on Arrett. They beat deep and thick in the mountains of the Giant's Teeth. They echoed softly through the green hollows of the Needsy Woods. They cursed harsh and violent in the cascading waves of the Delfin Sea.

Magicks in Arrett liked *trouble*. They stirred it up in every windsneeze, pebble, and toe.

Why, you ask?

It all started many years ago with the South Wind, who one day in his mischief-making found the heart of Arrett brimming with magicks alone in the middle of the sea. He demanded to know why Arrett wouldn't share. Arrett responded that no one could handle the weight of magicks, and so they bore the burden alone. But the wind called Arrett selfish and thought they had more magicks than they knew what to do with. So, the South Wind came up with a game.

The game was this: the South Wind would carry prayers from all around the world—from every green hill, half-stone, and child—and bring them to the heart of Arrett as tithes. If Arrett didn't fall in love (or pity) with these little magicks-less peoples living on the world by the time the South Wind had brought a thousand prayers, then the game was lost. Arrett could die from a magicks-congested heart for all he cared, and the South Wind would promise to stop running amuck and causing so much trouble.

But, if the South Wind won, then the heart would have to spill its magicks into the sky and share its great fortune with all the people who lived there. Arrett agreed immediately.

Now, Arrett's heart may have been selfish, but it was also delicate. It lost the game at the second story, a story about a small giant named Ovid.

With a loud hoot, the South Wind called upon the other three great winds and all their reckless little siblings to spread magicks to those with little hope or in great need. In return, the heart asked for nothing but more prayers. Prayers with enough weight to balance a curious heart.

Since then, the winds found purpose for their running. They traveled the world and traded prayers for magicks. To anyone, anywhere, in all corners of the cornerless world.

Until, of course, the prayers stopped coming.

The South Wind had forgotten that most hearts are self-ish. That hearts are often full of much *want* and little *give*. Arrett grew worried. They knew their magicks were too much for small hearts to bear, that the more a heart grew and grew but never gave back, the easier it would be for a heart to burst.

But we'll get to that later.

For now, I must tell you about the town that kept on praying—even though it had very little reason to and saw even less return on investment. It lay fractured and broken, a place that no longer sang or danced or made any kind of merry.

Shabby little West Ernost.[1]

As far as municipal districts go, West Ernost was not an interesting place. It was plotted with more roads than houses and housed more rice farms than trees. It was so boring that it was commonly considered worse than East Ernost, which didn't even exist. West Ernost was widely agreed to be a place for passing through, not for staying in. Which is unfortunate for a place teetering on the edge of the world: there's not much left to go to.

The most interesting thing about West Ernost was that it had developed a bit of a shadow infestation. No one was quite sure where these strange things, otherwise known as "gripes" and "gobblers," had come from, though many suspected that the witches had cursed the land right before the

---

[1] I must clarify, West Ernost was not that little. Or shabby. It was stuck with this reputation because that's what people called it. Names are particularly finicky magicks. West Ernost did not become little or shabby because it grew up that way. It became little and shabby because people told it that's what it ought to be. And it believed them.

last of them vanished. Although largely benign, the shadows had become pests. They tunneled through farms and made late-night snacks of herb gardens. They were harmless, shapeless bodies with nothing more than appetite.

But all in all, West Ernost was perfectly boring.

There did, however, live a funny little house on top of a flat hill by the edge of the cliff. His name was St. George's Home for Wayward Girls.

St. George's front door faced most of West Ernost, which consisted of rice terraces stacked on top of one another. Behind him was a smooth slope that led down to the cliffs of the Delfin Sea. St. George's boasted two floors, five and a half walls made of bamboo-slatted windows, a red-faded-to-brown thatch door, a squash garden, one sleeping moss-bull, fourteen orphaned girls, and an old headmistress named Doris Barterby.

When St. George's had been nothing more than a middle-aged broombranch tree, he had prayed to leave the Needsy Woods. He asked to be a boat. He wanted nothing more than to discover the sea's secrets, to trade his roots for an anchor and listen to Delfin sing her raucous songs.

One day, a funny little woman named Doris arrived in his forest. She had wiry hair twisted into a messy bun and a glint in her left eye. St. George's had never before seen a woman with head leaves so wild or a chest song so lively.

Doris came to his woods with nothing but a metal saw, a

green moss-bull, and a sled as wide as his very self. For an entire month, she put her saw to his trunk, determined to cut him apart piece by piece to make a house.

At first, St. George's resisted. This wasn't what he had asked for! When Doris climbed into his branches, he shook violently and threw her down. When she tried to draw lines in his bark for measurement, he stiffened and broke her pens.[2]

And yet, Doris never gave up. Day after day, she persisted and spoke kindly to him of the dreams she had. Dreams not of a boat to traverse Delfin's terrible seas but of a house with roots in place and walls sinking into the deep earth. In her dreams, there was a garden and children whose laughter would fill the rafters. She called it a . . . oh, what is that funny word again?

(A foster home.)

Oh yes, a "foster" home. I remembered all on my own with no help at all.

(Sigh.)

One day, in a moment of deep frustration, Doris threw down her instruments and finally asked for permission to turn this tree into a house. It shocked St. George's, and he took a whole day to consider the request.

He'd gotten to know this funny little person quite well, and hearing her plans made him think that maybe being a

---

[2] He'd never admit it, but he is immensely ticklish.

house might be more exciting than being a tree. Or a boat. So St. George's relented, and he gave his dreams to her. For a tree, this is what love is. And St. George's had fallen slowly, but surely, in love with Doris Barterby.

The next day he told his broombranches to leave and let Doris cut him down.

When Doris finished pulling him apart into dozens of pieces, he didn't worry. Not when the moss-bull pulled him out of the Needsy Woods, around Ahari's Creek, past the city-state of Nignip, and to the very edge of West Ernost. He didn't grumble when Doris hammered him into the ground or threaded needles through his roof or nailed his sides together. Doris even gave him windows that looked out toward the sea.

A tree's heart is his entirety, and he trusted her with every piece. Through everything, Doris never lost a single splinter of him, carefully putting him back together until he was a house.

After some time, he grew into a home.

Many years later, St. George's stood where he always stood, watching over his squash garden and Doris and the fourteen little girls with a wary, nervous eye.

Above him, the yellow moon sat peacefully atop thick layers of clouds. It was all a ruse. The clouds hid a secret.

Over the past few days, the sea had grown frantic and was reaching its arms up the cliff. Like it was trying to escape. A cold, unfamiliar wind blew through the unpatched hole in

St. George's roof. All the magicks in his timbers cried out in worry. Something strange—very strange—had awoken. And it was moving.

St. George's tried to listen. He tried to make out what it was he ought to be listening for. But he was still only a house. He could not warn Doris and the girls. He could not tell them to run far, far away. He could not tell them anything at all. The only thing he could offer them was the comfort of a place to sleep.

So instead, he sat there. He deafened the sounds of the world outside and whispered soft dreams into their little ears. For the first time in years, St. George's prayed.

CHAPTER ONE, PART TWO
good stories begin with troublesome girls

THE THREE SADDEST things in the world are a book without an ending, a broombranch without flight, and a child without dreams.

Milly without-a-last-name was a twelve-year-old girl trapped inside what she considered to be a horrible ten-year-old's body. She had irresponsibly curly hair, freckled brown skin, and a small button nose. She was only sometimes fond of St. George's. I often wondered if those feelings were mutual.

When you are a twelve-year-old girl, it is essential to feed your furnace of a heart on a steadily controlled diet of dreams, hopes, and aspirations. They're what keep the machinery going. However, if filled to the brim, a girl's heart is at risk of becoming a forest fire—wicked, selfish, and always hungry for more.

Milly did not have this problem.

"I have no need for dreams," she'd declared long ago. Now her head was a few years too old and her heart a couple sizes too big. She'd had the misfortune of growing up too fast. There were no longer any dreams large enough to fit her.

As St. George's oldest resident, she had more talent for

problem-solving than she did for dream-chasing. It's not like she couldn't hear the house's whispered dreams. In fact, she heard them better than anyone.

That's why she knew better than to listen.

She knew that no kid was worth anything if they didn't have a title. A job. An occupation. Maybe a career, if they were lucky.

Milly was assigned her title the very first day she arrived at St. George's. She wore it across her chest in careful, fragile letters: *big sister*. In fact, because of how frazzled Doris's mind had become, Milly was *basically* a mother. She only lacked the gray hairs.

Milly was the one who'd taught her sisters how to clean their dishes and braid their hair. She showed them how to tie their shoes and make rice noodles. She did this every minute of every day of her life.

Except for very, very early mornings—when the whole world was still asleep. Milly spent that part of her day in St. George's attic. Pointedly *not* dreaming. She couldn't dream if she didn't sleep . . . right?[3]

Downstairs the entire house lay wrapped in silence while she read *The Misfortunate Adventures of Tom Fool*. She pressed her back against the thin wooden slats of a

---

[3] The problem was never that Milly had no dreams. It was that if any of the adults ever found out what her dreams were, they'd tell her that her dreams were wrong. So she hid them so deep inside her own curiosity that even she didn't know how to find them anymore.

half-window and used the soft blue light slipping in to illuminate the text. Next to her were a number of books she'd read time and time again: *All Strange Things Live in the Dark, Jeddison Licks and the Magnanimous Balloon, Harsh Airs and Little Winds,* and *The Two Hundred Half-Moons of Tahena.* These were the splinters she fed to her ember of a heart: dreams of people she'd never met.

There was another book, however, hidden in the floor beneath the others. The thing that had awoken this particular morning. Milly put down the book in her hand and put her ear to the floor. She knew, logically, that everyone would be asleep, but she had to make sure.

Milly moved the other books aside and pried open the floorboards. She pulled out the hidden text: *A Witch's Guide to Rudimentary Magicks.*

Milly wasn't sure where it'd come from. She'd found it while cleaning out one of the rooms a couple weeks ago. Doris told her to get rid of it, but she never did. Obviously.

Milly ran her fingers over the cover. Intricate gold-laced patterns were engraved into the leather. Someone else had smudged two letters inside the cover, an inconsequential person with the initials *E.S.*

It smelled old. Musty. Most of all, familiar.

Milly looked around and sank into the floor. Witch literature had been banned ever since the Wizarding Wars. Ever since the witches disappeared. Ever since the wizards made being a witch illegal. She could never risk anyone thinking she might be a witch. Or that one of her sisters was one. Even—especially—if it wasn't true.

But though dreams didn't burn in her, curiosity did. She opened the book to the middle of Chapter 6: "How to Summon a Wind." On the right were sketches of currents twisting inside and around each other. On the left were a few broken paragraphs.

Winds are a volatile and persnickety assortment. They require much more patience to befriend than other beings of magicks. Many won't even give you the time of day.

If you wish for a wind's help, all you must (or can) do is ask. And use the magick word. Just don't do so expecting to receive anything in return.

Above all, do not—I repeat, do not—without exception, under any circumstance, ever, ever, ever attempt to tame one of the Four Winds. Many foolhardy wizards have seen the wrong end of insanity trying to control even the littlest winds. Many have lost their minds. Some have even lost their hearts.

Always remember that as a witch, it is never your duty to control the magicks you work with. They are not your servants. Your only goal is to—

"Milly? What are you doing?"

"HU—WHOOPS." Milly jolted and hit her head on a

wooden beam. She dropped the book and immediately sat on it, picking up *Misfortunate Adventures* as she did so. The back of her head throbbed.

The fuzzy top half of a little girl's head peeked out at her from the attic's trapdoor.

"Hi, Cilla," Milly said in as calm a voice as possible.

The little girl, Cilla, climbed into the crawl space with a stuffed blue borkoink squeezed under her left arm.[4] Half her hair stuck out to the side and her pajama sleeves drooped past her tanned brown hands. She sat down and rubbed at her eyes with her right sleeve.

"It's so early," Cilla said. "Why are we up?"

Cilla was six years younger than Milly, three pant sizes smaller, and two times the trouble. The other girls called her Silly, either because she talked to inanimate objects or because it was a not-clever play on her name or both. Milly tried very hard to call her Cilla.

Milly rubbed the back of her head with one hand while still pretending to look at the book in the other. "I was reading."

Cilla scooted toward Milly and looked at her over the book's binding. "Whatcha reading?"

"*Misfortunate Adventures of Tom Fool.*" Milly lowered the book and poked Cilla's nose. "You remember this one, right?"

Cilla squinted down at Junebug, her borkoink, then up at

---

[4] Sometimes they bork, sometimes they oink. Who knows what family of the animal kingdom these creatures belong to.

Milly. "Is this the one with the egg balloon that could fit a person inside it?"

"Yep." Milly shifted on her seat, very aware of the hard corners digging into her thighs. She put down the book and smoothed the spikes in Cilla's hair. "Why are you up so early?"

"We weren't tired. We—" Cilla stifled a yawn. "We wanted something to eat."

Milly glanced at the borkoink and raised an eyebrow. "Junebug seems pretty tired to me. Maybe you should have let her stay in bed."

"Is not." Cilla held up the borkoink and propped its little blue head with her thumbs. "She's plenty—*yawn*—awake."

Milly sighed. This act could be cute, but not that cute. "Come on, little one. Doris won't like it if she knows you're up."

"We won't tell her."

Junebug's button eyes glistened, as if it were whispering, *I make no such promises.*

Milly ignored it. "If I get you a snack, will you go back to bed?"

"What do you think, Junebug?" Cilla said. The borkoink's head drooped down.

"Ugh. Fine." Cilla stuffed Junebug under her arm and crawled back toward the trapdoor.

As soon as Cilla's head dipped out of sight, Milly slid out the *Witch's Guide* and tucked it in the floor panel beneath the other books. So much for a quiet spot to be alone. Milly blew a strand of hair out of her face and approached the trap-door. She paused when her fingertips grazed the edge. Down below was the world where half-chewed dreams gave way to the slow digestion of practicalities. She didn't want to start her day just yet; she wanted more time to read.

Too bad she didn't really have a choice.

Milly left her curiosities in the attic and jumped down, dressed in her unwanted title. It was time to be a mother again.

CHAPTER TWO
not everyone chooses to be a mother

OUTSIDE THE FOSTER home, Milly knelt on the ground with her hands in the mud.

A sudden shift in the wind lifted the brim of Milly's rice hat and sneezed water onto her face. She sputtered and reached up to pin her hat down with both hands, glaring up at the sky. She wanted to reprimand the bad weather, but another bundle of raindrops clattered against her teeth and she dropped her head back down.

"Ugh!"

Now even more cold and wet, Milly returned to the bucket she had been trying to wrestle out of the ground. Her forearms and every inch of her fingers were covered in mud.

She probably should have done this instead of reading earlier. Doris always said, "Better done in haste than done in waste."

Or . . . something like that.

Something rolled beneath her right foot and she slipped, falling backward into a mess of vines. The rain splattered onto her face while she lay in a patch of the squash garden.

She thought she heard a laugh.

Milly whipped her head around, flicking droplets from

her nose, but didn't see anything in the shifting walls of rain. Doris's old moss-bull lay on his side nearby. Snoring. Oblivious. Little pink wildflowers grew around his toes and legs. Years of sleeping had made him barely distinguishable from the landscape.

Rubbing her thigh, Milly got back to her feet. When she pulled her hand away, it was covered in the remains of a yellow-blue squash.

"Gross."

She tossed it aside, then pushed her sleeves up to her elbows and sloshed back over to the buried bucket. A small green grunkworm wriggled between one of the wooden slats into the dirt.[5]

"Okay," Milly whispered. "You need to come out. Right. Now."

She adjusted her grip around the edges—

"One . . ."

—dug her fingers in as best as she could—

"Two . . ."

—and set her two slippery feet shoulder-width apart.

"Three!"

It didn't budge an inch.

Milly gritted her teeth and mumbled, "Please just come out."

A small red spark flashed across Milly's knuckles and the

---

[5] Grunkworms are bright, luminescent creatures that glow only when the moon is out. Otherwise, they look like normal worms.

whole bucket flew upward into her arms. She shifted to keep from falling over with the sudden weight. An unbidden grin spread over her face.

Wait, did I do that? Milly frowned, then laughed, then frowned again, not entirely sure what to feel. Maybe she'd just . . . imagined it. Yeah, that was it.

She shook her head free of distracting thoughts. Knots of grass and dirt squished beneath her feet while she turned with the bucket between her legs. She waddled out of the garden and toward St. George's, squatting the entire time. The bucket's contents sloshed from one side to the other with each wide, unbalanced step.

Halfway up the slope to St. George's, she slipped against the mud. The bucket started sliding.

"No!"

Scrambling up, she sloshed to the bucket and held it from going any further with one hand. "Can you please let up for one moment?!" she complained to the sky. "Just let me in the house, and I won't come back out until you're good and finished. Promise!"

The sky flashed with lightning, followed almost immediately by thunderous fanfare.

Milly thought she heard laughter again, this time from behind.

She spun around and saw a shapeless shadow flicker in the rain.

"Hey!" she shouted. "Who are you?!"

She blinked several times to clear her vision as raindrops stung her eyes. When she could see again, the mysterious shape was gone.

Frustrated and a little embarrassed to be talking to no one, Milly kept one hand on the bucket and pulled it behind her. With a new sense of motivation, she trudge-slip-climbed the rest of the way up the slope to St. George's.[6] From outside, she saw all of St. George's wall-sized windows slatted shut against the wind. Except for the tiny window up in the attic, which she'd forgotten to close, and a narrow slit of light where she'd left the kitchen panels open. Milly could see the room lit up by a lantern on the center table.

She hauled the bucket up and into the house, then pulled herself up after it. With a loud exhale, Milly sprawled onto the floor, belly-side down.

Through the floor, she felt the faint vibration of approaching feet. The rhythmic tip-tapping grew louder until she heard two wooden slippers slap into the kitchen.

"Oh. Hello," came the disembodied voice of Doris. "Were you able to grab the last batch of fermented rice?"

"Yup." Without getting up, Milly knocked the bucket with her foot.

She heard Doris walk around her to retrieve it. "Thank you."

Milly shrugged, though she knew Doris probably didn't see it. She heard the sound of a fish's head slap against a

[6] Embarrassment can be a very powerful incentive.

chopping board, followed by the thud of a knife.

After presumably deboning and cutting several more fishes, Doris spoke. "Are you ready for the Happy Ghosts Festival?"

Milly shrugged again. "I guess."

"I'm glad for all your help," Doris said. "I know it's been . . . tougher than usual, with the shadows eating the crops, but I really am grateful. I've been thinking, maybe you should learn a trade next season. You like baking. I could ask Gimmy to take you as an apprentice."

Doris waited for Milly to answer, but Milly didn't want to.

"Some of the other girls are getting older now . . . I'm sure they'd be willing to take up some of your chores around the house. I'm sorry it's been a lot of trouble. I know how long you've waited."

The weight of silence sat between them.

And then, just as quickly as she created it, Doris broke the quiet. "I know you feel responsible for the other girls. Especially Cilla. But . . ."

Milly lifted her head and stared at Doris. *I dare you to say it*, she thought.

"You aren't their mother."

Milly shut her eyes and gritted her teeth. She didn't want to talk about this right now. She wanted to sink into the floor, or take a long shower, or sit in the attic and read the rest of her book. Anything, really. Just not this.

But Doris kept talking, and the words fell over Milly like

an itchy blanket she couldn't throw off. Doris meant well—
she always did—but no matter how many times Doris promised anything, Milly knew better.

Doris couldn't take care of the girls by herself. Milly
would remain their *big sister* or *mother* or whatever forever
and always. She'd watch Cilla and Nishi and Lissy and Ikki
find titles to chase, families to make their own, and then
she'd be left behind. Again. Stuck with St. George's and the
dreams she was never allowed to have.

A silent scream tore through her chest and she got up.

"I need to clean up," she sputtered, and ran from the
room.

⁓2

Milly sat in a wide barrel, staring into the foamy water that
had lost its heat long ago. She clutched her knees, studying
clusters of bubbles with glazed-over eyes.

In her mind, all she saw were ghosts. She imagined their
eyes were glossy black buttons, like Junebug's, peeping from
cupboards and beneath floorboards. Their skin stitched out
of the rough-hewn material Doris kept rice in. Their hands
made from long-bladed scissors.

She knew, of course, that real ghosts could never be that
ugly. Giving the unknown a mask to wear was just the best
way she knew to cope. If a ghost had a mask that was scarier
than its real face, it'd make seeing one easier. Right?

The Happy Ghost Festival happened every year in West
Ernost. It was how the village remembered everyone lost to

the Wizarding Wars, how they remembered all the children who used to live at St. George's, how they remembered to never trust witches again. No one else in Arrett really cared, so the people of West Ernost took it upon themselves to never forget. To always keep praying.

"Remember us."

A cold, gentle hand gripped her shoulder.

Milly gasped and jumped up, spilling water onto the floor.

"Geez!" Nishi pulled her hand back and fidgeted with two braids of hair. "I just came to tell you that dinner's ready."

Milly relaxed her shoulders, nodded, and stepped out of the bath.

Nishi grabbed a towel off the wall and tossed it at Milly. "You should probably clean first."

Milly caught it and blinked. "This is too small."

"It's for the floor."

Milly looked down at the mess she made. "Oh."

Nishi looked in a mirror, grinned at herself, and twisted on her heel. "See you downstairs!"

After wrapping herself in a much bigger towel, Milly slid open a panel, then stood up to pull on a large, hanging rope. The water from the bath rushed out in a thin, sudsy river along a little engraved pathway on the floor and streamed out through the miniature door. Milly held on to the rope until the entire bath drained, then slid the door shut with her foot and walked back to the barrel.

She dropped the towel Nishi had thrown at her and hopped

on it with both feet. One foot at a time, she slid around until all the water was soaked up. Satisfied, she glanced into the barrel once more to make sure nothing had been left inside. Two unpopped bubbles stared back at her, covered in her own shadow, like little glass eyes.

CHAPTER THREE
the living, the dead, and the in-betweens

EVERY YEAR, AS soon as harvest ended, Doris took her fourteen girls on a field trip for the Happy Ghosts Festival. Although not all the girls still believed in ghosts, they all had their own reasons for going.[7]

This year, they woke up with the sun and spent their day preparing a feast. Each girl had been given her very own job this year, while Doris stood in the middle of the kitchen blurting out names and sometimes getting them right.

"Lissy and Cilla, I need you two to collect banana leaves."

"Okay!" They (and Junebug) went outside and mostly played with green sticks.

"Gabby, I need you to rummage around in the spice cabinet and find me some cinnamon."

"'Gabby'? Milly, who's she talking about?" one of the girls whispered.

"I think she means Abby."

"Oh . . . wait. That's me!"

"Nenita," Doris continued, oblivious, "come here and

---

[7] The girls' top three reasons for participating in the Happy Ghosts Festival? 1) Honoring traditions, 2) respecting the ghosts, and 3) eating lots of really great food. Not necessarily in that order.

bring that sack of june-eyed beans with you."

Little Nene wobbled across the room, taking twice as long because she didn't want to step on any of the cracks in the floor.

"Nishi, can you keep an eye on that pot of rice?"

"Ugh." Nishi dragged Ikki along and forced her to stir the pot while she braided Ikki's hair.

"Mei, I need squash from the garden."

"Called it!" Marikit jumped out the door at the chance to go outside.

"Hey! She said I could do it!" Mei shouted, clambering after her with only one shoe.

"Aisha, please don't eat the pudding before it's ready."

"Aisha's not here today," said Aisha, with her pinky finger in the bowl of pudding. She licked it, then stuck her index finger in for another taste.

Meanwhile, Milly was in charge of nothing in particular. Which meant she was in charge of everything.

"Aisha, get your fingers out of that."

"I'm not Aisha. Today I'm Fahtma—"

"You knew exactly who she meant." Milly swung around. "Nishi, please stop making Ikki do your work."

"But I'm too busy."

"I'll fix your hair later."

"Really?!" they both said.

"Yes. If you do your jobs. I need Ikki to help me with these bean cakes."

"Go on, Ikki. I got this." Nishi pushed her sleeves up past her elbows.

"Fiiine."

Most of the morning continued like this, and they somehow made progress throughout the day. Slowly, the mess on the table transformed into an arrangement of platters and bowls. Little steamed packets of rice sat in a row, neatly dressed in banana leaf robes and twisted-grass ties. A large bowl of rice porridge with flowers carved along its wooden sides sat in the middle, cinnamon dusting the top. Round ovals were stacked on a plate, hard-crusted on the outside and filled with soft purple beans within.

When the sun began to set, all fourteen girls took a portion of this feast and packed their rice and bean offerings into little open-topped boxes. Doris lined them up and led them out the front door onto a small stony path that led away from the rice terraces and toward the Hallow at the edge of the cliff.

As they approached the Hallow, some of the farmers and villagers from the nearby Tugalong Town materialized down the road. Many of them were older without kids of their own, but they all had some ghost—some memory—to pay tribute to. Living in West Ernost meant you were haunted by the dead, and that was a fact of life.

Most of the girls were too young to remember who any of the ghosts used to be. For them, this was a chance to get honest, down-to-their-toes scared.

Every child wants to be terrified out of their boots every so often. Nothing's better than a monster at scraping down the walls, stripping the floors, and tearing down the doors that have locked up one's complacent heart. Fear has its way of startling the heart back into shape. It nips the heel. Stings the skin.[8]

As they marched toward the festival, the girls whispered among themselves stories of cruel fairies and ancient giants, mischievous dwarves and pale-eyed djinns. However, if they wished to be particularly scared, the definitive worst of the worst were the woesome, wily, wicked, and wasteful witches.

Nishi, as usual, was the first to bring them up.

"I heard they like to eat children," Nishi said, whispering over her shoulder at Ikki and Cilla. She licked her lips, wrinkled her nose, and took on a croaky voice. "Mmm, roasted bones."

"Teeth soup," Ikki added.

"Finger sandwiches!" Marikit exclaimed a little too loudly.

"That's not true," Cilla said. She had Junebug pinched beneath one arm while attempting to balance her boxed offering. "Witches aren't canned knee bulls."

"What?" Nishi made a face.

---

[8] This is not to say that all fearsome things must be hideous. Many of the best things in life are both beautiful and terrifying. There's a special holiness that comes with making friends with the monster under the bed. Of course, for most of these kids, being scared was just very good fun, and fun is a form of holiness, too.

"Canned. Knee. Bulls." Cilla repeated, emphasizing each word as she avoided the cracks in the worn path.

"You mean cannibals?" Milly asked, trying to be helpful.

"That's what I said."

"No, it's not." Nishi nudged Cilla forward. "Come on, you're so slow."

"I heard," Marikit said, "that they're the reason the ghosts can't pass on to the next life."

Ikki rolled her eyes. "Who told you that?"

"Old Man Tem-Tem. He says that's what all the shadows are."

"Well, duh." Nishi snorted. "That's why we had to get rid of them all."

"The shadows?" Cilla asked.

"No. The witches!"

Cilla squinted. "Are all the witches *really* gone?"

"Don't you know anything?" Ikki kicked a stray stone down the hill. "They made their last stand in East Ernost. And that's gone now. So what does that mean?"

"I don't know . . ."

"There aren't any more witches *anywhere*."

"Wizards got rid of the witches because they stole children," Marikit said. "And now the ghosts are all that's left of the children's souls."[9]

---

[9] Of course, that's not the real reason the few witches vanished. But stereotypes can be almost as powerful as names—it's because of them that West Ernost is little and shabby and witches are malevolent child-eaters.

Ikki nodded her head vigorously.

Cilla frowned. "I'm sure some witches are nice."

"Why d'you think that? Have you ever met one?" Marikit asked, eyes wide.

Nishi sneered. "Have *you* ever met one?"

"That's not the point!"

"Point is," Nishi said, "witches are scary and you should be scared of them."

"All witches have big noses to sniff out their prey," Ikki tried to helpfully contribute.

"And wrinkled hands."

"And smelly feet!"

Milly plucked a long blade of grass, then slowed down until she was walking next to Nishi.

"Why do you care about witches so much, anyway?" Nishi got closer to Cilla and lowered her voice. "You should be happy they're gone. If they were here, they'd probably catch you in a great big net. Then they'd bring you to their home and sing a wicked song while boiling water to cook you up in a—"

Milly tickled Nishi's elbow with the blade of grass.

Nishi screamed, almost dropping her box in the process.

Doris spun around, eyes ablaze. "*Shhhh.* Show some respect!"

All the girls hushed. Nishi glared at Milly and stuck out her tongue before finding a new place in the line.

Milly tossed the blade away and winked at Cilla. "Don't listen to her. No one's seen a witch in years, anyway."

But Cilla didn't respond like Milly had hoped she would. Instead, she looked down at her feet and kept walking.

Nishi looked like she wanted to say something else in retort, but Milly glared her back into silence. Instead, Nishi just exhaled through her flared nostrils.

Seeing an old couple ahead of them, the girls quieted and didn't say another word on their journey along the winding path.

The Hallow was a half-circle of stones that surrounded a large white tree growing out from the very edge of the cliff. Old Man Tem-Tem said that the tree had been consumed in a fire and lost its entire crown of leaves. Instead of dying, the tree was blessed (or cursed, depending how you thought of it) to grow for eternity. Even though it appeared completely dead on the outside.

Some nights, the villagers swore they could see little balls of fire still dancing in its branches. They claimed these dancing lights were the departed ghosts, and that if one were ever lost, all they had to do was follow these lights back to the tree in the Hallow.

They called the tree Elma.

When Doris and the girls arrived at the Hallow, they saw some of the villagers already laying down their offerings on the stones and whispering prayers for whoever it was they remembered or missed or wished would come back one day to visit.

Some of the girls had prayers already prepared, mostly for old parents to come back or for new ones to take them away. Others stared into their boxes with gurgling stomachs, wondering when they'd be allowed to get back to St. George's and eat.

As for Milly, prayers felt too much like dreams. She didn't really have any for herself. She knelt for a short while and placed her box down next to Ikki's. She had given up on asking for parents a while ago. She was almost thirteen, after all. Practically her own person.

She did, however, still keep a list of prayers for the others. Things like:

Please fix Doris's brain.

Please make Nishi shut up sometimes.

Please give Marikit a friend.

While she muttered her short, scattered prayers, she looked over at the others—some intensely staring at their boxes, others yawning into their fists. Cilla was mumbling something to Junebug.

Suddenly, a small shadowed hand reached toward Cilla's head from the nearby tree. Milly jumped up.

"Cilla!" she said.

The hand quickly pulled back.

Cilla stared at Milly, a very confused expression on her face. There was no sign of shadows around her.

Milly shook her head and sat back down. A cold wind blew across the sweat on Milly's brow as some of the others glanced at her, but she didn't look up. The wind brought with it the scent of something . . . burnt. An odd thought crossed her mind. She wished she could ignore it, but the idea was too strange. Too specific.

She closed her eyes and muttered one last request.

"Please don't let Cilla be a witch."

CHAPTER FOUR
the girl who talks to vegetables

IN THE EARLY dark, Milly sat in the library. The library was a circle of shelves and bookcases with very few actual books or scrolls to decorate them. At its center was the giant, winding bookshelf she climbed to get to the attic. Distinct footprints punctuated the dust that covered it from bottom to top.

On the side where she was sitting was a wall of large side-sliding windows that stretched down to the floor.

Whenever Milly needed to breathe or sit or hide or ponder, she always returned to the library. Usually, she'd climb up the bookshelf and find her place by the half-window, curl up with a blanket, and read by sundew or moonglow. She would stay in the stories for as long as she could, chewing up the words and mulling over the inky depictions of faraway lands that slipped between her teeth and tongue.

But today, the words that so often provided refuge felt suffocating.

Instead, she pulled open a wall-window and sat with her arms wrapped around her stomach, facing the breadth of ocean that lay past the sea of fog. She let her feet hang in the thick fog surrounding the house. The winds were especially ferocious today, almost blowing through her, pulling her hair back and daring her to jump.

The waves in the distance formed crests, momentary mountain peaks that rose for one second and crashed down the very next. It was their impermanence that made them so fascinating. That made them almost alive.

Milly had avoided Doris and the other girls since dinner the previous day and was taking time to be alone before she had to get back for breakfast. This was the kind of space she needed. Big space. Air too unruly to be bound by walls. Waves too wild to hold shape.

She didn't know why, but she wanted to feel small.

She closed her eyes and breathed in the salty air.

But, too soon, the world decided that she needed a rude interruption.[10]

Milly blinked her eyes open. She thought she'd heard noise from outside the house. She stood and poked her head out into the chilly air.

The most dangerous part of living on the side of a cliff wasn't the storm, but what came after: a large, rolling wave of white fog that came in from the seas and blanketed the ground all around St. George's. It swallowed up the green fields and hid the cliff's edges from sight, making it all too easy to tumble down. No one was allowed outside this soon

---

[10] Arrett may not be much of a stickler when it comes to the rules of narrative, but they are an impatient fellow and we're all on a tight schedule.

after a storm, especially not on this side of the house.

Milly began to sit back down. Maybe she'd just imagined the sound.

A girl's voice drifted from around the corner of the house. If one of the girls was lost in the fog, they might need her help to get back inside.

Milly dry-swallowed and looked down. She knew the ground was just a short drop from St. George's, hidden somewhere beneath the fog. But even knowing that, the ground seemed farther away when invisible.

She scrunched up her face.

Breathe.

Milly jumped down and landed on all fours with a jarring thump. She pressed her hands against wet grass and dug in her fingers. The blades tickled, poking out between her toes and against her shins like cold kisses from the earth.

She rubbed the dirt off her hands, then reached out to feel the familiar textured walls of St. George's. Slowly, she stood, until the fog came up to her hips. There was nothing but the house's wooden beams and the occasional sounds of a muddled voice to guide her forward.

Step by step, she made her way around the back of the house to the squash garden. She imagined how it might usually look. Vines roped beneath and over one another. Pinched leaves sticking out from the places she hadn't stomped over during harvest. Wild and always messy.

Instead, when she turned the corner, she saw nothing but a continuous wall of white. It was so thick she could bite it.

"Nasty fog, I wish you'd let me see *something*."

As if in response, a soft wind blew through and thinned the fog just the tiniest bit. Faint flecks of green revealed themselves before her. With renewed confidence, she let her fingertips leave the house behind and took larger, bolder steps until she saw the nearest corner of the garden.

And, next to the garden, Cilla, who was squatting. And talking to the plants.

Milly let out a huge sigh. That girl could talk the ears off anything, even things that didn't have ears.

"What are you doing out here?" Milly asked.

Cilla spun toward Milly, and a wide smile illuminated her face. "Oh, good! You can help us! We're trying to learn a new trick." She turned back around and muttered something.

"A trick?" Milly looked over Cilla's shoulder and saw a drawing of a squash. It looked familiar somehow. "Cilla, what are you reading?"

"We don't know. We didn't recognize it from your other books. It has cool drawings though! They looked like directions for growing plants."

Milly's took another step, and her chest tightened.

It was a page from the *Witch's Guide*.

"*Cilla*," Milly whispered. "Where did you get that?"

Cilla looked up at her, obviously confused. "It was in the attic with your other books." She looked down, then up again. "Is it yours?"

"No! I mean, yes. I mean—well, you can't use that one. Here," Milly said and reached out a hand. "Give it to me."

"Why?" Cilla grabbed the book and clutched it to her chest with Junebug. "I can read things, too! You didn't steal it, did you?"

"Of course not. I just need you to give it to me *right now*."

"No."

"Cilla—"

"No!" Cilla looked at the book's cover. "Everyone keeps saying magicks are bad, but this book isn't *bad*. It's helpful! It has directions for lots of useful things. Like gardening. And cooking! And, and—"

"*Please*. You're gonna get us in trouble!" Milly's whispers started to sound less like whispers.

Cilla dropped her gaze and wouldn't look at Milly, her eyes wet.

"Cilla." Milly softened her voice and put her hand on Cilla's shoulder. "Come on, let's go home and you can put that book back where you found it."

The girl kept her mouth shut and shook her head from side to side.

"*Cilla*." Milly said Cilla's name with a tone of *danger*. It was a voice she never practiced and rarely used. In fact, she could count on one hand how many times she had used that voice, and all but one of those times had been with Nishi. "You know you shouldn't be out here. Let alone reading about *witches*. Who knows who, or what, is out here listening."

Cilla opened her mouth to object, but Milly continued.

"You either give me back that book or I'm dragging you back to St. George's and telling Doris that you were out here in the fog."

Cilla's eyes widened. *"You won't."*

Milly lowered her voice. "I will."

Cilla's lower lip quivered and she looked out into the garden, her eyes darting back and forth. Then she ducked her head and whined, "I can't."

Milly's mouth fell open, but no words came to mind. Cilla could be stubborn, but never this stubborn. Milly put both hands on the younger girl's shoulders. "Cilla, look at me. I know you think this isn't a big deal, but it is."

"You don't trust me. You never do."

"I want to, but you have to trust me, too."

Tears formed in the corners of Cilla's eyes.

Milly exhaled, convinced the tears were an act. Cilla's theatrics wouldn't win her over this time. She grabbed Cilla's arm. "Come on. We're going back to the house."

"No!"

"Ci—"

"NO." Cilla twisted out of Milly's hand and tore into the fog.

"Cilla! *Oh, what have I done?* Come back!"

Milly tore after the girl. Her feet thudded against the damp clumps of grass and dirt. She searched for even a blue puff of Junebug. She saw nothing.

"*Milly.*"

"Cilla?!" she shouted. "Where are you?"

"*Milly,*" the voice said again. It came as a cutting whisper, as if from the wind itself.

Milly slowed to a walk, panting for breath. "Who—*gasp*—who is that?"

"*Milly.*" The voice came from ahead, distant and beckoning. It had gotten softer.

"Wait," Milly said, picking up her pace. "Come back this way!"

Something struck her shin. She tripped and put her hands out in front of her but found nothing to catch her fall. She tumbled somersaults down a steep incline, the air in her lungs escaping her like exploding bubbles, until she found the bottom of the slope.

Disoriented, she grabbed at tufts of grass and propped herself up. She was in a shallow pool, where the fog only came up to her wrists. Ahead of her she saw Cilla clutching the book in her arms. The wind whipped the hair around Cilla's cheeks and Milly heard the crashing waves somewhere nearby.

"Cilla!" she called, her voice hoarse and tiny. Getting to her feet, she stumbled forward once more. "Cilla, come back toward me!"

Cilla shook her head and took one step back. "We don't want to."

"Cilla, please. You have to trust me!"

Cilla shuffled her other foot backward.

Milly gulped and reached out her hand. "Cilla, if you're not careful you'll—"

Cilla's mouth dropped open in surprise.

Right before she fell off the cliff.

AN INTRODUCTION TO CHAPTER FIVE
the little winds

WHEN THE PRAYERS became quiet, so did the magicks. Not because Arrett wanted to punish anyone, but because Arrett knew that no person's heart could have magicks if it were also full of too much want.

The South Wind didn't understand. He demanded that Arrett give up their magicks once more, without the prayers. Arrett tried to explain the importance of trading prayer for magicks, how delicate the mathematical equation was that lay in every selfish heart, but the South Wind wouldn't hear of it. And so, Arrett had no choice but to consult Ovid, the smallest of the giants. Arrett asked Ovid to chain down the unruly wind.

Unfortunately, when the South Wind was involuntarily forced to retire, he left the world of Arrett in quite an awkward state. Suddenly, the seasons were skipping entire days and the calendar missed all of its important holidays. Snow tripped into summer, and the other winds forgot which direction hurricanes spun in.

In other words, the South Wind left some pretty big shoes to fill. Like, a size seventeen at least. These little winds, these young little upstarts, I don't think any of them could have been any bigger than a size three. Maybe four. And that's a very generous estimate!

Arrett needed to find a new South Wind. And fast. The immense pressure required all of the winds to stop doing their jobs and search. *Almost* all of them.

The exception I'm talking about is a little wind so young and so small he doesn't even have a name yet. After the war ended, the little wind never got the memo about searching for a new wind, and spent his time scurrying around the bottom of the cliff of West Ernost, doing his very best to catch the prayers of the locals and carry them to who knows where. Honestly, he's not very big and his arms are rather skinny, so most of the prayers fell through.

But one day, a little girl threw in a prayer so small it wouldn't have been noticed by anyone with bigger arms. Despite its size, the prayer she threw was so heavy that the moment this wind caught it, he didn't have the strength to carry any of the others he had collected. And before he had even made it away from the cliffside, another little girl tossed herself from the cliff and landed on his head!

She landed so hard that, quite by accident, the prayer passed into him. It's not generally a little wind's job to take on these prayers—only to carry them back to the heart in exchange for a little bit of magicks—but this wind had something to prove.

Anyway, good luck, little wind. Consider this a test run. A practical interview. An unpaid internship! It's quite the job for someone so small and untested, but don't worry. Sure, you might fail spectacularly, but at least then you can get back to your mundane routine as soon as possible.

CHAPTER FIVE
in which milly is definitely not a witch

"PLEASE DON'T LET *her fall please don't let her fall please don't let her fall.*"

Milly froze in place and felt a great surge of energy rush from her gut to her outstretched fingers. A bright red spark flashed into existence.

At the edge of the cliff, she sensed a presence. Something with power. Something with . . . magicks.

"Help me, wind," she begged. "Please."

The red spark grew until it exploded. The energy left her body, shot out, and hovered over the cliff's edge, filling the air with the smell of something simultaneously burnt and sweet. Milly watched as the air around her churned in visible patterns made of curling loops and flattened funnels, bounding in endless circles.

The drafts of air continued to run around, forming a tighter cone, until Cilla materialized out of its center and got sneezed directly back at Milly.

Milly landed flat on her back with a hard, brash cough. The impact left her lungs burning and her entire backside throbbing. Little dots splattered across her vision when she blinked her eyes open. It felt like those same little dots were tap-dancing all along her arms and legs.

"How?" Milly whispered with a coarse gasp.

"That was . . . amazing!" Cilla rolled off Milly and jumped to her feet without a scratch.

Milly sat up and twisted around, much to the displeasure of her ribs. She clutched the side of her torso, panting, and looked up to see Cilla staring down at something.

"Milly, you're a . . ."

Milly looked down and saw her palm covered in a black mark. She stretched out her fingers and gasped. Her hand had been stained with a broken moon. A deep dread filled the bottom of her stomach and she shook her head. "Please. Please don't say it."

Cilla opened her mouth as if to continue talking, then shut her mouth and grinned.

Milly propped herself up on her elbows and tightened her hand into a fist, silently willing the mark to go away. "Are you okay?"

Cilla patted herself up and down, then did the same to Junebug. "We're okay."

"Good." Milly fell back into the grass and closed her eyes. She was trying very hard to relax, but all her insides could do were somersaults and cartwheels. *What just happened? Did I just save Cilla's life? Was that . . . magicks?* She snapped her eyes open.

"Cilla," she said, scrambling to her feet. "What happened to the book?"

"Huh?" Cilla looked up from where she was now kneeling next to two little balls: one black, one blue.

"The book. We need to get rid of it."

"Oh." Cilla lowered her head. "We might have dropped it in the ocean."

Thank goodness, Milly thought.

"We're very sorry. We didn't mean to—"

"No, don't be sorry. That's okay." She stared at the black object crawling into Cilla's arms. "Um. What is that?"

Cilla lifted the creature up toward Milly. "Cat!"

It blinked at Milly from the girl's arms, then squinted its eyes and let out a very long yawn.

"Wh-what? How? I—where?"

"He showed up after we landed." Cilla hugged the cat, and he purred into her cheek. "Isn't he cute?"

Milly reached out to pet the cat, but he stopped purring and hissed. Milly pulled her hand back. "It's . . . all right."

"We want to keep him."

Milly couldn't believe her ears. "You almost fell off a cliff, and you already want to—" She shook her head and took a deep breath. "Know what? I don't care. Keep him. I just want to get back to the house before Doris wakes up." Milly looked around. Giant walls of fog stretched above her. She scratched her head and turned several times. "Um."

"Are we lost?" Cilla said.

"Yes," Milly said, trying desperately to keep her voice gentle and calm. (It wasn't working). "We are very lost."

"Is it my fault?" Cilla looked at the mud on her feet, then buried her face in the cat.

Oh. Milly turned toward her little sister and put her hands on the girl's shoulders. "No, Cilla. It's not your fault. We're gonna figure this out together, okay?"

"Okay," she mumbled through a mouthful of fur.

The cat seemed unimpressed with being in Cilla's arms. He wrestled himself out and fell to the ground, then started to walk away.

"Jasper! Where are you going?" Cilla exclaimed.

"Jasper?"

"The cat."

Milly opened her mouth to argue, then snapped it shut. There was no use trying to argue at this point.

Meanwhile, the cat kept walking until he disappeared into the fog.

"Jasper!" Cilla said. "Hey, Jasper, where'd you go?"

Milly sighed. "You probably shouldn't wander too far, cat. You might fall off the cliff."

"Jasper."

"What?"

"You have to call him by his name or he won't listen."

"That wasn't even his name until just a second ago!" Milly tried very hard to not roll her eyes.

Cilla glared.

"Okay," Milly said through gritted teeth. "Where did you go, *Jasper*?"

The tippy-top of a black tail appeared somewhere high up in the fog and wiggled its way back and forth down toward her until it disappeared. Soon enough, the creature it belonged to jumped out from the fog and onto a large stone somewhere next to Milly.

His fur was black from head to toe. He blinked his wide green eyes at Milly, opened his mouth, then promptly sat down and began licking his paw.

Cilla tugged at Milly's sleeve. "He wants us to follow him."

"How do you know? Follow him where?"

"Maybe he knows his way around here. Maybe"—Cilla paused and lowered her voice— "maybe he's magicks, too."

Milly walked to the cat and bent down. The cat stared at Milly, and Milly stared back. He returned to grooming himself.

Milly scrunched up her face. "I think he might just be a cat."

The cat looked up and glared at Milly, then turned around and walked off again.

"Told you he wants us to follow him."

"I don't think that's true."

Cilla huffed and marched off after the cat. "You always think you know everything."

Milly planted her feet down. "Cilla, if you fall off the

cliff again, I might not be able to catch you!"

The other girl kept walking without a word.

"Cilla, I mean it! Cilla? Cilla!" Milly stomped her foot down and ran after them. "I can't believe this is happening."

She followed Cilla, who was following the cat, who led them on a zigzag path to who knew where. Sometimes the entire cat was visible to them, almost as if he were walking on air. Other times, the fog was so deep that all they could see was his tail bobbing about ahead of them. Regardless, he seemed to *act* as if he knew where he was going and never once faltered or waited to see if the girls were following behind him.

After some time of climbing a particularly steep incline, Cilla stumbled and Milly caught her from behind.

"You okay?"

"Our legs hurt."

Milly looked up ahead and tilted her head. "Can we take a break, Mr. Cat?"

The cat's tail twitched, but he didn't slow down.

"I don't think he's in the mood for stopping," Milly said.

Cilla sat down in the wet grass and held her hands up.

"What are you doing?"

"We're tired."

"Do you want me to carry you?"

Cilla nodded her head and lifted her hands higher.

Milly looked up to see the cat getting even farther away, then back down at the little girl and her borkoink. "All right.

Come here." Milly bent down to lift Cilla and immediately regretted it. "Why. Are. You. So. Heavy?"

Cilla buried her face in Milly's shoulder and hugged Junebug tighter.

"Okay." Milly exhaled and glanced over to where the cat had been. "Let's see if we can find that cat."

She headed up the invisible hill one wobbly step at a time, searching for the black fur of the cat to materialize. "Hello? Helloooooooooo?"

Her voice got swallowed up by a fierce wind blowing in from the sea. Milly kept walking with Cilla in her arms, but neither of them saw any signs of life anywhere.

"Jasper," Cilla called, "Where'd you go?"

"I think"—Milly huffed her way up the incline—"I think he's gone."

The two girls made it over the crest of the hill and stepped into the soft glow of a waking sun. It spread its golden fingers from beyond the sea and cracked through the thick layers of fog covering the cliffside.

Milly looked out over the surrounding landscape and saw West Ernost waking up before her. The straw hat of a local farmer popped up through the mist not yet chased away by sunlight. A soft wind blew through the terraces, revealing the damp earth of the rice farms. A winding river curved through the farms all the way out into the far distance, where it disappeared into a forest of bamboo.

"Look." Cilla pulled at Milly's hair. "St. George's!"

And there it was, sitting on the hill closest to them. A light flickered on in one of its windows.

"Told you Jasper knew where he was going!"

"Looks like Doris is awake," Milly said, not fully hearing what Cilla had said. "I'm gonna put you down now, okay?"

Cilla groaned but didn't say anything when Milly lowered her to the ground. Full of newfound energy, Cilla bounded on ahead while Milly stretched her legs.

"Be careful next time."

Milly whipped her head around and saw the cat staring at her from a nearby rock. She mouthed "What" and took a step toward it, but the cat blinked once then jumped away.

"Come on, Milly!"

"Weird," she muttered, then opened her hand. The mark was still there, permanently etched on to her skin. She closed it into a fist, turned, and followed Cilla down the hill.

CHAPTER SIX, PART ONE
on the ineffectiveness of door-to-door marketing

THINGS AT ST. George's became quiet after our two friends fell off the cliff. Although Doris gave them quite the scolding, Milly and Cilla agreed never to speak of anything related to the cliff or book or anything magick of any sort. Cilla appeared more restless than usual, but Milly found herself very relieved that nothing more had come of the incident. And now that the book was out of her life, maybe she'd be less likely to stumble into magicks.

But every so often, her fingers would twitch and a little red spark would fly between them. Sometimes when she was washing the dishes or mopping the floor or weeding the garden, she felt her palm itch. It was weird, but she missed it. She missed the feeling of power. She kept wondering what it'd be like to use magicks just one more time.

But then she'd see a shadow flit out of the garden. Or around the edge of the house. And it reminded her of Cilla falling off the cliff, and she knew she could never risk being found out.[11]

---

[11] Most health experts will tell you that the very worst thing you can do is Take Risks. If you want to live a very safe, very easy life, then this is true and you

Because she was not in the mood for risks, Milly contin-ued with her life, getting increasingly bored and increas-ingly tempted and scrubbing her hand increasingly raw. Until, one day, while she was standing at the kitchen sink scrubbing her hand for the tenth time in a row.

"*Meow.*"

Milly looked up from the sink, still in a bit of a daze from the mental tug-of-war she'd been losing to herself. Sitting in the open window was the cat, watching.

"Oh, hello," she said. "Are you hungry?"

The cat just stared.

"Hm. I guess I'll come to you, then." Milly turned off the tap and walked over while drying her hands on a towel. She bent down to pet the cat. "Where'd you come from, little guy?"

The cat pulled his head back with flared nostrils. "Please do *not* touch me."

Milly froze with her hand in the air. "Did you just—"

"Speak?" The cat scratched his ear with a back paw. "Yeah, I figured out how. It's not as hard as you people make it out to be."

Milly fell back with a loud thud and opened her mouth to scream or babble or say anything at all, but nothing came out.

The cat tilted his head. "You okay there, little person?"

---

should listen. However, any seasoned adventurer worth their salt would argue that the best investment you can make is to save up a pocketful of Risks. How else would you be able to afford a decent Adventure?

"I— You— This— Talking cat! Talking cat? You're a—What?"

"Yes, yes, I know. I'm very impressive."

Milly rubbed her eyes with her fists several times and then reopened her eyes.

The cat sneered. "Still here."

"Okay, so this is real."

"Yes."

"This is a real thing that is happening to me."

"Yep!"

"This is real life and I am not dreaming and this cat is talking to me."

"I can keep saying yes if you like, but I'd hate to be redundant."

Milly exhaled and leaned back. "Okay. Okay okay okay." She looked at the cat and rubbed her clammy hands together. "First of all, name. What is yours?"

"Jasper, obviously." The cat's left ear twitched. "You should've known that already. You were there when your little friend first gave it to me."

"Oh . . . Sorry?"

"That's quite all right, little girl."

Milly scrunched up her face. "*My* name is Milly, by the way. And I'm not that little. The other girl's name is Cilla."

"It's possible I won't remember that, but I suppose that's good information to have."

Milly narrowed her eyes.

"What? It's not like you remembered mine either!"

Milly scratched her head and leaned forward. "I don't mean to be rude, but why are you here?"

"Right! Almost forgot." Jasper grabbed a thick, blockish object with his teeth and pulled it into view in front of him. He nudged it toward Milly. "You dropped this."

Milly looked down and saw the embossed gold letters of the *Witch's Guide* staring back up at her. Her eyes widened.

"Is that how you people look when you show gratitude? It's not as happy-looking as I expected."

"No, it's just—why did you bring it back?"

His right ear twitched. "I figured you'd need it, considering your upcoming circumstances."

" 'Circumstances'?"

Just then, Milly heard a faint knock at the door, followed by one of the girls shouting, *"Someone's at the door,"* immediately after.

"That was quick," the cat said and jumped out the house.

"Wait!"

"Good luck!" The cat disappeared over the hill.

She heard another knock on the door. In a panic, Milly kicked the book out the open wall-window and ran out of the kitchen.

"Coming!" she shouted, and hurried to the front door.

Whoever it was knocked again. Harder.

"COMING!" Milly blew a curl of hair out of her face and picked up her pace. "No need to be in such a hurry."

She pulled the door open to a complete stranger with his fist poised to knock again.

"Welcome to St. George's," she said. "Who are you and what do you want?"

"Ah, yes. Hello!" The stranger withdrew his hand and took off his hat—a very large, wide-brimmed hat with more feathers than a peacock. "I am the Great Wizard Charles Weatherman Hightop. I am here on, um"—he paused to fumble with one of his large blue sleeves and pulled out a tiny piece of paper—"official wizarding business!" He presented the card to Milly crumpled and upside down.

Milly squinted at it. It read:

> GREAT WIZARD HIGHTOP
> Resident Wizard of Nignip and Magicks Consultant to
> the High Council of Flying Broomsticks and Pointy Hats
>
> "Ask and We Shall Provide."
>
> *not a real business card

She shook her head and started to close the door. "We don't want to buy any of your black-market magicks."

Hightop stuck his foot in the door and winced when it collided with his ankle. He tried to chuckle the pain away. "*Little girl*, I am here on very, very official business. You may have heard of me? Hero of the Wizarding Wars? The guardian of Nignip and its neighboring realms? Tamer of the North Wind?"

Milly blinked at him in silence.

The man coughed. "Okay, well, I have it on good authority that a large influx of magicks recently erupted nearby." He sniffed the air a couple times and lowered his voice. "You wouldn't happen to know something about that, would you? Because if you do, you are legally obligated to tell me anything that might concern any unauthorized magicks."

Milly's throat became dry and she opened her mouth to respond, but the wizard wouldn't stop talking—mostly to himself.

"Of all the places to be, here? Really? Hasn't been a witch here in years! This place smells like rotten eggs stuffed inside an old gronkle's socks."[12]

At this point, Doris arrived in the doorway and placed her hand on Milly's shoulder. "Let me take care of this," she whispered.

Milly nodded and backed away from the door. She saw the other girls' faces peeking around the corner, all except Cilla's.

---

[12] Found among wet marshes in and around West Ernost, swamp gronkles smell as unpleasant as they sound. They are most easily compared to growling frogs with wider-set eyes and flat, stubby toes. Their pants are made of moss and their shoes of sunbaked mud. They are covered in so much green and brown that most people can't tell where their clothes end and their skin begins. Many a swamp gronkle has been known to use this to their advantage.

"Ah, yes, hello," Hightop said while trying to squeeze himself through the door. "I am the Great—"

"Yes yes yes, we heard all that already." Doris crossed her arms and stood in front of him. "You can conduct all your official business from *outside* the house if you please."

"Apologies!" He stepped back and held his hat between his hands, a forced grin embedded on his face the whole time. "I'm here to investigate any and all rumors, hearsay, and smells of magicks in the nearby area. I have reason to believe that a resident of this building may have witnessed an event."

Doris didn't budge one bit. "None of my girls would know anything about that, so you can be on your way."

"*Madam*, please." His smile wavered. "If you could just let me in so I can conduct some short interviews, I will gladly—"

"No." Doris took one step forward, forcing the wizard to take one step back. "You may not."

"But—"

"Good day!" Doris maneuvered herself behind the door and slammed it shut. As soon as she locked it, she turned around and stared directly at Milly. The very wrinkles around her eyes seemed worried. "Follow me," she said. "Everyone else, go to your rooms."

Milly locked eyes with Ikki before following Doris into the kitchen.

Doris spun around and put her two wrinkled hands on Milly's shoulders. "Please tell me you don't have that book."

"What book?" Milly asked unconvincingly. She glanced at the back of the kitchen. "I . . . lost it," she admitted, which didn't seem to be altogether untrue.

"Are you sure? Are you absolutely sure?"

"I—"

Doris closed her eyes and let out a long breath. She smoothed back stray strands of her graying hair with one hand. "I'm sorry, Milly. I believe you. I do. I just want to make sure you're safe."

"I am safe," Milly said. "Everyone is."

Doris looked at Milly, or through her, eyes glazed over as if she was remembering something, but then she shook her head and turned away. "Let's shut all the windows. I don't think it's safe for anyone to leave the house for a few days."

Milly nodded.

"Will you finish up in here? I'm going to check on the others."

"Okay."

"Thanks, dear."

Doris hugged Milly, then shuffled out of the kitchen. As soon as she was gone, Milly ran to the window.

The book was nowhere to be found. She jumped outside and scavenged around the back of the house but couldn't find it anywhere. "Where is it?" she whispered to herself. "Where did it go?"

After another minute (then two, then three) of looking, she gave up and walked back to the open window-wall. She was in the process of closing the slat when she looked down and remembered the cat's tiny pawprints leading away from the house. Following them was a set of little girl's haphazard footprints.

A tiny tuft of blue borkoink hair lay in the grass.

Cilla.

CHAPTER SIX, PART TWO
on the frightening appearance of a witch's nose

MILLY SAT ON the living room floor next to a lantern. The oil was almost gone. Doris had told Milly to stay at the house while she searched for Cilla, but that had been hours ago.

The other girls all slept in the same room. She tried to get them into their beds, but they all wanted to stay in the living room with her. Annie and Little Nene were huddled together, their limbs tangled in each other's blankets.[13] Marikit had made her bed (very uncomfortably) on one of the chairs. Abby had strewn several sheets over a table and snored peacefully from underneath.

If Cilla hadn't been missing, Milly might have enjoyed this impromptu sleepover. Instead, she huddled beneath a patchwork quilt and watched the front door with bleary red eyes.

Ikki crawled out of the pillow fort she'd been sharing with Nishi and Lissy and dragged herself over to Milly.

Milly blinked up at her. "You okay?"

Ikki nodded, then sat down. Milly lifted her arm and the

---

[13] Most children seem to agree that monsters and witches cannot attack them if they manage to keep all four limbs inside a blanket at all times. That's just science.

small girl crawled into the open space. She leaned on Milly's shoulder and closed her eyes.

After some time, Ikki whispered, "You think she's okay?"

Milly played with Ikki's hair absentmindedly. "I don't know."

"Doris will find her though, won't she?"

"I . . . don't know."

"Do you think she's really a witch?"

Milly's stomach tightened. "No. I don't think so."

Ikki rubbed her face into Milly's shoulder. "Do you . . . do you think it's my fault she left?"

This time Milly was certain. She knew who was to blame. "No, Ikki," she said. Firmly. "I am very certain it isn't."

"Okay . . ." Ikki said. "I hope she gets back soon. I kind of miss her."

"Me too."

Milly held Ikki until she fell asleep. When the lantern's light began to fade, Milly scooted out from the cover and lay Ikki's head down on a stray pillow. She stood up and stretched her fingers toward the ceiling. It was getting too late to stay up, but no matter how tired she was, she couldn't sleep.

If only she hadn't let Cilla see the book in the first place. Or let her run away. Or let her fall off the cliff. What a bunch of stupid things to do. Stupid, stupid, stupid.

Milly walked toward the hallway and tried to calm herself down.

"I wish I could do something," she whispered to herself.

"Anything. I can't even use magicks to help her. That's what got us in this mess in the first place." She wanted to cry. "Why can't I just . . . want the right things? Or do the right things?"

Why can't I just be the right thing?

A soft scratching noise came from the front door.

Who was that? It couldn't be Doris; she wouldn't have even knocked. Was it Cilla? The wizard? The . . . cat?

Milly crept toward the door. A strange green light glowed from the bottom, bleeding out into the hall. Milly froze.

That definitely wasn't Doris.

She heard a strange mumbling sound from the outside, and the door's handle twisted on its own. Slowly, the door opened, as if the wood itself was refusing—but failing—to let the stranger in.

The light faded when the door creaked all the way open, revealing the silhouette of an old, hunched woman with a very crooked nose.

A witch.

The air smelled burnt and old.

The witch wore layers of tattered fabrics like a crow that had collected the feathers of other birds. She leaned on a long wooden staff, and her skin looked like ash. Her hair came down in tangled cords. The ground around her was covered in shadowy hands and feet, but they didn't seem able to touch her or the house. She didn't seem to notice them either.

The witch raised her crooked nose and sniffed around. She spoke, but not *at* Milly. Past her.

"Where is she?" The witch turned toward Milly and tried to look deeper into the house. "Where is the witchling?"

Milly crossed her arms like she'd seen Doris do and tried to look brave and bigger than she was. She kept the hand with the mark tucked under her armpit. A shiver ran up her leg. "You're not welcome here. Please leave."

The witch continued to turn from side to side, sniffing the air. "Is it one of your little sisters?"

Milly gulped and tried to pull her shoulders back. It was getting harder to breathe. "You're . . . not welcome . . . here."

The witch cracked a smile, revealing her broken teeth. "Am I frightening you?"

Milly tried to say no, but her throat was getting dry.

"*Good*. You should be frightened." The witch drummed her fingers against the staff in her hands. "Believe it or not, I am actually here to *help* your little sister. I heard there was a wizard in the area looking for her. I thought I'd spirit her away. Keep her *safe*."

Milly felt her hands tighten into fists. "Why should I believe you're telling the truth?"

The witch's upper lip twitched. "You have no reason to. You have no reason not to. What makes you think anything you know is the truth?"

Milly shook her head. "Witches are liars. They keep secrets from people. They do things in the dark. They . . ."

Milly trailed off, realizing who it was she was describing.

The witch tossed her head back in a cackle. "I'm sure your sister isn't like that."

"My sister isn't a witch," Milly said.

"Ah, and how do you know that?"

"Because . . . because I just *know*, okay? She . . . it's impossible."

The witch jerked her head and lifted her nose again. She took a deep breath and grinned. "She's here. I can smell her brimming with magicks." She turned from the door and stepped out into the grass. "I'm afraid you're about to be very wrong, my dear."

Milly started after the witch, but she heard a creak and spun around to see Ikki's horrified eyes watching from the other room.

"Milly?"

"Stay here," she whispered. "Shut the door. Don't open it for anyone."

CHAPTER SIX, PART THREE
uh-oh

THE WINDS AND waves were quiet when Milly stepped outside. The very grass beneath her feet felt brittle, as if any wrong step would shatter the tension covering the cliffside. Up ahead, Milly saw the witch shambling down the hill toward an old woman and a little girl clutching her borkoink.

The quiet inside Milly broke, and she sprinted toward the three.

"Makisuyo," the witch said, "give us some privacy."

The air around the witch picked up in speed. It whistled toward and past Milly's ears, making it impossible to hear what anyone was saying. Milly saw the witch raise her hand. A green light flashed, and Doris fell to the ground. Cilla flinched but didn't move.

"Run!" Milly shouted, but her voice was swallowed up in the wind. "Run, please! Just run!"

Every single word was ripped from her mouth. Her legs grew heavy. The wind pressed against her, forcing her knees to the dirt. She tried to claw her way toward them, but all she could do was watch helplessly as the witch put a hand on Cilla's shoulder.

"Don't take her!" Milly tried to scream. "I'm the witch! *I'm the witch!*"

No one heard.

The witch raised her staff in the air, and a flash of light filled the sky.

Milly shut her eyes. Stars spotted her vision, and a loud thunderous crash reverberated around her. She grabbed fistfuls of grass. It felt like the whole world was being torn away.

When she opened her eyes, the wind was quiet again. Doris was clutching Junebug to her face.

Cilla was gone.

THE FIRST HIATUS
some girls actually can run forever

CILLA, SOME MIGHT say, was an expert at running away. She was never found unless she wanted to be found. She was never caught unless she wanted to be caught.

She really hated when the others told her to stay in place. It felt like they weren't taking her seriously. Especially Milly. It's not like she never came back. She always did. Eventually. Most of the time the others barely even noticed when she was gone.

There was a big gap between running *from* something and running *toward* something, but Cilla couldn't always tell the difference. She'd always known Milly was a witch, but Milly never seemed to want to be one. Cilla had heard plenty of stories about how bad the witches were, but they didn't seem true. If witches were really that bad, why was her big sister so good? And kind? And gentle?

(Most of the time, anyway.)

She was starting to doubt whether Milly was a witch, after all.

But then she saw Milly reading a book. One that she didn't want Cilla to see. And Cilla started to wonder.

Cilla waited until the dark of night, when even Milly was

asleep, before she crept into the attic. Although she couldn't read as well as Milly, she knew enough to recognize the word "witch." The book felt heavy in her hands. It felt old and full of magicks and . . . grown-up.

The first picture-spell she tried to replicate was making a flame appear.

"I command you to light up," she said to a nearby candle. Nothing happened. Cilla tried numerous iterations of the spell, but nothing she did could make magicks respond to her the way she saw them listen to Milly.

She tried one for making a puddle disappear, one for making grass tie itself into a knot, one for getting vegetables to grow faster. It was this last one she'd been attempting when Milly caught her with the book.

So Cilla, as was her specialty, ran.

You already know how that went.

When Cilla fell off the cliff and lost the book, she was devastated. All she'd wanted was proof that Milly could do magicks. All she wanted was for Milly to show her how to do it, too.

Instead, Milly stopped talking. Cilla now knew for certain that her sister was a witch, but knowing hadn't made a difference. If anything, it only made her feel more confused.

Cilla kept trying to do magicks on her own. She tried to do what Milly had done and talked to the winds. She talked to the flowers. To the soap bubbles and the dirt between her toes and to cobwebs and dust motes and milk squash and eggs.

Nothing responded.

Cilla didn't have any idea what she was doing wrong. So she decided to pray for something different this time.

As luck (or misfortune) would have it, the book fell back into her life.

This time she wouldn't waste her chance. She ran farther, far enough that not even Milly could find her, and spent the entire day talking to Junebug and attempting magicks. She found a bush of devil plums that she'd once stained Ikki's bedsheets with and drew moons on her own hands.

Late in the day, Doris found Cilla curled up on the ground next to a tree. Discarded plum pits lay around her, and she'd left a small drool stain on the page she'd been using for a pillow.

When Doris picked her up, Cilla didn't complain. She buried her face in the old woman's hair and breathed deeply while clutching the book underneath her borkoink. Doris carried her for hours in the quiet dark. She carried Cilla over the fields and beneath the stars. She carried Cilla until her arms couldn't do it anymore, and then she put the girl on her back and carried her some more.

Unfortunately, they had no idea what waited for them.

As soon as they stepped into view of the house, Cilla felt the book in her arms pull toward the witch.

Run. Get out while you can.

Doris put Cilla on the ground. "Stay behind me."

Cilla nodded.

"Makisuyo," the witch said, "give us some privacy."

Despite Doris's determination, the winds quickly pinned her to the ground, leaving Cilla standing alone. Cilla felt like wood, like her legs were made of bark and branch.

"Run," Doris gasped. "Leave the book and run." But Doris's voice sounded distant and empty.

"Hello, witchling." The witch reached out her hand. "I'm here to take you away. That is what you want, isn't it?"

Cilla froze. Was it what she wanted? In the middle of that cyclone of angry winds, the witch was offering Cilla everything she'd ever thought she wanted. A chance to run. A chance to be a witch. A chance to be taken seriously.

She saw Milly crawling toward her, and she turned to the witch with her crooked nose and broken teeth.

No. For the first time in her life, Cilla didn't want to run. She wanted to go home, to sleep in her own bed, to hug Milly and eat breakfast with Nishi and catch frogs with Lissy.

She wanted to run home.

But despite that, Cilla knew what she needed to do. If this witch was looking for someone with magicks, then that meant Milly was in danger. And her big sister had never been as good at running as her.

So Cilla showed the witch her plum-stained hands. And off they went.

CHAPTER SEVEN
sometimes home is the place you run from

MILLY CROUCHED BENEATH Elma with her arms around her heaving chest. She didn't know why she'd come here.

As soon as her limbs were able to move, she'd run from St. George's.[14] She didn't know why. She didn't wait for Doris to see her. She didn't go back to the house.

She just ran.

She ran and ran and ran and didn't once look back. She kept running until she couldn't run any longer. She ran until breathing hurt almost as badly as the shame.

Elma's branches rustled gently overhead, moving with the wind.

Milly blinked open her wet eyes to find herself in the middle of their boxed offerings. A beetle crawled over one of the ribbons. She wiped her eyes with a sleeve and looked out over the ocean. The waves were calm now, almost tauntingly so.

---

[14] "Run" is probably not the right word when you've been walking for hours and your legs feel like wooden pegs and you look like a possum who took a bath in a mudslide, but there aren't very many words which properly describe such an endeavor. Skip-hop? Slip-stumble? Tripped over herself thrice, fell on her face, and yet continued to move forward all the while? One of those things has got to be closer to truth.

"Please help me," she said. "I don't know what to do."

The winds didn't respond. She felt the same presence at the edge of her fingertips. But it was faint. And leaving.

"What good are you?!" Milly's voice cracked. "Why would you save her only to take her away?"

Low thunder rumbled in the far distance.

"Help me get her back!" Milly stared out at the sea, then spun around and pressed her forehead against the tree.

"What do I do now?" she whispered.

Unseen to her, a brief spark flashed at her fingertips.

"Maybe you could try crying some more."

Milly turned around. Angry.

There was the cat again, sitting on a large root protruding from the ground. She glared. She was so tired of being surprised by random strangers. "Go away," she said, and turned back around. "I'm not in the mood to talk."

"That's fine," the cat replied. "I can talk plenty for the both of us."

Milly felt a tail brush her arm as the cat made his way over to sit beside her.

She groaned and buried her face in her knees. "Why are you here?"

"You literally just asked for help."

Milly lifted her head slightly and frowned. "You can't do anything."

"How dare!" The cat's nose twitched. "I helped you when

the little one was in trouble, didn't I? And again when you lost the book. Humans are so ungrateful."

"You heard my prayer?"

"Heard it? Felt it, more like. Said you didn't want your sister to be a witch. Really botched that one, haven't I?" He spread his paws, as if ready to pounce on something.

"I don't understand. You weren't around when I said that."

The cat purred. "You read books, don't you? I'm pretty sure you do. The last corner you dog-eared—terrible habit, by the way—was even on summoning magicks."

"But I didn't . . ."

Milly stared at the cat, trying to figure out what he could possibly be talking about. The last chapter she read hadn't been about cats. It'd been about—

She gasped. "You can't be!"

"Can't what?"

"You're . . . you're a wind?"

"I am indeed. I am, in fact, *the* wind. The one your sister fell on, and the one you asked for help, and the one you just now asked for help a second time, even though I was very ready to be on my way and never have anything to do with this ever again. Very atypical for winds to get involved with little witchlings. Very atypical."

"But you're not a . . . wind." She couldn't get over it. "You're a cat!"

"And you are a witch. We can't all appear exactly as we are, can we? If I were to always be a wind, I'd be hunted down by the weather division of that magicks committee immediately. That means I am a wind that must sometimes be a cat, and you are a witch that must sometimes be a girl. We all do what we must to survive."

"But I *am* a girl."

"Exactly! The purrfect disguise."

Milly scrunched up her face.

"Don't like puns?"

"Not really."

"If you say so, little witch." The cat jumped to his feet and stretched his paws. "Well then!" he said abruptly. "No use moping around. I've got business to attend to, and you've got a sister to find." He charged at Milly and head-butted her.

She didn't budge. "What are you trying to do?"

Jasper continued to mash his head against Milly's knee. "Why are you so heavy?" he grunted. "Go get your sister!"

"How?" Milly asked. "I have no way of knowing where they've gone."

The cat took a break from headbutting and snorted. "You have a lot to learn. Didn't you smell the witch when she arrived at your house?"

Milly recalled the burnt scent that accompanied the old woman. "I guess so."

"Excellent. Did that remind you of anything?"

She tried to think harder. When was the last time she smelled anything burnt? "The cliff. But what does that have to do with anything?"

"Magicks leave a very pungent smell," the cat said. "Especially deep magicks. Like that book. It's how both the wizard and the witch found you here. Cilla has it with her. That means you can also—"

"Track down Cilla!" Milly leaped up, hands balled into determined fists.

"There you go."

"Can you still smell it?"[15]

The cat's eyes narrowed as he sniffed the air. "Faintly. You'd have to leave immediately if you don't want to lose the scent."

"Immediately?"

"Unless you want to lose your sister forever and ever. The trail is already very faint." The cat's tail twitched. "Don't worry. I'm sure you won't be gone too long. You'll have her back by this time next week!"

"Next *week*?"

"Or maybe tomorrow. Or next month. I can't predict the future. Point is, you'll find them. Then you'll have your sister and I can pretend this never happened and we can all get along with our lives."

---

[15] Anything touched by magicks is bound to sound funny or smell weird. Can't be helped. Everything in Arrett has a distinct sound, smell, look, or feel. Even lies.

Milly gulped and looked at the trail that led back to the house. Doris would have to do without her for a little while. She wouldn't be gone that long, right? Maybe she'd even like being away. Seeing the world. Learning more about magicks. And . . . witches.

She turned toward the cat. "One thing first."

"Okay. But make it quick."

"What did my sister ask for?"

The cat laughed. "That's definitely not within my parameters. But you can ask her when you see her again."

"Will you come with me?"

The cat frowned. "I don't think I'm allowed to."

"I can't go by myself!"

"Hm. Tough luck."

"I'm serious."

"I am too! You know what happened the last time a wind helped a human? It started a war!"

Milly bit the bottom of her lip and looked down at the moon on her palm. It itched. What was that thing about taming winds?

"Um." Jasper started to back up toward the edge of the cliff. "I really don't wanna know what you're thinking."

"I need your help." She stepped forward, avoiding eye contact.

The cat's ears flattened against his head. "I don't really think I can—"

"This is your fault to begin with. You brought that book

back into my life! You're the reason my sister was taken!" She paused. She knew none of that was true, but Milly couldn't stop blaming the cat once she started. "You've got to help me get her back."

She felt a great power burn from her palm. Though she had never cast a spell on purpose, Milly's next words came more naturally to her than meanness. "Wind, I demand your help to bring Cilla home. You are *tamed*."

"Blustering squalls, I'm outta here!" The cat turned and his body became ethereal. His limbs broke into soft currents and his whiskers twisted into smokey trails. A loud rush of wind almost knocked Milly off her feet as she watched.

But she stood her ground with her fingers outstretched. Just as the cat's front paws left the cliff, a red spark wrapped around his body and made his transparent cords flesh once again. The sparks continued to wrap around him and pulled him back onto the cliffside. Back into the form of a cat.

"What!" He looked back and forth, fur frazzled. "What did you do?"

Milly let out her long-held breath. She felt powerful and proud. Casting that felt so natural. She'd just tamed a wind! But seeing the disheveled cat at her feet, panting and confused, also made her feel a pang of guilt.

"I'm . . ." She shook her head. Now wasn't the time to be *sorry*. She could be sorry once she found her sister. "Okay, wind. You're going to help me find Cilla."

The cat rapidly shook his head as the red electricity faded

from his black fur. "What a rush," he said, glaring at Milly. "Okay, *witchling*. I guess I'll help you."

"You will?" Milly's heart lifted.

The cat laughed, but the glare never left his narrowed eyes. "You didn't really give me a choice."

CHAPTER EIGHT, PART ONE
a girl without a mother

MILLY AND JASPER made their way along the small upraised paths that crisscrossed through the rice fields. The paths were narrow passages made of tightly packed dirt just barely big enough for a grown-up to walk on. On either side of these paths was the partially flooded landscape in which the farmers grew their main grain.

The two had been walking for most of the night, and Milly knew it wouldn't be that long till morning. Overhead, the sky's deep blues were already shifting into a splotchy arrangement of purples and pinks.

Ahead of her, the cat trotted along with an annoying sense of certainty.

"What are we doing?" Milly would ask.

"Just trust me," he'd say.

"Do you even know where you're going?"

"Of course I do."

"So why do we keep changing directions?"

"Don't question the process!"

And so on and so on.

Milly passed her time by watching the reflections in the water and making shapes out of them. There, an ear of corn.

There, a rabbit. There, what she imagined an elephant to be.

Every so often, the cat stopped at a crossroads, lifted his little nose, and sniffed the air. Then he'd make an abrupt turn and take off down an adjacent path. The first time it happened, she was following him a little too closely and stepped on his tail. Jasper let out an ear-piercing yelp and jumped into the water. When he dragged himself back out, all of his fur was plastered to his bones. She didn't want to make the same mistake twice. Based on the occasional glare he threw back at her, neither did he.

Milly glanced up during their walk and saw that they had been inching closer and closer to the Needsy Woods, an endless bamboo forest that bordered the inner edge of West Ernost.

She gulped and stopped in her tracks to take it in.

The cat kept walking until he noticed she wasn't following behind him anymore, then backtracked to her.

"You okay, little girl?"

Milly looked down to see that the cat had sat down and, not for the first time, was attempting to groom the knots out of his fur.

"You look a little pale," he said. "We've come very far. No point stopping now."

"I know. It's just . . ." Milly hesitated. "I've never been this far from home before." For good reason.

"Something wrong with a couple trees?"

She shook her head. "Those aren't just trees. Those are

the Needsy Woods. I heard they were cursed by a witch after the war. They called her the Witch of the Wasted Woods. All the farmers told stories about how she lured children into the woods to eat them . . ." Her eyes widened. "You don't think she's the one who took Cilla, do you?"

The cat choked in the middle of licking his back and made an awful wheezing noise.

Milly looked down at him. "What's wrong with you?"

The cat threw his head back and continued to wheeze.

Milly realized what the cat was doing and glared. "Why are you laughing?"[16]

"Witches don't eat children." His eyes shone with mischief. "You don't have nearly enough meat on you. They'd rather eat a half-giant!"

"I'm serious!" Milly said. "For all we know, this could be the witch that took Cilla. She's supposed to be dangerous. She could even be where all the shadows came from."

"Eh." The cat licked his paw and ran it over his head. "Doubtful."

Milly picked up a clump of mud and threw it at the cat's head.

The cat ducked and stared. "What was that for?"

"If you're not gonna take this seriously, I don't want your help." She started walking again, stepping over the cat and toward the forest.

---

[16] Cats are not generally known to have a great sense of humor, so they were never given all the proper working parts to express themselves fully.

"Hey! Watch it!"

Milly kept stomping onward.

"Little girl," the cat called. "Little person! Hey, girl. Hey, little—*I knew I should have remembered her name. What was it? M-something. Mildew? No, wait. Milly?* Milly! Come back!"

"No, thank you."

"You have to listen to me, you know. I'm older than you!"

She whipped around, eyes ablaze. "Oh, yeah? How old are you?"

"Forty!"

"Forty years old?!"

The cat chuckled. "Not quite."

"Forty *what*?"

". . . seasons."

Milly ran the numbers in her head. "Forty seasons in years is forty divided by four, which equals ten . . . so that means . . . HEY, I'M OLDER THAN YOU." She kept walking.

"Do you even know where you're going?"

"Nope!" She was now halfway to the woods. Seeing something flutter up ahead, she stepped off the last dirt path and onto a long stretch of clumped moss leading to the tree line.

She heard the cat scramble to his feet and chase after her. "Hold up!"

Milly kept walking.

"Did you forget that you're the one who needs *my* help?"

he said, falling into pace beside her. "You can't even smell the magicks. How will you find your sister? Besides, *you* tamed *me*. I can't very well untame myself."

Milly let out an exasperated sigh and pointed up ahead. *"That's* how I'll find Cilla." There, in a clump of bushes, was a white page fluttering against the wind. "I release you from your oath or whatever. Go on and be free to do . . . wind things."

"That's not how this works," Jasper said, stopping in his tracks. "I'm stuck with you until we get your sister home! This is very deep magicks you're working with; it can't just be undone."

She felt her stomach tighten with guilt. "Oh. I . . . didn't know that."

"Oh, no. I'm *sorry*. Is this your first time *taming a wind?"* the cat teased.

"This was all your fault, anyway!" Milly blurted out. "I can't talk to you right now."

"So what? You're just gonna leave me like this? I have reason to want to find her, too, you know. I can't stay a cat for the rest of my life!" The cat-wind *mrrow*ed. "Come on, I didn't mean it! Milly!"

Milly ignored him as she bent down to grab the torn page. It was a drawing of a carrot. She smiled. *Don't worry, Cilla. I'll be there soon.*

She looked up ahead to see another page and continued into the forest, picking up each piece of the trail. She'd been walking for a long time before she realized it had gotten very quiet behind her. When she turned, the cat was nowhere to be found.

Oh well. Who needed him?

A long while later, Milly found another piece of paper barely hanging on to a branch. This was the second page she'd found that was too high for her to reach. She'd realized early on that the papers must have been dropped from somewhere above the trees. Which meant that Cilla and the witch had to have been . . . flying?

Milly maneuvered her way through clusters of bamboo. The tighter the trees became, the harder it was to see or move forward. Overhead, a soft wind rustled the leaves. She shuddered.

Slowly but surely, the sun spilled through and dappled the floor as the trees rippled back and forth. It made everything, even the trees, glow white. Milly squinted her eyes. She thought she saw another page a little way ahead, but they were getting harder and harder to see, so she couldn't be sure.

Milly balled her fists and pushed through the trees until she could reach it. It *was* another page. Good—that meant she was still headed the right way.

She snatched it up and stuffed it into one of her pockets along with a dozen other crumpled sheets of paper.

"Oh, boggins." Looking up, Milly realized that she'd gotten herself stuck in a little ditch.[17]

With a loud grunt, she tried to pull herself up with one of the nearby trees. She shuffled up onto it and felt it bend beneath her weight.

"No no no no."

The tree continued to bend. She held on until it got stuck on another cluster of trees.

"Okay, listen. You can do this. It's just gonna take a lot of . . . focus."

Milly scooted up an inch at a time, gritting her teeth every time the tree below her shivered. "Almost . . . there . . ."

She heard a loud *snap*.

The tree she was balancing on fell, and her stomach briefly felt like it had left her body. She landed on a bed of bamboo and tumbled to the ground.

"Oof. That one was so bad I can't even laugh at it." *Jasper.*

She lay on the ground for a few seconds and put her arm over her face. "Why," she grunted, "are you here?"

"I needed to make sure you were all right," he said. "It's okay. I forgive you."

---

[17] If you are an inhabitant of Arrett, your parents might wish that the word "boggins" had been censored. However, like many bad words, it is not inherently bad. It is, in fact, the name of a very real creature. Bogginses are orc-like, bulbous creatures that like to loot through people's drawers. They are responsible for mischief like making only one sock in a pair go missing, which is why they earned a spot on Nignip's list of minor curse words.

"Forgive me?" Milly slid her arm down and scowled at the cat with one eye. He was sitting nearby with a big old smirk. "I didn't say sorry."

"Didn't have to! I'm just *that* charitable." His tail swished across the forest floor and he took a short sniff. "You're losing them, you know. I can barely smell that book anymore."

Milly groaned and pushed herself back up to her feet. "I was doing perfectly fine before you showed up."

Jasper grinned, as much as a cat *could* grin. "Oh, I know, I've been following you for a while now. You've been doing *just fine*."

Milly took stock of her surroundings and started heading in the direction she thought she'd been going originally. "I still don't want your help."

"You sure?"

"Yes."

"Then I'm sure you'll realize in your own time that you're headed in the wrong direction."

Milly stopped as she stepped on one of the fallen branches from the tree she'd just cracked. She wiped the sweat off her forehead and snorted, then spun around and walked past the cat in the opposite direction.

"You're welcome, little person."

"Thanks," she mumbled.

"What was that?"

"I said THANKS." Milly stomped through the bamboo

toward another piece of paper. "And my name is MILLY. Not 'little girl' or 'little person.' M-I-L-L-Y. *Milly*."

"Names are so boring. Fine. Whatever. If I call you Milly, will you let me help you finish your quest?"

"Do whatever you want. I don't care anymore. I just want to get my sister back."

"All right! Jasper and Milly, at it again!" The cat fell into step beside her.

She snorted again and kept walking.

After a while, the cat ran ahead to a slight incline and paused at the top. "You know," Jasper said, "there might be an easier way to do this."

"What do you mean?" She wrestled to squeeze between two trees and snatched another paper.

"What I mean is, you have witch blood. Why don't you, you know, use it?"

Milly shook her head violently. "I'm not a witch."

"That's not what you said earlier." Jasper sneered. "Anyway, it's too bad you feel that way. Would have made this much easier. And it's not like you had any problems using it on me."

"Made what easier?" She climbed up next to Jasper and looked in the direction he'd been staring. She gasped.

There, in the middle of the bamboo forest, was a large, magnificent tree with a trunk as wide as a house. In fact, maybe it was a house. A knot of wood that could have been a doorknob protruded from the base, and several openings that could have been windows were carved into its bark.

That, however, was not what had caught the attention of our two friends.

Circling around the top of the tree were dozens and dozens of flying broombranches. They shook their yellow straw leaves as they whistled by, rustling and making their own sort of percussive music. They flew around and under and between one another, diving in the air and looping around the tree's larger branches.

For a moment, Milly wondered why the tree's shape looked so familiar. Then she realized: it looked just like Elma! Is this what Elma had been like before the war? A broombranch tree?

Milly shifted her weight and something snapped underfoot.

The broombranches all instantly darted out of the sky and into the tree's canopy. Their knotted ends twisted perfectly into the tree's branches and they preened their leaves until they looked like a normal tree from a distance. In a fraction of a second, the entire scene had gone silent. The only sound came from the faint teasing of the winds above, wondering why their broombranch friends had stopped dancing with them.

Milly remained frozen. She glanced down at the cat and whispered, "You don't think the witch lives here, do you?"

The cat sniffed. "I don't know. This tree should practically reek of magicks, but I don't detect anything. It smells like nothing, like it's not even there."

"This is very strange," Milly said. "I don't like it."

"Me neither." The cat wiggled his haunches, then jumped down. "Oh well!"

CHAPTER EIGHT, PART TWO
a world without boundaries

"*JASPER*," MILLY HISSED. "What are you doing?"

"I'm gonna ask a broombranch for a ride," he answered matter-of-factly.

"Jasper, stop." Milly scrambled after him. "I don't want to ride a broombranch. I don't even know how to fly!"

"You're a witch, aren't you? If there's anything I've heard you humans say about witches, it's that they serve their cat masters and only travel by broombranch."

"That's not true. What would you know about witches?"

"They're all you humans ever talk about. Every year I wait for prayers to drop from that cliff of yours and all I hear are things like *'Please don't let the witches come back'* or *'Keep me safe from the witch in the woods'* or *'Bless the wizards for banning all the witches forever and ever, amen.'* You're a very fearful lot, you know. Actually, your prayer in particular was very interesting. It wasn't very big, but it sure was the heaviest one I've ever caught. There was something rooted in there, something even heavier than fear. It was almost—"

Milly cut him off. "Okay, okay. Let's get a broombranch." She didn't want to know whatever it was that'd made her prayer so heavy. Milly squinted. "What was your plan gonna be?"

"Ask one politely?"

Milly rolled her eyes.

"What?"

"I don't think they talk."

"You didn't think a cat could talk either."

"But you're not a real cat."

The cat shrugged. "Never know until you try."

"Doubtful." Milly looked around the small clearing for something with which to get one of the branches. Something at the edge of her vision skirted around the tree.

"What was that?" she whispered.

"What was what?"

She put her finger to her lips and made a *shh* sound, then tiptoed toward the tree.

The cat followed behind. "What are we doing?" he whispered a little too loudly.

"Quiet, please. I thought I saw something."

The two crept around the tree and saw a single broom-branch peek out. When they spotted it, it ducked back out of sight.

"Did you see that?" Milly said.

"Sure did."

"Maybe we can—"

"Talk to it," Jasper said. "Catch it," Milly said at the same time.

"Wait, what?" They both paused.

Jasper twitched his nose. "*Catch* it? A broombranch? You're going to use magicks on this too? Tame another living creature with your special powers?"

Milly felt her cheeks burn. "No . . ."

"What are you going to use? Your bare hands?"

"I mean . . ." Milly scratched her palm nervously. "I use my hands for everything."

"I really don't think that's a good idea."

"Yours doesn't sound much better. What if we scare it away? I think we should try to catch it off guard."

"Fine." Jasper snorted. "We'll do it your way. Just don't be offended when I say *I told you so.*"

"I won't have to. I'll be the one saying *I told you so.*"

"If you're wrong, I demand . . . hmm, what is it that cats eat again?"

"Mice?"

"Ew, no. Not that. I demand a cake."

"Can you even eat cake?"

"Beats me. But I hear enough prayers about it that I'm dying to find out."

"Okay, if I'm right, you have to stop calling me *little person.*"

"Ooh, that's tough. This means I'll have to remember your name."

"Exactly."

The cat twisted his nose. "I suppose that's fair."

All the while they'd been arguing, the broombranch had floated closer and was watching them with either apprehension or, more likely, curiosity. In fact, it was near enough that either one of them could have reached out and touched it if they had noticed.[18]

It wasn't until a moment later, in the middle of a sentence, that Milly finally noticed the branch and froze.

"Hi there," Jasper said.

The branch immediately shuddered and tried to fly away. "Grab it!" Milly shouted, and jumped toward it. Her fingers brushed its tail end as it fluttered out of reach and she landed in the mossy grass.

"With what?" Jasper scoffed. "My *mouth*? I think I'll leave this to you."

"Thanks a lot." Milly scrambled up and held both her hands out in a placating matter. "All right, come on over."

The broombranch quivered, taunted her, and shifted from side to side.

"It's teasing you!" Jasper made his awful laughing noise. "How delightful!"

---

[18] *Rules and Regulations of Being a Wizard, Chapter 4.* How to catch a broombranch: Hunt it at night while the tree is asleep. Do not try to wrestle or cut it off, especially not with a knife. The smoother the branch, the younger it is. Attempt to find one with a few knots. Middle-aged trees go through their own midlife crises and are thus unmotivated to run when you hunt them. We suggest these as the easiest option for beginning broombranch hunters.

"I can see that!" Milly said through her teeth. She lunged forward again and the broombranch hovered sideways, just barely out of reach.

It rustled its brittle leaves happily.

"It's too fast!" Milly said.

"Oops. I wonder what other options we could have possibly had."

"If you're not gonna say something helpful"—Milly swung and missed—"don't say anything at all!"

"There's no fun in that!"

The broombranch led Milly in a haphazard dance around the tree. They danced over roots and around patches of dirt and over clumps of vegetables and—

"What are you doing?!" came a woman's voice.

The broombranch abruptly stopped.

Milly saw her chance and grabbed on with both hands.

"LET GO OF THAT BROOMBRANCH!"

But Milly did not let go. She held on even harder as the branch lifted her off the ground and took her in a half-circle round the tree. As she spun around, she saw a woman covered in green running toward her with an outstretched wand. So a witch did live here—just not the one that had taken Cilla.

"It's a witch!" Jasper said.

"Grab on!" Milly shouted.

Jasper wiggled his butt and jumped toward her as she

flew by. He landed on her back and clawed his way up to her shoulder, pricking her every inch of the way.

"Ow! Ow! Careful!"

They climbed higher and higher as the witch flailed her arms beneath them and the broombranch picked up speed. From up here, Milly realized she'd been chasing the branch around an entire garden all this time. All the rows of un-grown seeds had been trampled. By her.

The witch grabbed at her headscarf with both hands, too distraught to know what to do. "My cabbages! My daisies! My *home*!" She raised a pointed finger. "I don't know who you are, but I want you to come down here and clean up this mess!"

The broombranch became more and more frantic as it climbed higher in the sky until it suddenly shot off in a random direction, trying to fling Milly and Jasper off.

Milly held on for dear life as they sped over the treetops, her knuckles white with fear.

"Where are we going?!" Jasper said.

"I don't know!"

On and on they flew, bucking to and fro as the broom-branch grew increasingly manic.

"Let go of that broombranch!"

Milly looked back between her arms and saw the witch following them on her own broombranch.

"It's only a child!" the witch said.

Milly's arms were growing tired too, and she gasped as her lungs burned with the air whipping by. "Please," she said. "Please let us down!"

A very agitated voice entered her mind: *"Only when you let go!"*

Milly nearly let go from the shock of it all. "You talk!"

"Of course I do!"

"Why didn't you say anything?"

"I did! It's not my fault you don't speak tree!"

"Sorry!" Milly said, palms sweaty. "Please let us down, and I promise I won't try to ride you anymore!"

"Yes! Yes, please!" Jasper shouted. "I'm not sure how well this body would sustain such a long fall!"

"Fine by me!"

"Fine!" Milly said.

"Fine!" Jasper repeated. "We all agree. Just stop already!"

"Let go of that branch!" the witch shouted.

The broombranch divebombed into a tangle of trees until it was wobbling just above the ground.

"GET. OFF."

The broombranch came to an abrupt halt. The momentum sent Milly and Jasper tumbling onto the ground. When they had stopped long enough to get a sense of their bearings, Milly looked up and saw that they were almost at the very edge of the woods—somewhere opposite West Ernost.

The broombranch shook itself like a wet dog. *"Stupid*

human," it said, then shot up and toward the witch, who was still headed in their direction.

"Um, Jasper?"

"Run!" the cat said, already on his feet and sprinting toward the edge of the tree line.

Milly's entire body felt shaken, but she got up anyway and sprinted after the cat.

"Wait! Stop!"

Milly glanced back to see the witch dismounting ungracefully from her broom. She tripped onto the ground, and her head covering fell back to reveal shockingly green hair. She leaned against one of the bending trees, trying to compose herself. "You can't leave this forest!"

Oh, yes I can! Without a second glance, Milly spun on her heel and tore into the woods.

Milly didn't have to run long before she saw a bright opening in the trees. After all that had happened in the past two days, her legs were burning something fierce. She didn't know how much longer she could keep running from everything.

"Don't leave the woods!" the witch cried. "It's not safe for you there!"

Milly gritted her teeth and tried to run faster.

"Stop!" The witch sounded farther away, her voice tired. She started to mutter unfamiliar words but stopped abruptly.

Milly looked back and saw the witch standing in place,

heaving, one hand holding her side, the other hanging by hip. Shadowy hands and feet stood between Milly and the witch.

Was this the edge of the witch's domain?

She locked eyes with Milly, then turned toward the shadows.

With a breathless scream, Milly put on an extra burst of speed and broke out from the woods. Near-white sunlight blinded her momentarily. She slowed to a stop and shaded her eyes with a hand. After blinking several times, she realized that the brightness came from a nearby creek. The sun bounced around on the water in broken pieces.

Milly slowed to a walk and giggled—she couldn't help it. She was just so relieved to be back on the ground. She took her shoes off. Holding them in one hand, she jumped in the water, splashing the cat.

"No! Stop that!"

Milly ignored him and closed her eyes. She waded further and stuck a hand in. The ice-cold currents swam between her fingers and toes, soothing her sore muscles. Frothy bubbles popped like laughter.

When she opened her eyes, she found the cat sniffing angrily at the water on the other side. His fur glistened with a couple drops of water and the ground around him was dotted with tiny damp patches.

"How can you possibly enjoy that?" He glared at his own reflection.

"How can you not?" she responded. She waded out of the water toward the side he was on and collapsed into the grass. She stretched every one of her limbs. She never wanted to fly again. Or run, for that matter.

Jasper let out a long exhale. "Well, I suppose, all things considered, that didn't go as badly as it could have."

"Go ahead. Tell me you *told me so*."

"Told you so."

Milly sighed and kept her eyes close. "I don't even care. I'm just glad we're out of that forest." Then she opened her eyes and looked around. "Where are we, anyway?"

The cat took a whiff of the air, then pointed his tail in a direction parallel to the river. "I think I smell something over thataway. The smell is very close, but it's not particularly strong. Stay here for a minute."

Without waiting for a response, the cat disappeared into a nearby thicket.

"Jasper," Milly whispered. "What's going on?"

She saw a bush rustle and then heard his voice soon after. "Over here!"

Milly ran through the thicket, yearning but nervous to know what the cat had found. She found him dragging a soggy *Witch's Guide* out of the river. The book had half its pages ripped out.

"Where are they?" she asked, breathless.

"It's just the book." He spat a couple times and stuck his tongue out. "Ugh, gross."

"Can you smell them?"

He shook his head.

Milly grabbed fistfuls of whatever pages were still intact. "We failed!" She ripped out the wet pages and flung them into the river, one clump at a time. "All of that was for nothing!"

"Milly . . ."

"I'm so useless!" she said. "I was supposed to protect her! I was supposed to be her big sister. But *I'm* the reason she's gone. The witch came for *me*."

"Milly." The cat bumped his head against her shoulder. "Look up."

"Leave me alone."

"Stop moping for a minute and just look, will you?"

Still holding the torn pages in her hands, Milly sniffed and lifted her head. Her mouth fell open.

"Nignip," she whispered.

Down the river stood the great city-state. Long, stretched-out walls rose from the ground, made of many chopped trees lashed together. Round holes had been cut into their sides, and the walls themselves were dressed in banners and flags of all shapes and colors. Behind them, Milly saw the faint heads of houses peeking out, stacked upon each other in mismatching colors. And of course, rising above all that proudly stood a tall, crooked tower with a half dome for a hat.

There was no doubt about it. That was Nignip, home to

all sorts of creatures and music and magicks and foods.

"Come on." Jasper's tail brushed against Milly's shin. "Maybe we can find answers there."

Milly gulped and turned back for a moment. She searched past the river and beyond the congested forest they had just escaped. She searched for the familiar hilltops that she knew must still be behind it all. Somewhere, St. George's was waiting for her, and Doris and Nishi and Ikki and all the other girls.

But not Cilla.

Milly let the pages fall out of her hands—faded images of a forbidden text she knew she shouldn't be familiar with— and put her shoes on. She wiped her nose and threw the book back into the river. She didn't need it.

CHAPTER NINE
a good witch always follows her nose

ONCE THEY PASSED the outer walls, the collective voices of the city's inhabitants flooded Milly like a boisterous wave. The deeper she got, the louder they grew. Milly soon realized that the residents there must have been from the southern countries because none of their clothes looked like anything she'd seen before. Some had metal scales pinned to their chests. Others wore colorful hair made of plucked feathers.

Everywhere she looked she saw people like she'd never seen before. Living in West Ernost felt like sitting on a boring blade of grass next to a busy anthill; Nignip was the anthill. Except instead of holes in the ground, it had a wild mishmash of wayward streets. And instead of a queen in the middle, it had its very own residing wizard as self-proclaimed protector.[19]

---

[19] *Jeddison Licks and the Magnanimous Balloon, unknown chapter*: Nignip is a fantastic place, if you like headaches and toothaches. I swear, if they serve a meal at my funeral, I want them to serve two hundred Nignip cakes and a barrel of firefly rum. As far as formalities go, this hoity-toity place is "protected" by some guy who refuses to be called king. He much prefers "The Great Wizard Weatherman Hightop" because: 1) "I am not a king," and 2) I guess wizards are vastly more fearsome than kings. If you ask me, his head's gotten too big for his buttons ever since the war, but you didn't hear that from me.

She ducked beneath the arm of a sleeveless giant. The giant's skin was dark gray and her muscles rippled like liquid boulders. In the giant's raised arm, she held an empty fishing boat.

"Move!" Jasper grabbed Milly's sleeve with his mouth and pulled her to the side as a troop of long-bearded gnomes scuttled by. Their square spectacles sat atop their blockish noses, which stuck out from their boxlike heads. Even their robes were covered in golden lines and rectangles. Despite the fact that the tallest of them barely came up to Milly's shoulder, they all looked very important, and none of them looked anyone in the eye.

"What are they?" Milly whispered to Jasper.

"Gnome wizards." The cat hissed. "From the look of their attire, they're probably members of the High Council. They're supposed to regulate all things magicks, but most of the time they just boss people around. They really, *really* don't like my kind. Or yours."[20]

Right as he said that, the gnome with the longest beard came to an abrupt halt. All the other gnomes bumped into him from behind. Clearly annoyed, he repeatedly tapped his left foot against the ground. A little cloud of dust rose.

"Ahem!" he said to the giant lumbering on in front of him. She seemed oblivious to the tiny gnomes.

---

[20] Officially, the High Council came to places which most needed their help. Unofficially, they only came to places where they could get the least amount of work done.

"A-HEM," the little gnome repeated, and whacked a stick against the giant's ankle.

"*Hrrrrrm?*" The giant scratched her head with her free hand, then swung around. The hull of the boat scraped against the roof of one of the smaller houses, sending tiles clacking to the ground.

The little gnome stared up at the giant and ground his flat teeth together. "You're in our way!" He twisted the stick around in his hand.

"Ah'm sorrrrrry," the giant said. "Ah'm gurrt."[21]

"Move to the side and let us pass."

The giant looked from side to side. "No roooooom."

"Well," the gnome said, "make room!"

The giant frowned but curled herself into a ball so that she could fit between two buildings. She balanced the boat on top of her head and pulled her chin down. She looked like a small hill with a crooked hat.

"Better," the head gnome said. He led the other gnomes past the giant. The youngest gnome, who hadn't a lick of gray in his beard, whacked one of the giant's toes as he walked past.

---

[21] There aren't any equivalent words for this in human terms, but I will translate as best as I am able. Guurt: half noun, half adjective, occasionally a verb; to feel rock-congested or sedimentary, like the feeling you've had after taking a gravel bath and leaving too early because you forgot to scrape the mud off your toes first. Evidently, this is a common enough occurrence among giants for them to need a word for it.

Milly gasped and stepped forward to confront them.

Jasper bit her sock and tried to pull her back.

"Stop! You'll get us in trouble," he said between clenched teeth. He spat out the fabric. "Your feet stink."

Milly glared at the cat. "We can't just do nothing."

"Do you want to find your sister or not?"

When Milly turned back around, the gnomes had already vanished and the crowd swarmed back into the street as if nothing happened.

Milly looked up and made eye contact with the giant. She wanted to say sorry or . . . something. But the giant shook her head, uncurled herself, adjusted the boat onto her other shoulder, and continued lumbering along.

"Come on," Jasper said. "We need to get moving."

Milly fiddled with her fingers and glanced back.

"Hey! I'm serious. You need to forget all that. Now that you're a *you-know-what*, this is something you'll have to get used to. It'd be even worse for you if you got found out."

She didn't want to get used to it. But she followed along anyway.

Most of the rest of their walk was uneventful, even though the streets only continued to get busier and busier. Whenever she was able to see past anyone's heads, she could see that they were getting closer and closer to the crooked tower.

"We should look for Hightop," she said.

"Who?"

"The one who visited St. George's. He's supposed to be some well-known wizard who lives here, I think." She pointed at the tower. "That's the biggest building. We can probably find him there."

"Not your worst idea. That's a very presumptuous-looking building."

"Thank you."

She took two steps before the scent of a spiced roast wafted up through the crowd. She bent over in the middle of the street, clutching her stomach. She hadn't eaten in such a long time. All the hunger she'd been ignoring suddenly stabbed her at once. "Or maybe," she said, "we can find food and then find Hightop." She grimaced, looking down.

"Keep up," she heard the cat say.

She looked up but didn't see him. He weaved through the crowd much more easily than she could.

"Jasper!" she shouted.

But her voice was swallowed up by the noise.

"Jasper!" she tried again.

Nothing.

She pursed her lips to the side. Looking up, she could see the top of the tower. It didn't look far.

The scent of the roast returned, and she clutched at her gurgling tummy. Her legs trembled. Okay, no. It'd been too long. She needed food, and she needed it now.

"Sorry, Jasper," she whispered. "I'll only be a second."

The smell led her to a side street next to a place called the Quacking Dragon. Her mouth watered.

The alley's damp pavement and dilapidated walls felt like a completely different world from the main streets of the city. There were still people walking between these little side streets, of course, but their jackets weren't as colorful, their shoes were missing buttons, and not all their mouths had a full collection of teeth.

Up ahead, she saw a red-faced gnome sitting at a doorstep. He had beside him a bucket full of flutterwishes. They didn't look any bigger than the size of someone's palm. Beautiful white feathers lined their chests, complementing their tiny beaks, and they had their tiny blue wings pinned together with iron clothespins. Milly watched as the gnome sold a flutterwish to a man dressed in a tattered suit.

"And what d'ya wish for, good sir?"

"I wurna be made of money!"

The gnome grinned. "This one's on the house."

The man grinned back when the flutterwish was dropped into his open hands, revealing a mouth full of rubies for teeth. He then promptly shoved the entire wish into his mouth.

Milly gagged.

The man leaped into the air and vanished in a puff of smoke, leaving behind nothing but a pile of jewels clattering to the ground. The gnome laughed, clapped his hands together, and got on his knees to pocket the jewels.

Milly tried to walk past as quickly as she could, but the gnome caught sight of her and whistled.

"Hey, girlie! Come here and buy your heart's desire!"

Milly froze, then turned and stared at the gnome. He didn't have a long beard like the others, and his face wasn't as rigid or squared. In fact, from his ears to his belly, everything about him was round.[22]

"You're not a gnome."

"Right you are! Name's Ned. Ned Culligan. And I'm a gnob!" Getting back on his feet, he stomped his left foot down. "Not many people can tell the difference, but it's clear as secrets to us gnobs." He stomped his foot again.

Milly walked closer and looked into the bucket. "Why do you keep their wings pinned?"

"They're sneaky little rodents. Can't have them flying away," Ned said. "Want one?"

She shook her head. "You made that man disappear and stole all his money."

The gnob laughed, and his round cheeks grew even redder. "Nah, girlie. Tall-legs did that to himself."

Milly tilted her head and looked down at the flutter-wishes. One of them made eye contact with her and started chirping. "What do you mean?"

---

[22] And when the narrator says round, he quite literally means *everything*. A gnob's nose is a button, and his eyes are portholes and his ears doorknobs, and even his belly is shaped like a barrel. Round isn't just what they look like. They are defined by the very meaning of roundness.

"You can't just wish for anything," he said. "Hey, shut up!" He kicked the bucket to subdue the chirping. "As I was sayings, you gotta wish proper if you want one of these. It's gotta come from deep, deep down in your heart. Tall-legs wished honest, but stupid. Got what he deserved." His voice lowered, and he leaned in close. "But you knows what you want, don't you, girlie? I can smell the hunger off you."

Milly pulled back. The gnob's breath was horrible.

What did he mean? Did he know she was hungry, or did he mean hunger in a different way? Maybe she could wish to find Cilla? When she looked back into the bucket, the thought of eating one of the creatures was enough to make her sick.

"No, I don't want to hurt them."

Ned shrugged. "Suit yourself; they're only flutterwishes."

Now Milly felt her cheeks flush. Something about seeing the flutterwishes's wings pinned made her insides burn. She was angry.[23] And she knew exactly what she wanted.

"Help us."

Milly's eyes widened. She could understand them, like she did with the broombranch.

"Can I take one without eating it?"[24]

---

[23] More than that, she felt guilty. And sometimes guilt and anger are two siblings that hit with the same fist.

[24] We must not be fooled by the appeal of instantaneous wishes. Milly realized just now that wishmaking, like many things in life, isn't easily bought. Only a rare and lucky few get their dreams without consequences. For the rest of us, it requires a steeper price.

His eyebrow bent upward, and a wry smile tugged at his lips. "Now, girlie, what would you want to do that for? They're useless without their wishes, ya know."

"No, they're not," Milly said.

"Hmm." He stroked the stubble on his chin, tapped one of the red jewels against his teeth, and counted his fingers twice. "You ain't got much, have you? But I'm sure you have lots of dreams in your head that are right young and vibrant."

Milly tried to resist smiling. Little did this gnob know that all her dreams had shriveled up long ago. She forced her mouth into a frown and turned her voice soft and quiet. "Oh, but I can't give up my dreams, sir."

"Can't ya? I'll give you two flutterwishes for a dream. How 'bout something you wanna be when you grow up? Or a kiss from your first Prince Charming?" He laughed. "Maybe even your first couple Prince Charmings?"

Milly pretended to think long and hard, but really, she was counting how many flutterwishes were left in the bucket. She counted five heads.

"How much for all five?"

"All five!" He laughed so hard he fell backward and hit his head on the door behind him. If it hurt, he didn't seem to notice. "Little girl, for that you'd have to sell me your own mother."

"Okay."

He wiped the corners of his eyes, laughter fading. "I'm

not stupid." His voice grew dark now, and his eyes were tinted with threat. "I know you haven't got a mother. Maybe you haven't got anything. Deal's off. I can find better customers round here."

"I'm not leaving!" Milly reached forward and grabbed the bucket.

"'Ey!" Ned stood up and gripped the other side of the bucket. "You best let go, girlie."

Milly stared defiantly and yanked harder.

The bucket cracked between them, and all the flutterwishes fell to the ground.

"Get out of here!" she yelled. "Go on! Run!"

Ned snorted. "They can't run. And they can't fly or swim or tunnel away, either. Them's magick clothespins. Only way to free them's if I wants to."

Milly reached for his feet and clung. "Let them go!"

"Gerroff!" The gnob tried to pull away, but she wouldn't release him. "Off, I says! Why's it matter to you, anyways? Stop meddling!"

Milly thought back to the giant, then the broombranch, then her sister.

She refused to do nothing.

"No," she said.

Milly felt a strange power rise from within her chest, and a red flash of light appeared between her fingers. Milly let go, tumbled back, and stared at the light in her hand.

"Y-y-you," the gnob stuttered. "You're a witch!"

"No, I'm not." She continued staring, then jolted up. "I'm not!"

The light remained.

"A witch!" he cried. The gnob tried to back away with the flutterwishes in his arms but tripped over the broken bucket. "Help me! There's a witch!"

Milly watched the light in her hands, scared of the growing heat. She didn't know what to do with it, but maybe she could use the gnob's fear to her advantage.

"Let them go," she said.

"W-what?"

"Let them go"—she paused—"and don't tell anyone about me."

"Don't make me do that. They's my livelihood, see? You understand."

"*Please.*" Milly raised her fingers. "Let. Them. Go."

"What'll you do?" His lips quivered.

"I don't know," she answered honestly. "We probably don't want to find out."

His red cheeks puffed out like balloons. "Fine! Have 'em!" He tossed them at Milly's feet. "Us gnobs know when we's beat!" He stomped his foot. "Just lets me alone!"

Milly nodded and lowered her hand. The light still hadn't faded. "Y-you should probably leave now."

"S-s-s-sure thing." And, just like that, the gnob was

gone, slipping and sliding his way from the alley.

Milly kneeled next to the flutterwishes. Their wings were still pinned. She looked at the light and exhaled. "Be free," she whispered, and pulled at one of the clothespins. It dissolved into the flame.

Her mouth hung open.

Her hand trembled.

"That worked," she stammered, still not quite believing it.

She moved from one flutterwish to the next, removing each of their shackles one by one. When she was finished, the red light vanished.

"Go on," she whispered. "You're free. Get out of here."

"Thank you, witchling."

Each of the flutterwishes chirped happily and flew lazy eights around her, teasing her hair and tickling her ears. She laughed as their feathers brushed against her skin.

"We're so happy you're here," they said. *"Life has been so much harder without witches."*

"What do you mean?" she said.

But they didn't answer. Instead, they shot upward and vanished into miniature clouds that had appeared out of thick air.[25]

---

[25] The whole notion of people pulling things out of thin air is a lie concocted by fake magicians who are too scared to reach into thick air. Thin air is the place where white lies and half-forgotten whispers drift about. *Thick* air is the home of deep hopes and heavy secrets.

She felt quite proud of herself, but also terrified. Milly stared at her hand. There was no more sign of the strange fire. No tingling or unfamiliar residue.

Milly snapped her fingers.

Nothing happened.

She pressed her fingers together to snap again.

Suddenly, two large hands grabbed hold of her—one on her shoulder, the other over her mouth. She tried to scream, but the hand was bigger than her entire head. Whoever it belonged to muffled her voice and pulled her into a wall.

No, not a wall, she realized. A face materialized above her, and she saw it was a small giant.[26]

"Not safe," the giant said. "Witches not good. Shadows come. Must hide."

And with that, the giant picked her up and tossed her into a giant-sized lunch basket. She landed in a half-eaten bowl of salad the size of a bed.

The basket must've been big even for the small giant, because he picked it up with both hands and carried it at a crooked angle.

The motion sent Milly slipping deeper into the bowl. She was tangled in a mess of cabbage leaves the size of her body and sliced carrots as big as her legs. Jostled back and forth, she tried to reach up and peek out of the basket. She saw that the giant was carrying her down the alley, away from

---

[26] Which is to say that he was still taller than even a large-sized man.

the tower, toward the outskirts on the other side of the city.

"Hey," she called out. "We're going the wrong way!"

"Hush make," the giant said. "Must hide."

Milly watched the townscape fly by through a thin crack in the weave, including the sight of a large roast pig being turned over an open fire.

She groaned, remembering her hunger, and dropped back down to the bottom of the basket. Sinking against the wall, she propped herself into place with her feet and tried to nibble on a whole floret of broccoli. She could barely get her teeth around it.

Frustrated, she pushed it to the side, lay down, and curled her arm around her head.

Maybe she shouldn't have followed her nose.

CHAPTER TEN
dinner with strangers in a house made of puzzles

WHEN THE BASKET hit the ground, Milly fell against a lone cabbage leaf and heard it crunch against her ribs. Tiny shafts of light leaked through the basket. She slipped her fingers into the holes and tried to peek through.

She heard voices. Then smelled feet.

"Horace, what are you hiding in that basket?"

"Found witchling."

"Found a what?!"

"Witchling. Girl child. Help hide."

"And you put her in your basket? My heavens, let her out. She must be suffocating in there."

The basket tipped wildly, and Milly grabbed for the edges.

"Horace, be careful with her!"

Milly screamed when she tumbled out of the basket, along with the massive veggies, onto someone's floor. Suffocating darkness surrounded her, and she whirled around to look for any source of light.

A large hand lifted the giant bowl off her head, and a smaller hand appeared in front of her face.

"Hello, dear."

Milly took the hand and was pulled to her feet. She wobbled for a moment, and the walls around her spun in circles. When she gained her footing, she could see the room she'd fallen into was the living room. Or the bathroom. Or a kitchen?

Actually, it didn't look like any of those.

And the walls wouldn't stop spinning.

"Don't worry. You're not seeing things—everything here is swirly." The woman giggled and twirled her finger in a circle.

Eyes adjusting to the light, Milly looked at the person who had helped her up. It was a woman with light-brown skin and short, wispy, bright-pink hair.

No, it was purple.

Now it was blue!

"Welcome to my house. Whole thing's one big puzzle." The woman grinned and spread her arms wide. "Like it?"

Milly looked around and realized that the room wasn't one room at all. It was a dozen rooms, all constantly folding into each other. Some walls ended where the roof began, floors acted as tables, chairs folded into cabinets. The back wall rotated, and a door appeared where a painting had been. The sink collapsed into the floor, replaced by several large cushions.

"How?" Milly said. "How do you tell what's what?"

"Easy!" the woman said, "Blue's for kitchen, green's for

bed, purple's bath, pink's the workshop, and so on and so forth."

Milly realized now, in the midst of the furniture moving and shifting, that everything was color-coded. And yet . . .

"It still doesn't make sense."

"Of course it doesn't! Makes it all the more fun." The floor shifted beneath them, and both the woman and Milly fell backward into seats. "Oh, I guess it's dinnertime!" A wall fell crashing down between Milly and the woman and the giant. An entire meal awaited them upon the newly set table. There was some sort of fried fish and sliced carrots the size of discs and broccoli heads the size of actual heads and grains of brown rice the length of noodles.

"You can tell me all about yourself while we eat. Dig in!"

The woman picked up one of the rice grains with her hand, popped a piece of fish on it, and shoved the whole thing in her mouth. She ate with one knee up on her chair and stared at Milly expectantly.

"It's guhd," she mumbled through the food, and gestured with her chin.

Milly glanced over at Horace, who was carefully picking up one of the carrot discs with his large fingers. The giant's hands and head looked too big for the rest of his gangly, relatively normal-sized frame. Normal if he were about twice his age, anyway.

He smiled shyly and picked up the plate so he could offer it to Milly. "Orange?"

Milly hesitated. What if the food was poisoned or something?

But the smell of it was too enticing. She tugged one of the oversized carrot pieces onto her plate. It took up the whole space. She scratched her head, then picked it up from both sides and took a big bite. It was much softer than the ones in the basket. It practically melted in her cheeks.

She sighed loudly, swallowed, then followed the woman's lead and tried some of the fish and rice.

Who cared if it was poisoned? It tasted *delicious*.

Maybe it was the hunger clouding her judgment, but she thought this was the best meal she'd ever eaten. Although the salt and pepper flakes were as big as her teeth, the flavor didn't seem the least bit overwhelming. She closed her eyes and enjoyed the taste and the warmth and the glorious smell that reminded her of ocean and wind and grass.

"So," the woman said, "who are you and why are you here and what did you do that would make Horace here call you a you-know-what?"

Milly swallowed, and all the warmth flooded out of her. She opened her eyes again and stared at her hands. They were quivering. "I—he tried to sell me wishes, so I freed them."

The woman scratched absentmindedly at a mark half hidden by her sleeve. "You mean Ned? He tried to get you to buy flutterwishes?"

"Horace saw." The giant made extravagant motions with his hands. "Girl use fire. Save them."

"Is that so?" The woman giggled. "Very interesting."

Milly stared at Horace, trying to figure out what he was doing with his hands.

"Tell me, little one, what's your name? Mine is Emm. It's short for something, but I don't remember what. I'm Nignip's registered puzzle-maker and resident mystery lady. I am *not* a witch." She winked.

"My name is Milly. It's not short for anything," she replied. Then, after a moment to think: "Is your house made of . . . magicks?"

"It's very nice to meet you, Milly. And yes, it is! It's very happy that you noticed." The house's gears churned out faster for a moment. "It was already magicks before the High Council set up their ridiculous zoning regulations, so there's nothing they can do about it!" She cackled. "Horace said you needed a place to hide. You're more than welcome to stay here as long as you like, though I don't recommend staying very long." She paused. "People aren't very keen about you-know-whats here. Say they're to blame for the shadow infestation."

"Shadow infestation?" Milly shook her head, thinking back to the hands and feet she kept seeing. "What is that, exactly?"

"No one knows." Emm picked at her teeth with a long branch. "Shadows started showing up after the war ended. Lots of people think it means the witches are coming back"—she winked again—"but that couldn't possibly be it. Have you seen a witch lately?"

Milly scratched her arm. "I'm not really sure if . . ."

Emm put the branch away and leaned forward. "Maybe I should ask that again. My dear Milly, have you seen a witch lately?"

Milly glanced at Horace, then back to Emm. Her hair was now a deep, dark red. The color of secrets.

"No?" Milly said.

"Didn't think so!" Emm's hair flashed to a bright white. She leaned back in her chair and put both her feet on the table. The wooden surface split apart and the floor spun a circle. When everything stopped moving, Milly saw that they were sitting side by side, facing a fireplace.

"Tell me, Milly," Emm said, pausing to pull out a block of wood and a small chisel. "Why are you in Nignip? Sightseeing? We are home to the world's most lopsided egg museum, if you're into that sort of thing. Whole thing sits on top of an empty tortoise shell."

"No. I . . . I'm looking for someone."

"Just any old someone?"

Milly didn't know how much information she should share. "My, um, sister."

"Ah." Emm nodded her head. "Always wanted to have one of those."

"She's not my real sister. We're orphans."

"Is there a difference?" Emm cut into the wood with a flat-edged knife. "Anyway, bad idea to nose around here. Dangerous place for witches, not that that would matter to you. Dangerous everywhere really, but especially here. High Council's really fussy."

Milly let out a long breath and finally asked the question she'd been wanting to ask this whole time. "Why do people hate witches so much, but not wizards?"

"One of life's great mysteries." Emm tossed the back of her hand against her forehead in exaggerated protest and sang: *"Witches like danger and strange happenstance / Wizards like borders and order in chance"*—she jumped up in her chair and grew louder—*"Witches like ends, friends, and bending bad rules! / Wizards like projects, profit, and tools / OH, PEOPLE OF NIGNIP, YOU SAD SILLY FOOLS / THE WIZARDS WILL ONE DAY TURN MAGICKS ON YOU!"* She fell back in her chair with a frown. "I shouldn't have improv'd that last line. The rhythm's all wrong."

Milly shook her head. That didn't answer her question at all. "Do you think they'll find out I'm a . . . you know?"

"Witches in Nignip?!" Emm gasped. "I've never heard anything so absurd. Have you, Horace?"

Horace stepped through a wall with a washcloth in his hand. "No, ma'am." He then returned to the other room, which looked like it was filling quickly with bubbles.

"Anyway, I doubt they notice much of anything nowadays. Seem they've been more focused on stopping the shadows than hunting—ahem, I mean *relocating*—any witches lately."

"But..." Milly sighed. This was so frustrating. "I thought you said the shadows came because of the witches?"

Emm rotated her wood block, and Milly saw that she was making some sort of small token. "Maybe they did, maybe they didn't. Or maybe they came because there aren't any witches left to stop them."

Milly stared at her.

Emm went back to her chiseling.

"Are the shadows good or bad?"

"Now that"—Emm paused to study the token in the firelight—"is an interesting question."

Milly waited for an answer, but Emm never continued. Instead she kept working on her project while Milly stared into the fire.

Milly stared for a very long time until she started to nod off. She felt her chin drop a couple times and would jerk up before nodding off again. All she could think about was shadows now. Slipping in and out of the garden back home, sometimes hanging outside the windows, but never coming in. The seat beneath her grew soft. She leaned back into it with a savage yawn. The arms of the chairs twisted into bed frames, and the back collapsed into a mattress. Her eyes started to flutter closed as the house grew dark. Before she knew it, she felt a large blanket cover her body.

Milly dreamed she was in St. George's garden, sifting

through ears of corn during the harvest. She glanced down over the countryside and saw the little heads of farmers with their ankles in the waters, tending to their rice farms. She turned her head toward the moss-bull and smiled.

Two pink bamboo blossoms had sprouted between its closed eyes.

She walked up to the moss-bull and pressed her forehead against his. He was so very soft and so very warm. She wondered if he'd ever open his eyes again.

"*Wake up.*" A soft breeze brushed against her exposed feet and she dug them deeper into the grass.

"I don't want to," she mumbled. "I'm so tired."

"*This is no place to sleep, little one. Wake up.*"

"Let me sleep."

"Milly? Milly, wake up!"

Milly snapped her eyes open and saw a long shadow-beast hovering over her. Now she saw not just hands and feet, but a face set in the middle of the creature. The thing had coals for eyes and what looked like dry, withered grass covering its body like many threads of hair.

Standing at the other side of the room, Emm held a crooked branch in one hand and the token in the other. Her sleeves had been pulled back to reveal bright, white stars on both her wrists. "Stay away!" she cried. Her hair burst into strands of aquamarine as a similar blue light erupted from her wand and knocked the beast into the walls.

Milly looked down. There was no blanket around her

feet, but a large transparent shadow covering her legs.

"Umalis makisuyo."

A little blue strand of light broke through the shadows, and they dissipated into the floor.

Milly scrambled up and climbed onto a nearby table. "What are they?!"

"No idea!" Emm picked Milly up off the table. "Horace! Come, you need to get Milly out of here."

Horace fell through a hole in the ceiling with his lunch basket in hand. "Horace sorry."

"Not your fault." Emm lifted Milly into the basket. "You let Horace know where it is you were headed."

"I—I need to see Hightop."

Horace gulped. "But he—"

"No buts," Emm said. "If that's where she needs to go, you take her there. And if you have to, be ready to do a lot of running."

"Yes, ma'am."

Milly grabbed the edge of the basket. She pulled herself halfway up. "Hold on. What about you?!"

Emm looked back. The shadow rematerialized, liquid-like limbs re-forming out of the wall. "You, my dear, are going to find your sister." She pressed the token into Milly's hand. It was carved in the likeness of three wind currents braided together. As soon as it touched her skin, the moon on her hand faded away. "And then the two of you are going right back home."

Milly picked it up with her other hand and put it in her pocket. As soon as it left her fingers, a faint outline of the moon started to re-manifest itself. She raised her head. "Will you be okay?"

Emm smiled, then pushed Milly's head gently back into the basket. Her hair had faded into a dull gray. "I'll be just fine."

The basket's lid shut, and Milly felt herself get pulled off the ground.

"Get out of here, Horace!"

Milly felt the basket swing high and over the half-giant's shoulder, then heard Horace's large footsteps stomp through the house. She peeked through a hole in the bottom of the basket. The shadow had grown larger and towered over Emm's now black-haired head. The fireplace held no light. The gears of the house groaned.

Emm raised her wand once more. A large flash of light exploded.

The house stopped moving.

CHAPTER ELEVEN, PART ONE
we're off to see the wizard!

MILLY POKED HER head out of Horace's basket as he trundled down the streets.

From this high up, the city's glass lanterns floated past at eye level. Their transparent orbs were filled with dozens of dancing, cool-colored lights bouncing to and fro. One glowed like burnt amethysts, the next like kernels of sapphire.

Over Horace's shoulder and past the lanterns ahead, Hightop's strangely leaning tower stared down with empty windows. A single cloud sat in the sky just above it. Licks of lightning crawled through the white puffs every so often, but there was never so much as a peep of thunder.

The closer Milly and Horace got, the more the tower seemed to lean, the bigger the cloud appeared, and the darker the streets grew.

Shadows. All along the ground.

These didn't move, not even when the nearby lights flickered. They appeared to stretch out from the center of the city, as if they had gotten frozen while crawling out of the tower itself. Milly couldn't tell whether it was her imagination, but they looked like hands and feet.

She shuddered and sunk deeper into the basket.

"You think Emm's okay?" she asked.

"Emm fine," Horace said, and though she didn't believe it, Milly was grateful for the lie.

Eventually, they neared the tower and the mysterious cloud. Now she could see that the tower wasn't just leaning. It was crooked, like a pencil broken in three pieces and then stacked back together very poorly. From beyond the tree line, an orange bead of light split the sky and painted the city in its soft glow. The people of Nignip awoke, unaware of the shadows that dissipated into the earth.

Horace shuddered. "Spooky house."

Milly patted the half-giant's shoulder. "You don't have to come with me if you don't want to."

Horace straightened his shoulders and shook his head. "Horace come. Horace brave."

Milly paused. "Thanks."

He nodded at her.

Horace put the basket down, and Milly climbed out. Holding his hand, she marched toward the tower. The half-giant lumbered just behind her until they arrived at the entrance. It was a large, oak door etched with drawings of what looked to be the wizard's exploits. There was one of him lassoing a wind. Another of him meeting with a coven of witches. There was even one of him sitting on top of a giant, lopsided egg.[27]

---

[27] The artist who designed this door had taken some very serious creative liberties.

Milly tilted her head. "He seems to think very highly of himself."

"Hightop proud. Hightop"—he pointed at a picture of Hightop fighting a giant—" '*hero.*' "[28]

Milly shivered. This was the person she needed to help her find Cilla? What would he do if he found out Milly was a . . . ? No, she couldn't think about that right now. Right now, her priority was getting her sister back.

"Here goes nothing," she whispered, and raised her fist to knock on the door.

"*Psst,*" a familiar voice said.

Milly looked up and saw Jasper's furry head poking out from a nearby window.

"Jasper!" she said, surprised by how happy her own voice was. "What are you doing here?"

"What am I doing here? Why are you so late?! Do you know how long I've been sleeping on this windowsill waiting for you to show up? Where have you been all night?"

"I . . . got hungry." Milly felt her cheeks burn.

"Oh." Jasper wasn't as scathing as she expected him to be. "I forgot food was a thing you humans needed. Sorry." Then he coughed and straightened up a bit. "All right, not

---

[28] History can be an ugly creature. Contrary to belief, it is not objective. It changes its skin every few years the same way a snake sheds his. Because of this, history has a hard time knowing the difference between good and evil. Or truth and lies. It feeds on the tales told by whoever is still living and gets fat on only the stories that get told.

about to get used to that. Who's your new friend?"

"This is Horace!"

Horace put his hand up, like he was waiting in school for the teacher to call on him.

". . . Yes?" Milly said.

"Who talk to?"

Milly scratched her head. "Oh, sorry. This is Jasper!"

Horace blinked. "Jasper is cat?"

"Yes."

"And cat talk?"

"Yes?" Milly glanced at Jasper, then back at the giant. "I'm sorry, can you not understand him?"

Horace shook his head. "Girl talk. Horace talk. Cat meow."

Jasper laughed. "Well, isn't this delightful! Our inability to communicate must be a byproduct of *someone* turning me into a *permanent cat*! Hello, Horace. You're a half-giant, aren't you? You speak grass tongue really well."

Milly tried to ignore the first half of that spiel. "Jasper said you're really good at speaking grass tongue."

Horace smiled wide. "Horace grow stone. Horace go school. Horace learn grass."[29]

---

[29] The giants of Arrett always referred to themselves as stone people because they came from the mountains and to almost everyone else as grass people because they came from the hills. Most giants found grass tongue very hard to get accustomed to, but Horace—being only half-giant—took it upon himself to speak both languages. Even if his grass father hadn't been around to teach him.

"Good for you, buddy." Jasper turned toward Milly. "Ready?"

Milly nodded.

"Good. Ask the big guy to lift you up to this window."

"What? Why?"

"So we don't have to bring him along, obviously. No offense to him, but we're trying to stay quiet. We can't have an entire half-giant wandering around with us."

Milly crossed her arms. "He's coming with us."

"Little person—"

"*Milly.* My name is Milly. And this is Horace and he is my friend and he's coming with us."

Horace was looking more and more uncomfortable as the conversation went on. "Horace want talk."

Milly and Jasper both turned to him.

"Jasper thinks you should stay here. I want you to come." She chewed on her bottom lip. "I guess I should have asked what you want to do."

Horace was quiet for a long time. He looked down at his hands and something in his eyes hardened. "Horace promise keep you safe. Horace stay. Keep watch. Wait till done." The half-giant stood beneath the window and turned around. "Climb up," he said. "Horace wait."

Milly hugged him tightly, then climbed up the half-giant's back and into the window. "Thank you," she said. "I promise we'll be back soon."

"Okay." The half-giant sounded nervous. "Quick please."

CHAPTER ELEVEN, PART TWO
a very unlikely favor

THE INSIDE OF the tower was very, very dark. Milly and Jasper snuck up its winding staircase with tentative steps. Along the walls were paintings and statues and busts of famous wizards and sorcerers and enchantresses and conjurers. Hightop had amassed quite the collection over the years. He'd even commissioned works of art in his own likeness. Milly paused by a rendition of Hightop riding a tornado. It glistened with various knife and brush strokes of oil layered on top of each other.

Milly rolled her eyes. The sooner they could be done with this, the better.

Our two friends passed by several rooms as they climbed. One was full of strange-looking spheres, all orbiting around a giant glowing orb in the middle. Another was a library with no floor, and bookshelves that stretched all the way around the wall. There was even an entire garden in one of the rooms, which Milly found fascinating until a small plant opened its petals to reveal tiny teeth and ate its much larger neighbor.

By this point, Milly's legs were starting to feel very stiff. With the exception of last night, Milly had been on her feet nonstop. She felt like a lumbering turtle. Made of lead. That had just finished an entire plate of eggplant lasagna the night before. Nevertheless, her frustration gave her energy to keep on keeping on, and that was all the motivation she really needed.[30]

After a considerable amount of time, the two finally made it to the top. They kept going until they found a door at the end of the stairwell, slightly cracked open. They heard someone curse from inside.

Milly and Jasper exchanged a look, then peeked through.

The tower's ceiling was split open, and a gnome sat on a broombranch above Hightop's head. Ned the gnob paced back and forth beneath him while Hightop sat in a chair occasionally tapping his foot against the floor.

"—I'm telling you! I saw a real live witch! She blasted me in the face, she did, and ruined my business."

"Your *illegal* business, you mean," the gnome said. "It's no secret that you've been engaged in black-market magicks for years. How do we know you're not just blaming your bad fortune on an innocent child?"

Ned jumped on a table and stomped his foot against it. "I may be dishonest, but I never lie! I knows what I saw. She was a witch. Her fingers were on fire and all."

The gnome sighed. "I suppose I can file it with the other reports, but you know nothing will come of it."

---

[30] "Keeping on" is a hard skill to master. It is not for the faint of heart or the slow of feet. Perhaps the worst part is that it's a survival skill. You only get to practice when you don't want to.

Hightop stood from his chair and drew his wand. "Hold on, friend. Let's give the man a moment. Tell me more about what you saw. What did this witch look like?"

"She was small. Wiry," Ned said. "Brown-skinned, with a ferocious look in her eye. Almost like a wild animal."

"And where did you say the fire came from? Her hand?"

"Yes, yes! There was a moon on her palm. Glowing red."

"And did you smell anything off? Any hint of something burnt?"

"Hightop—" the gnome said.

"Shh. Let me work."

"Now that you mention it, there was something funny. Like wet toast."

Hightop laughed. "It's all right, Mr. Gnob. We'll get all of this sorted out for you right quick."

"Hightop?" The gnome's voice squeaked. "Hightop, what are you—"

Hightop's wand came cracking down, and the gnob froze still. Milly gasped, covering her mouth with both hands.

"Hightop," the gnome said. "You know that the High Council highly disapproves of this methodology."

"The High Council doesn't need to know, Finnegan. And you aren't gonna tell them."

"Okay, but *if* they knew—"

"Stop worrying." Hightop pulled the wand back from the gnob's lips, and a long string of some strange purple substance came with it. "He'll be perfectly fine. He'll just be a little scatterbrained for a while. Here, hand me that bottle, will you?"

The gnome looked flustered, but he flew to the other end of the room and came back with a tiny glass. "I don't like this one bit."

Hightop shrugged. "Sometimes good guys have to get their hands dirty." He put the gnob's memory into the bottle and corked it, then quickly hid the wand in his sleeve. "There we go. All done."

Ned blinked and looked around the room. "What happened? Why am I here?"

Hightop smiled. "It's all right, sir. We'll have that problem sorted for you right quick! Now, if you would, the door's over there. I'll send the bill your way soon."

"I . . . um. Thank you?"

"Not at all." Hightop ushered him toward the door. Milly and Jasper pulled back and pressed themselves against the wall. "Have a good day, sir!"

Ned passed by Milly and Jasper, eyes glazed over. "Must be going mad," he muttered to himself. "Why the boggins would I come to Hightop, of all people? Oof, maybe it's this stomach. I feel queasy. I hope he didn't charge me too much for whatever this is."

When the gnob had turned the corner, Milly and Jasper exchanged a worried look, then edged forward to continue eavesdropping.

"—I'm sorry, Hightop, but the council simply cannot

endorse this venture of yours. We cannot allocate any more funds to this witch relocation project. You know that."

"But what about West Ernost? What about the witch in the woods? These gripes and gobblers have been infesting all of Arrett. You heard Ned. They're still out there! We need to make sure they're *all* accounted for."

The gnome narrowed his eyes. "They *are* accounted for. You said the puzzle-maker had been taken care of—"

"And the shadows came to her house anyway, yes, I know. But I don't think they found *her*. I think they were following someone else."

"What could possibly make you think that?"

"The puzzle-maker hasn't been trouble for years. I doubt she even remembers she used to be a witch."

"*Hightop.*" The gnome's voice dropped to a whisper. "Don't be so careless with the words you choose."

"What, 'witch'? Witch witch witch witch. You all need to stop being so scared. The shadows will be easily taken care of. It's these witches you need to be worried about."

"These . . . *witches* haven't been the problem lately. In fact, I've heard rumors in the council that we might need to reinstate them."

"What?! Why?"

"I think you know why."

"It's because you're scared, isn't it? You're scared of a handful of shadows."

"It's because the High Council is starting to doubt you've made any progress in this expedition of yours. Because maybe *certain people* realize it was a mistake to ban the witches to begin with! You ever think about that?" For the first time in the conversation, Finnegan grew stern. "How do we know the shadows and witches have any connection at all?"

"I told you that I was closing in on the case, didn't I? You've just got to give me more time."

"You've had time!" The gnome sighed and lowered his voice. "Look, Charles, we appreciate what you did for us during the war. We really do. But it's high time you realized that we don't need heroes anymore. We need consistency. And you, old friend, are bad at consistency. We can't continue to support this little crusade of yours."

"You mean *you* can't."

The gnome shrugged. "I'm just a messenger."

"So what does that mean? I'm irrelevant?"

"Exactly that." The gnome shook his head. "I know it's hard to hear, but maybe you should take some time off. Relax. Find a *new* hobby that isn't just chasing down winds and sniffing out witches. They've learned their lesson. I know you've got personal business in this—"

Hightop pointed one of his fingers in the gnome's face. "Don't."

The gnome backed away. "I know you *care,* but why don't

you leave them be and let *us* deal with the shadows?"

Hightop groaned dramatically. "If you just give me a little more time, I can—"

"*No!*" A loud chorus of voices boomed out from the cloud above them like a thunderclap.

Hightop's shoulders slumped. It seemed all the fight had left him.

"You heard them." The gnome turned his broombranch around. "Goodbye, Hightop. Take care of yourself. If anything changes, I'll be in touch."

The gnome shot up through the ceiling and toward the singular cloud that had been sitting above Hightop's tower. Milly squinted and held her breath. It wasn't a cloud. It was a giant, floating castle.

There was a sign on its archway that read *The High Council of Pointy Hats and Flying Broomsticks: Ask and We Shall Provide.* Those golden words had been plastered over something much older, words engraved into the stonework that said *Be kind and do no harm.* As soon as the gnome disappeared behind the gates, the cloud made a loud rumbling sound and trundled away.

"That's fine! I was done talking anyway! Don't come crawling back to me when the shadows eat holes in your bedsheets!" Hightop shook his fist, then halfheartedly swung his hand in the air. "Whatever." He collapsed onto his back in the middle of the table and picked up a handheld mirror to commiserate with himself. "We had a good run. Still got our looks, so that's something. And free drinks at the Quacking Dragon for life. And . . . well, I guess that's it. BAH." He cast the mirror aside and let it crack against the floor. A second later, the mirror pulled all its glass shards back together and was good as new. "I just need a way into the forest," he muttered. "That witch's magicks are too strong, but maybe if I . . ." He stopped midsentence, jolted up, and froze with his mouth pried open in a crooked posture.

"*ACHOO!!!*"

His sneeze echoed through the entire room. Hightop searched for a tissue and blew his very red nose. "Why are my allergies acting up? There's no— *achoo!*" He locked eyes with Jasper, then Milly, and fell backward off the table.

Milly winced at the sound. She pushed open the door and ran over. "You okay?"

Hightop waved his hand several times "I'm fine. Perfectly, perfectly fine." He propped himself up and squinted at Milly's face. "Do I know you? Did you try to sell me mint pastries last week?"

Milly shook her head. She opened her mouth to explain, but he interrupted.

"Oh, were you the intern whose application I rejected? Gracious, aren't you the determined one."

"No, I—"

"Of course! An autograph. That's what you want." He

unwrinkled the paper he'd blown his nose in and tried to scribble his name across the bottom. "Here you go."

"Gross," Jasper said, finally having made his way across the room.

Milly jerked away from it. She fiddled with the token in her pocket. "I'm not here for your snotty autograph! I'm here because I need to save my sister!"

"Your sister?" Hightop looked her up and down, and the light of recognition finally filled his eyes. "Oh. You're from that ragged little orphanage. I'm sorry. All you kids look the same. Amazing! What are you doing all the way out here? And how'd you get through the woods? You're not a . . ." He narrowed his eyes and took a long, hard sniff. Suddenly, his gray eyes darkened and he grabbed Milly's wrist. "Aha!"

Her blank palm stared up at them.

"Let go of her!" Jasper hissed.

"Damn it all!" Hightop didn't acknowledge the cat, but he did let go. "You're not a witch."

Milly pulled her hand back and continued clutching the wooden token Emm made in her pocket. Her wrist throbbed. Was Hightop not able to see the mark? Did he not smell the magicks off her?

She swallowed, but her throat was day.

It didn't seem to matter. The wizard had already gotten distracted and was rummaging around the room for something.

"You were hunting the witch," she said. "I need your help to find her."

The wizard chuckled. "*Hunting* is such a primal term. I prefer *procuring*. Much more sophisticated. Why do you need my help? It seems like you've done a pretty good job getting all the way out here yourself."

"I lost the trail," she replied. "Out by the river."

"Oh?" The wizard's eyes gleamed for a second. "Oh! The *river*. Yes, you mean the forest river? You know, little girl, on second thought I think we might just be able to help each other. I also lost her, you see, but I know exactly where she is."

"So the reason you haven't gotten her yet is . . . ?"

"Let's just say that I, for reasons I don't feel like getting into, am currently incapable of retrieving her. But!" The wizard jumped up and patted Milly's head. "As someone completely lacking in magicks of any kind, you are a prime candidate!"

He ran over to another side of the room and started fidgeting with some of his instruments.

"Wait," Milly said. "What does that mean?"

"I—*achoo!*—please keep that cat away from me." The wizard swung a broken umbrella at Jasper.

Jasper hissed before retreating to the door. "Obviously, I'm not needed or welcome here," he said. "I'll wait for you outside. Scream if you need me."

Milly opened her mouth, but the cat had already departed. She sighed and followed the wizard around the room as he constructed a haphazard contraption of metal objects collected from random nooks and crannies. He talked all the while. "Your sister's in the Needsy Woods."

Milly felt her throat tighten. Cilla had been there all along?

"I can't explain how I know, but she got away from that old ragged lady and fell in. I'd go in there and get her myself, obviously, except I can't. There's a witch in those woods, more malicious and powerful than any I've ever heard of, who has used powerful magicks to keep me out—I've been trying to get her to move for years, heard she's protecting the last broombranches or something. I don't know how, but that's that. You, however! You managed to walk through the woods without so much as a scratch. At least—" He paused. "I assume you walked."

Milly wondered if she should elaborate, but she only nodded.

"Excellent. That means whatever magicks that witch is using to keep me out don't work on you. Though I can't explain why—"

"Sounds like there's a lot you can't explain."

"I'm ignoring that. See this?" He pointed at his own face. "IGNORING IT. What matters is you can get in and destroy her magicks with *this*." Hightop held up the contraption he'd been making. It was a multi-edged blade, sticking out in several twisted directions from where the handle was. "So how about it?"

"How about what?"

"Will you do me a favor?"[31]

She didn't answer, not sure why this powerful wizard was asking her for anything.

"You want your sister back, don't you?"

She nodded. Reluctantly.

"And I'm the one you came to for help, aren't I?"

She hesitated, then nodded again. "What do you want me to do?"

"Excellent!" He wrapped the blade in a cloth and handed it to Milly. "Now, you be extremely careful with that. It's not something you should just be swinging about willy-nilly. It's dangerous. You'll have to find the heart of the woods—it's inside a giant tree, you can't miss it—and you'll plunge that deep in there. Make sure to twist it a couple times for good measure. Hopefully that'll be enough to break the magicks and let me come in. Then we can take care of your sister and whatnot."

---

[31] Favors are a dangerous business to get into. Most businesspeople in the Favors industry like conspiring with Shady Dealings and delegating in Strings Attached. Many of them are white-collar criminals, playing with the Gray Market and selling Favors back into the economy for half their market value. If anyone ever asks you to deal in Favors, hold one firmly in your hand and make sure it's real. Bite on the edges with your teeth if you must. Study it under the brightest light you have.

"Will my sister be okay?" Milly held the object tightly, but warily.

"I'm sure she'll be more than fine. Hopefully. Who knows what that witch would do if she's found her? That's another thing!" The wizard stopped everything and held Milly's shoulders. "You must make sure to never, ever talk to the Witch of the Wasted Woods. She is powerful and dangerous and will do whatever she can to make you think she's your friend. But she's not. She's a *witch*. She's a liar and a fraud and *must* be dealt with."

Milly's brow started to sweat. "A-are all witches bad?"

Hightop stared deep into her eyes. "Your sister isn't a witch, is she?"

"Of course not!" She felt her cheeks burn.

"It's okay if she is." Hightop smiled. "If she hasn't awakened her power, there's hope for her yet. I'll bring her to the High Council, and we'll make sure to take *very good* care of her. Okay? All witches can be unmade if we start early enough. Besides," he mumbled, mostly to himself, "most wizards were witches once . . ."

Milly nodded timidly. She knew what she should have said, but she was too scared.

"Anyway! I believe in you, little one. All of Arrett does!" He lowered his voice. "Don't let us down."

CHAPTER TWELVE
the house of a witch terrible and beautiful

UNDER HIGHTOP'S INSTRUCTION, Milly, Jasper, and Horace scurried around the perimeter of Nignip in order to avoid being seen by anyone from the High Council or a particular gnob. Milly definitely didn't want to see Ned, whose befuddled brain she felt a little responsible for.

"It's not that you'll get in trouble," Hightop had explained when telling her the plan. "It's just that I'd rather anyone not ask questions."

"I won't tell anyone."

"Good. Not even that half-giant napping outside my window."

"Why not?"

"Secrets must *always* be kept. You can trust me. I'm an adult."

Considering that she didn't really feel like answering questions either, Milly was more than happy to comply, even if she didn't feel good about it. Something about the way Hightop said "secrets" made the word feel dirty. But she needed to get Cilla back, and she'd do anything to make that happen. Even if it meant keeping one sad adult's stupid secrets.

Besides, she also wanted to avoid making Horace's life any more complicated. She glanced over at him. The half-giant had been quiet the entire day. She was pretty sure she was the reason the shadows had chased her to the witch's house; it seemed like everything she did only made things worse for everyone around her. She hoped she could make it up to him when this was all over.

She felt inside the messenger bag at her waist, clenching the padded blade with one hand and pinching the token between her fingers with the other.

First she had to save Cilla. Through any means necessary.

The three of them arrived at the edge of the woods by midday. Milly had given the half-giant multiple chances to stay behind, but he kept insisting on coming along. At first Jasper complained about it, but Milly felt obligated to let him tag along. It was kind of her fault he didn't have a house anymore.

Clouds had obscured the sun from sight, and a light mist filled the air. It was hard to see very far into the woods because of the fog settling between the trees. Milly looked from her friend to the cat.

"Are you guys ready to do this?" she asked.

"Absolutely!" Jasper said. He jumped forward and stretched his legs.

Horace looked down at the cat with a confused look, then grunted.

"I think the big guy said yes."

Milly let out a big breath. "Here we go."

Jasper led the way, followed by Milly, then Horace. Jasper's tail popped out of the fog, which came up to Milly's knees and Horace's shins. Our little train of vagabonds wove through the bamboo, deeper and deeper into the forest. Jasper tried to sniff out any trace of magicks, but he couldn't find anything, so he had to lead by instinct.

Milly spent most of her time watching the trees, constantly on edge, wondering if the shadows would come for them.

She knew she must be a witch. There wasn't any way to keep denying it. Those shadows hadn't come for Emm. They came for her. The old witch didn't want Cilla. The old witch wanted *her*. If anyone knew who she really was—*what she really was*—who knew how they would react? She didn't want to be a witch. Magicks had done nothing but make her life worse at every turn. She couldn't help but feel as if something deep inside her was very, very wrong. Broken. Sick. Maybe evil.

She didn't want Cilla to have to live with that. Not even the assumption of it. The idea that people were hunting Cilla down for something she wasn't almost felt worse than if her sister had been the witch all along.

Milly took in several shallow breaths and tried to calm her rapidly beating heart.

Maybe Cilla was okay. She'd gotten away from the witch on her own, after all. Who knew what else she was capable of?

"We're here," Jasper said.

Milly looked up and saw the giant tree. It wore such different clothes in the mist. The cold air framed its hanging branches like hollowed-out ghosts and made the holes in its bark look like grimacing mouths, as if the tree was eternally mourning. None of the broombranches made so much as a rustle. Milly wondered if they were sleeping or if they were scared.

Now that she had the chance to properly study the tree, Milly saw the vines clawing pathways up its trunk. The base where the door was looked almost like a stone planted in the ground. A wild stone that had been watered and given moonlight and care, grown like a plant, twisting upward and outward with the rest of the tree.

She wasn't really sure what to do except walk up to the front door.

"You two stay here." The weight of the blade pulled down on her shoulders. "I need to do this alone."

"What?" Jasper said, "Don't be stupid. We can let the half-giant keep watch if you want, but I should at least—"

"Horace come."

Milly sighed. "Do whatever you want."

She turned toward the house, looked both ways, and stepped out from the trees. A loud *thud* came from behind her, and she looked back to see that Horace had tripped over Jasper.

"*Shh!*" she hissed, ushering them backward.

The half-giant scuttled back into the woods sheepishly and gave her a thumbs up.

Jasper huffed. "I suppose I'll keep watch."

Milly waited, but no one came out from the house. She held her breath and stepped out again. This time she was careful with her feet. She noticed the garden she'd trampled over last time had been replotted, and several stalks were being held up by support stakes. It wasn't until she'd gotten close to the door that she heard the soft singing of the witch drift toward her. She tiptoed around the tree and saw the witch kneeling in the dirt, gardening while she sang:

> *"Skin and bones, eyes and toes*
> *In my soup, the whole thing goes*
> *Hairs and nails, not for me*
> *Don't like things stuck in my teeth*
> *Fingers, ears, noses, tails*
> *If you get desperate, eat a snail . . ."*

Milly shuddered and snuck to the back door, which had been left open. She stared into the house. It smelled much nicer than she expected. There was incense burning from somewhere inside, filling the house with a thick, oaky smell.

Milly covered her nose with her shirt and breathed through her mouth. She didn't know if the smell itself was enchanted, but she could never be too careful.

She crept through the first hallway. Two doors lined it on

both sides. She opened the first one and found a tiny study full of books and plants and crystals and dishes. No sign of Cilla. The next door led to a staircase made of twisted tree limbs leading up. Where would a tree's heart be? Probably in the opposite direction. The next door she opened was a black, shapeless void. A rush of wind tried to pull her in, and she propped herself against the doorframe.

"Bad bad bad," she said to herself, and shut it.

The last one looked like the oldest of the four doors. Dust covered the handle, and a soft blue light came from beneath. She turned the handle and the door groaned open, revealing a strange tunnel full of gemstones. A large, luminescent cobweb lay across the pathway.

Our brave, scared hero studied the hole. It seemed to angle downward, leading somewhere below the house.

Milly almost wished she'd hear a wind or see a ghost or . . . something. Anything but the total silence that closed in around her thicker than any blanket ever had.

She groaned.

Of course she was going in. The curiosity burned through her like a piece of hot coal in a bed of ice—and perhaps there was some clue to where her sister had gone through here.

Milly entered the tunnel and tried to push the web to the side. To her surprise, it moved like a curtain. When she had passed through, the web fell back across the entrance unbroken.

The girl gulped but continued. The passage wound around

a few times, twisting and turning and always leading further down. Its insides were lit by large clusters of quartz crystals glowing with an inner light, ensuring that the entirety of the floor was visible.[32]

The longer she walked, the less uncertain she became. This had to be where the heart of the tree was.

After what felt like more than enough walking, Milly arrived at a dead end with a trapdoor. She knelt down and blew at the engraving in the floor, revealing lines cut deep into the stone beneath all the dust.

It read: *What's the Magick Word?*

Magick word? What magick word? That could be literally any word!

She cycled through some of the words she thought she'd read in books before, but she had no idea how to even pronounce any of them.

What was the word she kept hearing the witches use?

"Makisuyo?"

The door creaked open.

A ladder dressed in glowing silver dust led to the floor below. Milly climbed down.

Roots twisted between each other in the ceiling and the walls. Various shelves wrapped around the room, covered in

---

[32] By this point, Milly had more than mastered the art of Keeping On. Even so, she was glad that she didn't have to face the even more horrible art of Walking in the Dark. There are some fears in life that we can beat with enough time and experience. Others have the unfortunate habit of sticking around.

all manner of vials and bottles and jars, all differing shades and shapes and colors. And there, in the center, was a giant pulsing gem. It sat in the tangle of roots spreading outward. She wasn't quite sure what color to call it. It was pink and blue and purple and green all at once. Nor was she sure what shape to name it. It looked like both a flower and a stone. All she knew was there could be no doubt about what the gem was.

It was the tree's heart.

Milly searched through the shelves leading to the center of the room. The glassware had been labeled according to names of people and places. One shelf was dedicated to Nignip, one to Delfin, one for West Ernost, another for East Ernost.

Milly blinked. East Ernost's shelf was entirely empty except for four very old, very tiny bottles. Three of them had been tied together and shared a single parchment label.

The last vial said *St. George's.*

Milly gulped. What did this all mean? How was this witch connected to St. George's? To Hightop? To the shadows?

Why was there was a bottle with her home's name on it?

Milly walked to the shelf and stood up on her tippy-toes. She grabbed the one that said *St. George's.* The bottled memory—for that's what these were, memories—was ice-cold and dark as mud.

Flecks of dull green swam around in the liquid. She wiped the dust from the bottle with her thumb and stared into her own reflection. Her eyes were large and sad. Her hair tousled.

Bottom lip cracked. It hadn't even been one week since she'd left St. George's, but she already barely recognized herself.

She wondered if the others were okay.

Milly stuffed the bottle in her pocket and turned her attention to the heart of the tree.

"Okay," she said to herself. "I can do this."

Milly drew the unwieldy object from her bag and unwrapped the blade. The gemstone pulsed before her, steady and calm. Her palm began to itch. She gulped. The broken moon started to manifest itself, burning back onto her hand. She reached for Emm's token but as soon as she pulled it out, a sliver of light spilled from the gem and made the moon shine even brighter.

Vicious green leaves flew from the heart and melted into her skin, as if the heart was trying to ward her off.

But Milly barely noticed them. She closed her eyes, ignoring the guilt worming through her stomach. She needed to get her sister back.

The longer she held the blade, the more her hand burned.

She gritted her teeth.

She raised her hand.

She plunged the blade into the heart. But it barely pierced through.

A quiet rage filled Milly. She couldn't let this stupid tree get between her and her sister. She pulled the blade back and pushed again. Again, something kept it from reaching the center of the heart.

Milly raised the blade above her head one more time.

"Give me back my sister!"

She stabbed the heart, and this time the blade pierced through. Milly closed her eyes so she didn't have to see her handiwork, attacking it over and over.

She could feel the heart weaken beneath her hands, its light dimming with every blow.

"Milly?"

Milly's eyes snapped open, and she dropped the blade. She spun around and saw a face staring out at her from beneath the ladder. It was her. Same mussed-up hair. Same sleepy eyes.

"Cilla!"

THE SECOND HIATUS
some broombranches just really want to play

AFTER SHOWING THE witch her stained hands, Cilla felt a rush of wind pull her and the witch up into the sky. The force ripped Junebug from her arms. For a brief second, she hovered in the moonlight, neither rising nor falling. Then . . .

A broombranch rocketed beneath them and carried her off with the witch.

She held on to the branch with one tight fist and on to the book with the other. She could see that the broombranch had letters engraved into its wood. *H.C. . . . something.*

Cilla held her breath to keep from screaming as they tore through the sky at a frightening speed. The ground beneath them vanished into a blurry patchwork of colors. She heard the witch's laughter fill her ears as they ripped through a cloud. The soft impact left her clothes damp.

Cilla shivered against the harsh winds. They were wild and violent, tearing and pulling. It was like they were trying to yank her off. The broombranch buckled beneath them and ducked below another cloud. She saw that they were approaching a forest.

The witch sitting ahead of her cursed at the broombranch

as it struggled to fly. Cilla tried to see if the witch would notice, then bent down and ripped a page out of the book with her teeth. She dropped it and looked back to see it fluttering toward the ground. Cilla grinned, then started to rip out more pages, determined to leave a trail.

All of a sudden, something whipped by them.

The witch cursed again.

Cilla tried to figure out what was going on, but they were going so fast that all she could do was keep ripping pages and hope she wouldn't fall.

Whatever it was whipped by Cilla's head, tossing her hair.

"Leave us alone, you pesky branch!" the witch said.

Cilla looked up just in time to see a wild broombranch whip around them. The one they were riding bucked in response, as if it wanted to join in the fun.

"Those liars told me this branch was already domesticated!" The witch pulled out her wand and wove a wicked spell. "I command you to ignore that branch and *take me home.*"

The branch shivered beneath Cilla, and she saw its wood darken between her fingers. It was . . . changing. It was in pain.

The other broombranch made a loud rustling noise and flew at the witch.

The witch ducked and aimed at the branch. "Now for *you.*"

Cilla finally found her voice and grabbed the witch's arm. "Leave it alone!"

"What the—unhand me, child!"

The two of them corkscrewed through the sky, neither in control as they wrestled over the wand.

"*Let go!*" the witch said.

"You'll hurt it!"

Cilla let go of the book and pulled at the witch's wand with both hands. "Ha!" she shouted, tilting too far and falling from the branch.

"Aaaaaaaaaaaaah."

She looked down to see the forest approaching fast.

There was no one to catch her this time. Was this how she'd die?

The forest rustled violently for a moment. Dozens more broombranches flew out of the trees and surrounded Cilla in their wild flurry of yellow leaves. They brushed by her cheeks and arms and legs, slowing her fall until she landed with a very soft *plop* in the shallow part of a creek.

She laughed as the broombranches rustled around and above her before darting away and toward the witch. They clacked and chattered angrily.

Something tapped against her foot. She looked down and saw the book she'd dropped had drifted down the creek. Almost like it had followed her. She picked it up and stared at its soggy cover, then let out a frustrated growl and threw it into the deepest part of the waters.

"Stay out of my life!"

Cilla watched until the book floated out of sight, then nodded to herself. That was that. She looked up and saw the witch now busy with the dozens of broombranches attacking her. Cilla pulled herself up out of the creek and ran into the woods.

Like I said, some girls are just really good at running.

CHAPTER THIRTEEN
in the heart of the woods

THE TWO GIRLS held each other in a tight embrace for a very long while. By the time they let go, Milly had run out of *I'm sorrys* to give, and Cilla had soaked through Milly's shirt with tears.

"What are you doing here?" Milly managed to say. "Are you okay? Is the witch keeping you captive?"

Cilla shook her head. "No, she's a good witch. Like you! Her name is Edaline. She's been keeping us—me—safe."

"Safe? From who?"

"The witch who took me! Her name is Lilith. She's not nice at all. But she can't get into the woods. Edaline sent broombranches to chase her away. She said that as long as I stay with her, I'll be fine."

Milly's stomach tightened. "But we have to go home, Cilla."

"Why? I like it here. I think you would too. There's magicks all over the place. Maybe Edaline could teach you how to be a better w   "

"Cilla."

Cilla frowned. "What's wrong?"

"We can't stay here. I need to bring you back."

"No." Cilla's breathing quickened. "Edaline treats me seriously. All anyone at home wants to do is treat me like I'm stupid. Or wrong. I don't want to go back. I want to be a witch, too! I want to . . . I want to belong."

"But, Cilla, St. George's *is* where you belong."

"Do you feel like you belong?"

Milly sighed. "Don't be silly. You know we have to go back."

"You can't make me!" Cilla turned away. "You'll never understand me."

Milly didn't know what to say.

The blade clattered onto the ground. Milly spun around at the noise and saw a large gash in the tree's heart. She gulped.

Cilla stared at the blade and sniffed. "What were you doing?"

Milly felt her throat tighten. "I was trying to rescue you."

"But why—"

"I was just trying to—"

Cilla glared. "You were trying to kill the tree, weren't you?"

"I . . ."

"You were!" She turned around and ran. Right into the Witch of the Wasted Woods.

"Oh my!" The witch, who'd just finished climbing down

the ladder, looked taken aback. She put her hand on Cilla's head. "What are you doing here? Why are you crying? Are you . . . ?" She trailed off when she saw Milly and the tree. Her jaw visibly tightened. "Is this your sister?"

Cilla nodded into the witch's shirt.

"Cilla, do you want to head upstairs while I talk to your sister?"

Cilla nodded again, wiped her face across the witch's garments, and then climbed up the ladder.

The witch didn't seem to notice the snot now on her clothes. Instead, she simply stood and studied Milly for a long moment.

Milly stood and watched too, unsure what to do. The witch was much younger than she'd expected, barely even ten years older than Milly.

The witch gave a deep sigh and gestured toward a stool. "Would you like to sit down?"

Milly crossed her arms to distract herself from her throbbing palm. "I'd like to stand."

The witch scrunched up her nose. Milly couldn't tell if she was angry or amused. "If that's what you prefer." She leaned on the table opposite Milly and studied the blade on the floor. After she breathed deeply for a few moments, her face softened.

"Did Hightop send you here?" the witch asked, her voice much gentler.

Milly didn't respond. She studied the witch, waiting for her to try to cast a curse or something. The witch didn't seem to be bothered. In fact, by the sad resignation in her voice, it sounded like she was used to being treated this way.

"It's okay," the witch said. "You don't have to answer if you don't want to. Although if you try to hurt my broom-branches or their mother again, I'm afraid I will have to ask you to leave." She fidgeted with her sleeves, revealing markings along her wrists that disappeared down her fore-arms. "I won't hurt you, but you should know that these woods are important to me. I can't let you do anything to wreck them."

Milly didn't know what to say, but she did feel a little bad. "I'm . . . sorry," she managed. "I didn't know the broom-branches were alive until one of them talked to me."

The witch nodded. "His name is Ash. I'm sure he'll for-give you if you ask. But please don't do that again. Many of the young broombranches have never been ridden before."

Milly gulped. "I'm also sorry for ruining your garden."

"Apology accepted." The witch dipped her head. "Thank you."

Milly started to relax her tight shoulders, though she didn't let her guard down. Why was she apologizing so much? Even when she thought she was doing good, she couldn't help but feel guilty. "Cilla said your name is Edaline?"

Edaline smiled. "Yes. And you are Milly?"

Milly nodded.

"It is very nice to meet you. Cilla talks a lot about you. She said you're a witch."

At that, Milly's muscles tightened again. She felt her hand burn and clenched it tight.

"Cilla also told me you don't really want to be a witch." Edaline frowned. "Which makes sense. I guess you haven't been given reason to want to be."

Milly still wasn't entirely sure what to say, but it felt wrong to stay silent. "Witches destroyed my home. Witches brought the shadows."

Edaline's voice sounded hurt. "Is that how the stories go?"

A dozen thoughts raced through Milly's mind. *Why am I still talking to the witch? Hightop told me not to. I should just get Cilla and leave.* "Can you tell me none of it is true?"

"Would you believe me if I could?"

Of course not! But what if she has answers? What if every-thing I learned about witches is wrong? What if it's possible for me to be a good witch? Milly faltered, not sure if it was safe to keep asking those kinds of questions. "I don't know."

Edaline sighed and glanced down at the floor. "Witches have taken the blame for most of this world's problems because there aren't enough of us left to say otherwise."

She doesn't seem evil. She seems . . . hurt. Sad. "It was a witch that took my sister."

The witch took a long breath. "I know. I'm sorry. I don't expect to change your mind about us."

I don't want to feel pity! I want to be angry! Milly stared for a moment, then nodded. "What about Cilla?"

"What do you mean?"

"She needs to come back to St. George's, but she wants to stay here with you and be a . . . witch."

"She's safe here, if that's what concerns you. I know you care about your sister, but I also can't, in good conscience, let you take Cilla out of these woods if she doesn't want to leave."

Milly's panic returned in full force, and she reached for the blade.

Edaline put her hands up. "Sorry, I won't stop you if you want to leave. But I just think you should talk to Cilla first and figure out what it is that she really wants. Anyways, it wouldn't be a good idea to leave immediately if she's still being hunted, even with that charm you're holding."

How did she know?! Milly tightened her fist around the braided-wind token. "How did you know?"

"I'd know her work anywhere. I used to dabble in charms too, but Emm's always been better at them. Would have made a fine enchantress if they'd let her." Edaline smiled. "That one's quite effective. I didn't catch a whiff of you when you snuck into my house. I bet it worked on Hightop too."

"You know Emm?"

Edaline's smile remained, though her eyes dimmed. "Yes, she's—well. I guess there's no point in hiding it. Emm's my sister."

Guilt settled in Milly's stomach like molasses. What was she supposed to say now? Maybe Cilla was almost right. Maybe not all witches meant to be bad. Maybe witches were cursed to be bad no matter how hard they tried to be good. Could someone be born bad? It certainly felt like she was.

"If you don't mind me asking, how was she doing when you saw her?"

"I think . . . I think you should talk to Horace," Milly said.

"Oh, is he here?" Edaline's eyes lit up. "I haven't seen that boy since he was practically a pebble. He probably won't remember me."

Milly slowly nodded. "He's outside."

Edaline stood up from the table and extended her hand. "Is it okay with you if we head up?"

Milly paused, then walked forward without taking the witch's hand.

Edaline pulled her hand back. "Oh, before we go, may I ask you to please put that awful thing away? I don't want the broombranches to be scared."

Milly looked back at the metal blade. It shimmered on the ground, stained in a myriad of colors. She picked up the cloth and wrapped the blade. The weight of it felt like death in her hands. She stuffed it back into her bag; she deeply hoped she'd never have to use it again. She glanced back at the heart. "Did I—Will it be okay?"

Edaline ran her hand over the heart. It glowed softly against her fingers. She answered without turning toward Milly. "I'm sure she'll be just fine."

Milly had no idea what to believe anymore.

CHAPTER FOURTEEN
a good witch is nothing without regrets

MILLY SAT ON the upper half of the bunk bed she was sharing with Cilla. Cilla hadn't talked to her all day. Talking to Edaline had given Milly a lot to think about, but it didn't do anything to change her mind about Cilla. She needed to take the younger girl home. Doris would be worried sick about them.

On the opposite side of the room, Horace sprawled across the floor. (There hadn't been a bed big enough to fit him.) Once he'd told Edaline about the shadows attacking her sister, Horace had been quiet, too. The only one who continued talking to Milly was Jasper, which felt oddly comforting and lonesome all at once.

For the past hour, Milly had been staring at the ceiling made of moving broomsticks, fiddling with the bottle she'd taken from downstairs. She knew she probably shouldn't try to open it, especially if the memory didn't belong to her, but she didn't know who was telling the truth anymore. She didn't even know if she was telling the truth to herself.

Maybe, just maybe, the answer lay in this bottled memory.

Milly had been wrestling with what she should do ever since the others went to bed. Every conclusion she came to felt wrong.

But her curiosity burned stronger than ever.[33]

The bottle smelled of deep, old magicks. For the first time in her life, Milly felt like she could actually understand what it was she was smelling.

But that didn't mean she should open it, did it?

She groaned into her pillow. She wished she could ask someone for help. Anyone.

She lifted her head from the pillows and looked at the bottle again. Its dark liquid appeared even blacker now. Almost like ink.

Milly sat up and looked around the room. Horace snored loudly from the floor. When she peeked over the edge of her bed, she saw Cilla curled into a ball. Over by the open window, Jasper stared out into the woods without a word. The wind rustled against his fur.

Milly withdrew beneath her sheets and popped off the cork. It didn't smell as horrible as she thought it would. It was like an overripened banana, on the cusp of becoming rotten but not quite. Perfect for making banana bread.

Here goes nothing.

---

[33] You've likely heard it said that "curiosity killed the cat." It's often given as a warning to prevent you from taking unnecessary risks in your life. You know, like touching hot pots or crossing the road without looking both ways. But there are three universal truths that we don't say: 1) Curiosity is very convincing, sometimes more so than death. 2) Girls are incredibly curious, sometimes more so than cats. 3) Curiosity doesn't always result in death; sometimes it ends in something worse.

She tilted the whole thing into her mouth and swallowed before she could regret it.

The memory tasted as sweet and brisk as an ocean of apples stirred by warm summer winds. It sent a happy chill down Milly's throat, cool and warm all at once. But then, halfway through, it turned bitter. As if the apples had been picked too late, as if the winds had been bitten by an autumn chill. By the time the memory settled in her gut, it sunk like a cold stone.

She dropped the empty bottle onto her mattress.

Scenery faded in like watercolors spilling shapes onto a blank canvas. First a woman's crying. Then the smell of old bread. A ceiling with painted moons and stars. A window. A crib. A cold breeze.

"Milly, come here, please," said a voice.

Milly felt the head she was peering out of turn toward the voice. She saw a woman with brown skin and curly hair and eyes just like hers. She realized this wasn't Edaline's memory.

It was hers.

The woman motioned with her hand. "We have to go."

Milly turned back toward the crib. A baby reached up with tiny, wandering fingers.

"Can I hold her?" Milly said.

"Okay, but be careful. She's still very little."

This past version of Milly reached down to pick up a baby Cilla. Clutching the child to her chest, Milly followed the woman toward the door.

"Where are we going?" Milly said.

"Across the border."

"Why?"

"It's not safe here anymore."

Milly felt the woman's hand on her shoulder. She heard a woman crying from behind, but the memory wouldn't turn to see who it was. Milly's mother opened the door. A howling wind, the source of the cold, rushed in, and a bright light flooded her vision.

When she could see again, she was standing in a different time at the opening of St. George's. Her mother's hand was no longer on her shoulder, and she was holding Cilla in a thick blanket.

Her legs ached. She felt a thick weight pressing down on her shoulders. Before her stood a young Doris with hair the color of a dull fire.

"Who are you?" Doris said.

"Milly."

"Where are your parents?"

"I . . . don't know."

"Are you from East Ernost?"

Milly nodded.

Doris held out her hand. "Come in. Quickly."

Milly shuffled toward the house. As she did, she saw three heads peek out from over Doris's shoulder. Edaline, Emm, and . . . Hightop?

This time the rushing wind pulled her in. As soon as she passed through the doorway, the memory shifted again. Now she sat cross-legged in St. George's library with a teenage Edaline. The two of them huddled over something in Edaline's hand.

"What is it?" Milly asked.

"A memory," Edaline said.

"Where'd it come from?"

Edaline laughed. "My head."

"Why did you take it out of your head?"

"Don't worry. It's still in there." Edaline tapped her temple. "I just pulled a copy out because I needed to process it better."

Milly scratched her head. "I'm confused."

"It's something the witches in my old home taught me. To help us deal with sad feelings."

Milly watched the liquid swirl. "Can you show me?"

A loud creak came from the door, and the two of them turned toward the sound. No one was there.

Edaline tucked the bottle away in one of her sleeves. "Maybe I'll show you when you're older. I know Doris doesn't mind, but we should probably not talk about witch-related things here."

"I thought the wizards and witches were friends."

"I did too . . ." Edaline put her hand out. A small tattoo adorned her wrist. "Come on, I promised Doris I'd help her with dinner tonight."

Milly took Edaline's hand and followed her out the door.

The memory turned red.

Milly found herself in the living room. Everyone around her was frozen still. She saw an older Hightop standing above her with hands reached out and locked in time. A couple years must have passed since the last memory. He glared down at her, dark green flames at the tips of his unmoving fingers.

Milly looked down at her own hands stretched out in self-defense. She was shaking. She looked around the room and saw Doris in a corner with Cilla in her arms. A young Nishi and Ikki. A toddler, probably Abby.

Milly realized she was the only one able to move.

Did she cast this spell?

Edaline burst through the door and ran toward Milly.

"Are you okay?" Edaline gasped.

Milly felt herself wanting to talk, but this past version of her could only tremble.

Edaline looked around the room and then at Hightop. "I trusted you!" Edaline shouted at him. "How dare you come after Milly!"

The frozen wizard couldn't reply, but his gray eyes darkened.

Edaline stood in front of Milly and raised her hand against the wizard's temple. "You will forget this," she said. "In all your days of searching, you will not know Milly. Even if she stands beneath your very nose, you will not remember her! But, for as long as I live, you will remember me. My name will forever fill you with guilt and shame and regret." Edaline pulled her hand back. "Now sleep."

A white tendril spilled from Hightop's forehead into Edaline's cupped hand, and everyone in the room fell to the ground.

Edaline tightened her fist and the memory in her hand dissipated into nothing. When she turned back around, Milly hugged her legs and shivered.

"What if he remembers?" Milly said.

"He won't." Edaline knelt and put her arms around Milly. "I promise."

"What now?"

"I have to leave. It's not safe for me here anymore. It hasn't been for a long time."

"Can I come?"

Edaline smiled, but tears were slipping down her cheeks. "I wish you could."

Milly trembled. "Please don't."

Edaline stood up and gently put Milly's arms back down to her sides. "I'm sorry. I'm so sorry."

Milly buried her face against Edaline's clothes.

"Don't worry. It'll be like I never left." Edaline put the palm of her hand against Milly's forehead.

The memory started to fade, disappearing back into an empty canvas.

The last words Milly heard were: "Makisuyo[34] forgive me."

---

[34] When Milly heard the word ricochet around in her mind, she finally understood the full weight of it. It wasn't a curse. It wasn't a spell or hex or even some kind of jinx. It was an old word full of courtesy and gentleness and urgency and hope. Not because it was inherently powerful. Because it was alive. It was the world's simplest and oldest word. Older than "sun" or "love" or even "no." It simply meant *please.*

CHAPTER FIFTEEN
the loud sound of silence

MILLY WOKE IN a dark room, tangled in an unfinished wrestling match against a blanket. The blanket was winning. She twisted to shake it off and sat up to find herself completely alone in the room. Almost.

Edaline sat cross-legged by the wall of leaves next to Jasper, looking out through a thin opening which let a single shaft of light into the far side of the room. Jasper was curled up next to her, his black fur absorbing the sun.

Milly jumped down from the bed, wrapped the blanket around her body, and approached the two. When she got close, she saw that the witch was wearing a long-sleeved shirt and loose pajama pants. Her headscarf was loose too, barely covering her long black hair. Steam rose from the cup she held between her two hands.

Milly shivered, not sure what to say, but Edaline looked up and smiled, then shifted over to make room.

Jasper didn't even stir.

Milly sat down next to the witch, and together they watched the world wake from its slumber.

The sun's slow path up the sky began to melt away the mist. Every so often a tree would rustle. A wind would blow.

A bird would sing. But that was it. It was if the entirety of the woods had decided together that today was a day for sleeping in. For being quiet.

The aftertaste of the memory was thick and murky. It left behind a sulfur-like residue. Her mind felt worn out. Her throat felt dry. It tasted like she'd just drunk something forgotten in the back of a cupboard for many years. Worst of all, the flavor was stuck on her tongue like a thin layer of lint. It sat in Milly's mind as she filled with anger. And hurt. And guilt.

Not at Edaline, though. At Hightop. At the loss of her home.

At herself.

After the mists had almost fully dissipated and the tea in Edaline's cup had run dry, the witch gestured at the door and the two of them stood up. They shifted past Jasper, who only dug his head deeper into his body, and walked down to the kitchen.

In continued gentle silence, the two made breakfast.

They cracked eggs into a cast iron skillet, boiled a pot of rice, diced garlic, plucked basil leaves, picked green tomatoes, and prepared themselves a fine meal. Which they also ate in silence.

All of breakfast went by like this.

Edaline didn't seem in any hurry to talk, and Milly—much as she hated to admit it—enjoyed having a normal day where she could do nothing at all. But the uneasiness quietly ate away at her. Who was Edaline? Who was *she*? Was this how Doris felt? Like there were missing pieces in her brain, just waiting to be put back in the right places? Every time she worked herself up to ask about the memory, she put it off. Every time she wanted to say she was sorry, the words inside her fell apart.

Milly still wasn't sure what to believe, but she knew whatever she'd believed before was very, very wrong.

Instead, after breakfast, she wandered about the house. Apparently, Horace and Cilla had gone outside to tend to the garden, so she was able to explore the entire place by herself. In one room, she found a small indoor herb garden full of clay pots hanging from the ceiling. In another, she found a little water pump and a bucket. Edaline had left a new towel and bar of soap next to it, along with a fresh set of clothes a couple sizes too big. Milly spent the rest of her morning scrubbing every inch of her skin and untangling her mess of a hair-helmet.

Once she was back downstairs, Edaline broke the silence and asked Milly if she wanted to help her make lunch for the others.

She nodded her head.

Jasper joined them while they were slicing tomatoes and meowed loudly. "Anything for me?"

Edaline looked up. "Oh, hello, Jasper. Are you hungry?"

"Very!"

"You can understand him?" Milly asked.

"It took a while to find the right spell, but we managed,"

Edaline said. She poured milk into a shallow platter and put it on top of the table. "We had a very good conversation about his life as a wind."

"Thanks, E." The cat jumped up, sat down, and lapped it up gladly.

Milly transitioned to cutting cucumbers, taking as long to slice them in even pieces as she possibly could. She kept hoping Edaline would say something first, but she never did.

After some time, the cat sat up and meowed.

Edaline gave him more milk and he shut up again. It was the quietest he'd been since Milly met the creature.

But that didn't last long.

Halfway through his second saucer, the cat walked up to Milly and sat next to her while Edaline went over to do the dishes. He whispered, "So, you guys talk things out yet?"

Milly shook her head.

His eyes narrowed. "Why not?"

Milly glanced over at Edaline and silently mouthed, "I don't know what to say."

"Never stopped you before."

"It's different this time," she murmured.

"Did something happen?"

Milly shrugged.

"Well, you'll have to do something. She's obviously waiting for you to say something first. She's very nice, by the way. Good at boundaries."

Milly raised an amused eyebrow. "Oh yeah? Is that your opinion?"

"Better than you." The cat snickered.

"Why are you even still around? We found Cilla. You can go now." Milly made a waving motion with her hand.

Jasper stared intensely.

Milly made a face. "What?"

"Your exact words were, oh—what was it again? 'Bring Cilla *home*.' Does this look like home to you?"

Realizing how insensitive she'd been, Milly reached a hand out. "Oh, I didn't mean to—"

"It's fine. At least E feeds me." The cat jumped off the table and returned to his milk.

Filled with a renewed pang of guilt, Milly watched the witch wash the dishes. Now she could see the resemblance between Edaline and Emm. They shared the same hands, the same noses. But she also saw the differences. Edaline was thinner; her shoulders drooped. A couple stray strands of gray had even infiltrated her long black hair.

Milly took in a deep breath, then asked Edaline the question which felt both the safest and the worst.

"Why doesn't your sister remember you?"

The witch turned off the tap and put down the wooden bowl in her hands. Her wall of silence had lost its last stone. "I'm guessing you found your lost memory."

"Yes," Milly said—carefully. "Did you take Emm's, too?"

"I understand you have many questions, but . . ." Edaline nervously met Milly's eyes. "Would you like to go for a walk?"

―――②

The two left lunch on the table for the others and walked among the trees. They followed the river and, when they were within sight of the forest's edge, Edaline turned and walked parallel to it along some invisible line that she refused to cross.

Milly walked beside her, wondering why they had to walk or if they were going anywhere in particular. Jasper had said he was going to keep watch over the house, but Milly figured he was just too lazy to come.[35]

Their path brought them to a clearing in the trees where there were nothing but stumps. These were nothing like the bamboo shoots. These stumps had once been large, broad trees. Time had carved many rings into their centers, and scorched broombranch leaves lay scattered on the ground. Scorched and white. Like Elma.

"Why are we here?" Milly asked.

Edaline rested her hand on one of the stumps and traced the rings with her fingers.

---

[35] On the contrary, Jasper was exercising the most self-control he possibly could at the moment. He wanted nothing more than to eavesdrop and offer his commentary on the entire conversation. But as a little wind, a profession which dabbles in the greatest of secrets, Jasper also knew exactly when *not* to listen to people's conversations. Unlike most winds, he had boundaries.

"People didn't used to be able to fly." Edaline looked up at the sky. "No amount of magicks could change that. There used to be a time when only the winds and the birds and the broombranches were familiar with that feeling. For a time, for a long time, we were okay with that."

Milly stood next to the witch and clutched one of her arms close to her body. What did any of this have to do with Emm?

"The very first witch on Arrett was a miracle. Or an accident. Many, many years ago, there was a mother whose child was very, very sick. She prayed for help. The East Wind heard her prayer and carried it to the heart of Arrett, who had such compassion for the child that they did something unheard of. They *gave* the child magicks and, with it, the ability to commune with all other magicks. A miracle child, the first witch. So old I don't even know her name. She taught others how to speak magicks. How to befriend a fire and dance with a tree. She used her magicks to bring together the stone and the grass. Arrett was happy, and the winds amused. At least, that's how the legend goes.

"The first wizard was the result of a choice. He too asked for help, but Arrett, seeing the selfishness in his heart, would not grant it to him. So he stopped praying. He decided there were other ways to find magicks, ways much more easily . . . controlled. It was a wizard that tamed the first little wind, interrupted this wind in its duties and broke Arrett's heart and stole magicks for his own."

"What did he ask for?"

"No one knows. Whatever it was, whatever the case, wizards and witches have been at odds ever since. Arrett's heart grew quiet. Wizardry became popular among the people of Arrett, once they realized that they could have control of magicks without asking—which is all that prayer is. They wanted to take with nothing to give in return. And they became very good at it. Many witches became wizards out of convenience. They developed spells and schools for taming many things. The winds became too dangerous, too angry, and so they turned their attention to other things." Edaline stopped and gestured toward the clearing.

"Charles—sorry, *Hightop*— never really cared about the witches. Most wizards don't care about the witches. Not like they used to. They only cared because there were powers in this world they couldn't control and there were people stubborn enough to prevent them from doing that. And it was easy for them to villainize us. People fear what they can't control. These broombranches were the last straw. When the wizards said they wanted to clear out the whole forest, the witches couldn't stand it anymore, so we put up a fight. We were doing well until they found East Ernost—home of the witches, where the East Wind brought magicks to the first child. No one knows how, but they made it disappear. They made us disappear."

Now she sat down on the stump and pulled her knees up to her chest. It was a strange reminder to Milly that Edaline used to be a kid, too. Maybe, in some ways, she still was.

"Where I come from, a faraway land called Tahena, we learned how to bottle our own memories in order to understand and process our emotions better. It was a way my people dealt with things like anger or grief. It was how I dealt with leaving my home. We never used it as a way to forget. And we never used it on other people. Never.

"When I took Charles's memory, I broke something. Deep magicks that had been asleep for many years. The gripes and gobblers—the shadows—noticed. Hungered for it. A witch is never supposed to use their power to dominate another person. And I did. It took a while, but eventually Charles discovered how I took his memories. And he twisted those magicks into a weapon. I thought I was using those magicks to protect, but he started using them to hide his mistakes.

"Maybe I could have stopped him. I don't know. I didn't even try. I was too scared. With his help, the wizards cut through the woods. I bound myself to the very last tree to keep the forest alive, but by then most of the broombranch trees had already been lost. By the time they were done, I was stuck here. Amidst all this 'wasted wood,' as they called it. They've turned this forest into a place of rejects. Broken broombranches are sent here when they're done with, and I take them in.

"Charles took my sister's memory from her, and I couldn't do anything about it. I thought that would be enough to keep her safe. Eventually, I was the only known witch left. I thought that'd be okay. Maybe I thought so long as he never found you again, it'd be okay. I was wrong."

Now she looked at Milly, face tortured. "I thought that maybe, in spite of all my mistakes, I could at least protect you and Cilla. That even if all the rest of us had to hide away, they wouldn't be able to find you. That was why I took away your memories. I thought if you didn't know who you were, you'd be able to keep your magicks a secret. That they would believe there were no more witches. But I only made things worse for you. I'm sorry."

Milly didn't respond for a long time. The older witch stared out into the woods while Milly sat next to her on the stump and traced the rings in the tree with her finger.

"Does that mean . . ." Milly stammered. "Did the shadows get worse because of me? Because I'm a witch?"

"No." Edaline shook her head. Fiercely. "Gripes and gobblers are as old as Arrett itself. They don't hunt witches. They feed off guilt and shame. They come every time a member of the council remembers what he's done. Every time Hightop feels regret for his actions. They've been watching me for years. No one really knows what happens if they catch you. They've never been aggressive, until now. Something must have changed." Edaline put her hand on Milly's shoulder. "None of this is your fault. Okay?"

"Okay," Milly said, though she didn't completely believe it. How could Edaline possibly know how much Milly hated herself? Not just for being a witch. For hating the idea of being a witch for so long. For hating what she was born to be. For being so, so stupid. So scared. "Hightop is looking for me, isn't he? Because I'm from East Ernost."

"Yes."

"But why did he mistake me for Cilla?"

Edaline jumped off the stump and paced back and forth. "It must be that book from the orphanage. I thought I burned them all." Edaline shook her head. "I'm sorry, Milly. I didn't know Hightop would ever notice West Ernost again. Or Lilith. I didn't even know Lilith was still alive. Maybe Lilith thought she could protect Cilla from Hightop. But that doesn't make any sense—why she would steal her?"

"Hightop won't stop until he's found her." Milly balled her fingers into tight fists. "But he doesn't need her. He wants *me*. He wants me and he can't even *see* me."

"He won't find you here, if that's what you're worried about. You and Cilla are safe in these woods."

"No, I want—I *have* to be found."

"Milly." Edaline's eyes widened. "You can't."

"You thought you could protect everyone by keeping them hidden away. But now no one is safe. As long as I'm still hiding, other people will be put in danger. I can't just stay here and do nothing."

"It's too dangerous." Edaline put her hands to her temples and closed her eyes.

"Cilla needs to go home. And the only way she can do

that is to make sure Hightop never has reason to hunt her down ever again." Milly put her hand on the witch's arm. "Please. I don't want to run anymore. I'm not good at it."

"I don't agree, but . . ." Edaline looked up. When she spoke again, her voice sounded broken. "How do you want me to help you?"

Milly swallowed, suddenly afraid of her next words. She looked around at the clearing of lost trees and wasted woods.

She turned back toward Edaline, sure of what she wanted.

"Teach me how to be a witch."

CHAPTER SIXTEEN
it's a bird! it's a plane! it's . . .

WHEN MILLY SAID those words, her hand lit up in orange-green flames. It felt like something had been taken from her, like someone ripping buried secrets out of her chest and dashing them against the floor. It felt like shattered clay and broken plates. It felt like getting old and growing up.

She didn't like it.

When the flames disappeared, her hand continued to throb. A new mark lay there. That of a white waning crescent moon.

Edaline glanced around the clearing. Shadows lurked between the trees, their fingers long as branches, toes like squared-off stubs.

"They're here," she whispered.

Milly grabbed the older witch's trembling hand and ran.

The shadows continued to watch them, not bothering to chase them down. But Milly didn't stop for anything.

Just ahead, more gripes appeared in the trees. Milly pulled Edaline with her to cut around them, but with every turn, she saw more fingers and more toes reaching for them. If they got close enough, Milly swore she could even see the flash of a gobbler's crooked teeth.

It felt like running through a maze with walls made of shadows. Forcing Milly and Edaline into narrower passages. Forcing them into a trap.

The deeper into the woods they ran, the worse Milly's hand throbbed.

And the darker the forest grew.

A loud rustling approached from above, and Edaline dug her heels in to bring the two to a jarring stop.

"Milly, wait."

Milly glanced to the side; the gripes were so close she could hear them breathing.

"Edaline," she gasped, "we need to—"

The rustling stopped.

A shower of leaves exploded above them as two broom-branches shot down and plucked the two witches right off their feet. Together, the four of them shot back out of the hole the branches had made in the shadows and flew above the tree line.

Milly hugged her entire body against the branch as wind whipped by her cheeks. To its credit, the branch flew a mostly straight line over the trees despite the novice rider it carried.

Green blurred with blue, and Milly shut her eyes.

"You don't have to hold so tight if you lock your ankles."

Milly repositioned her legs around the branch. "Who said that?" she said, keeping her eyes closed.

"The branch you're choking."

"Oh!" Milly peeked open her eyes and loosened her grip a little. "It's you!"

The branch shook itself like a wet dog and continued to fly onward. *"Hello again."*

Milly sat up a bit and saw Edaline flying just ahead. When she did, she noticed that the broombranch she was riding had been splintered at its end. H.C. PROPERTY had been etched into its surface.

"I'm not . . . hurting you, am I?" Milly asked the broombranch.

"I am fine. So long as you don't try anything stupid this time."

"I'm sorry. I really am."

"I believe you." The branch leveled out and slowed to a glide.

Milly's breathing started to return to normal. She glanced back and saw that the shadows were shrinking into the distance. When she turned around, she loosened her grip and locked her ankles into a more comfortable position. "What's your name?"

"I am—" the broombranch made a sound halfway between a walnut cracking and a cricket's wings clapping.

Milly stared blankly.

"You can just call me Ash."

"Thank you, Ash."

"Thanks for not trying to drive."

⸻

The sun had already begun its descent by the time Milly and Edaline flew into the roof of the house. As soon as they landed, the broombranches returned to their perches and Edaline ran down the stairs.

"What's happening?" Jasper asked from a nearby chair.

"The shadows are here!"

Our two bewildered friends followed Edaline downstairs.

They ran past Cilla and Horace, who were eating berries in the kitchen. The two glanced at each other, then joined the growing train of people.

Edaline led them deeper still, down the hall, through the tunnel, all the way back to the room with the tree's heart. She dashed to the center of the room. And stopped. She brushed her fingers over the tree's heart where Milly had left the large gash.

The heart's light was dim. Black cracks had appeared along its surface. It was clear the tree was dying.

Milly's stomach twisted into knot after knot after knot.

Was Edaline angry? Would she give Milly over to the shadows? To Hightop?

She imagined the weight of that cursed metal in her hands. She remembered how cold it felt against her skin. How lifeless.

Edaline approached Milly, and Milly shut her eyes tight.

The footsteps got closer.

And then—

"May I hug you?"

Milly blinked her eyes open to find Edaline kneeling in front of her.

Milly nodded.

Edaline extended her arms, and Milly walked into them. Tears dripped down Edaline's face. "I'm sorry," the older witch whispered. "I am so, so sorry."

Slowly, carefully, Milly lifted her arms until she was hugging Edaline back. With her memories of Edaline partially restored, she suddenly remembered that they had once been friends. The memories were faint, just barely out of reach, but they were there somewhere. Floating on the fringes of her mind. Memories which had previously been hazy now had Edaline in them. Teaching her how to cook. Showing her magicks. Making her happy to also be a witch.

Milly started crying, too.[36] "I'm sorry I hurt your tree."

"It's not your fault—"

"Yes, it is!" She pulled back. "I'm the one that stabbed it! I shouldn't have listened to Hightop. I should've . . ."

Edaline wiped the tears from Milly's cheeks. "You didn't know any better."

Milly returned to Edaline's arms and sobbed until she couldn't cry anymore.

"Milly, these shadows are going to come for you—for

---

[36] We mustn't judge Milly too harshly for how she reacted. If you've spent any amount of time among grown-ups, you know that they have a hard time looking at children as Actual Persons, regardless of whether they're a gnome or gronkle, giant or tree. And Milly had spent so much of her entire life not being seen that experiencing it for the first time proved quite overwhelming.

us—no matter where you run. We don't have much time,"
Edaline said softly, "but I promise to make the most of what
we have."

"Make the most of what?"

"Your training." Edaline pulled back and stood to her
feet. "First thing tomorrow morning."

"What's happening?" Cilla asked.

"We're going to teach your sister how to be a witch."

"*Oh!*" Cilla glanced in Milly's direction, a smile partly on
her lips, then something else. Cilla spun around and climbed
up the ladder. Horace shrugged and followed her up.

Milly made to follow them, but Jasper jumped onto
her shoulder and whispered, "Don't freak out, but look at
Edaline's neck."

Milly looked over and saw that part of the witch's headscarf had slipped down, revealing something coarse where
her skin used to be. Whatever it was spread out in vein-like
patterns, just like the cracks that had appeared in the heart
of the tree.

"I don't know what's going on," the cat said, "but she
wasn't lying. She doesn't have much time."

AN INTRODUCTION TO CHAPTER SEVENTEEN
rules and regulations of being a witch

HERE'S A SECRET: It was not magicks that saved the first witch. When the East Wind first heard the prayers of the mother of the first witch, the wind was too late. When they returned bearing the gift of magicks, the child was too sick for anything to bring healing. The child was already too near death. The magicks was too weak.

So the mother did what any loving mother would do. She sailed across the sea herself and carried her child directly to the heart of Arrett, desperate and afraid. No heart is full of more want than a mother's.

In return, Arrett did the only thing they could do; they gave part of their own heart to the child. They spoke life into the child, asking only that the child speak life into every other living creature that she met thereafter. The heart of Arrett spread through the use of magicks, want given direction, prayers given form. This was what it meant to be a witch.

For generations, the main tenets of being a witch were passed down through tradition. These governed how witches were to treat their fellow beings, nurture the earth, make peace with magicks, and speak life into all things. At last, once paper had been invented, the great Dragons Master Jyllan Iffrydt Yyllsyf condensed them into three core guidelines. They are translated into grass tongue as follows . . .

CHAPTER SEVENTEEN, PART ONE
ask and you might receive

"OKAY." EDALINE PULLED her hair back and twisted it into a bun, then rewrapped the scarf around her head. "Follow me. Take notes. Obviously, we don't have time to teach you every rule and regulation of being a witch, but I can at least give you the basics." Edaline chatted her mouth off as she led Milly and Jasper up the stairs, past the library room, and to the very top of the house. "There aren't many books left after they were all burned, and the ones I have are probably too complicated, so we're going to start with something hands-on."

The staircase narrowed and forced them to walk single file until they arrived at a platform suspended in the air. The room was utterly dark. Edaline pressed a blade of grass in front of her lips and made a loud bird-like whistle. The dark around them shattered into a thousand pieces. Broombranches flew in frantic circles, darting in and out of the light that now broke into the house, all around and below and above and beside the platform.

Edaline turned to Milly with a wild gleam in her eye. "First lesson: tame a broombranch."[37]

---

[37] *A Witch's Guide to Rudimentary Magicks, Chapter 2.* How to befriend a broombranch: Becoming a broombranch's partner is one of the first lessons

Milly tried to follow the branches whipping back and forth, but that soon proved impossible. "How?!"

"I wish I could tell you, but I'm afraid Rosas insisted you learn this on your own."

"Rosas?"

Edaline gestured toward the tree.

Milly felt her entire body shrink.

"Sorry," Edaline mouthed. She whistled once more and one of the broombranches split off from the others. The staircase below them vanished. Edaline mounted the branch and smiled. "You've got this."

And with that Edaline left, leaving Milly staring downward and Jasper, with flattened ears, pressed against the platform.

"How is this helpful?" Jasper howled. "Also, why am I here?!"

"I don't know," Milly said, then looked back up. "But we captured a broombranch once. I'm sure this can't be that hard."

Oh dear, how very wrong she was.

Jasper shut his eyes and dug his claws deeper into the

---

a young witch must learn. Like all things brimming with magicks, broombranches are living, sentient creatures with their own desires and wants and even language. We recommend treating them with the utmost care and patience. The best way to befriend a broombranch is to learn its language. Many broombranches are quite willing to partner with a witch, so long as the broombranch has matured to the point of detaching from its mother tree. Never try to cut an unwilling broombranch from its tree.

platform. "Just tell me when this ordeal is over. I never thought I'd say this, but heights are not nearly as fun when you're a cat."

Milly turned her attention back to the broombranches. In most situations, she might have been scared. But she'd had a good amount of practice with falling now, and her mind was far too occupied to have the time to be scared.

A loud rustling echoed from the base of the tree, sending vibrations through the platform that Milly stood on.

Okay. Maybe she was a little scared.

She reached out her hand, the one with the moon, toward a nearby broombranch and tried to construct a spell the best way she knew how. "Please come over here."

The branch started to come close, then darted off, making a weird chittering noise.

Jasper peeked an eye open. "I'm pretty sure that branch was laughing at you."

Milly snorted and tried it again. "Broombranch, I summon you." She stared at the mark on her hand, willing a spark to appear, but nothing happened.

This time several branches were laughing. She didn't need Jasper's commentary to hear them.

"They're never going to come here, are they?"

"After the stunt you pulled last time? Not likely."

Milly sat on the platform and watched the branches flit about. Most of them had begun to calm by now and were drifting idly. They ignored her for the most part. Instead, they rustled their thin-yellow leaves at one another and flew lazy circles in the patches of sunlight that poked through.

That's when Milly saw the one broombranch that hadn't moved. The one with the splintered end and claw marks.

She waved. "Hello, Ash."

The broombranch drifted closer. *"Hello, little twig. May I ask what it is you're doing?"*

"I'm supposed to tame a broombranch."

If the broombranch could, it would have scoffed in disgust. *"Yes, I see that part. Why?"*

"Well . . . I'm a witch now. This was supposed to be my first lesson."

"Would you like it if I tried to tame you?"

"Of course not," Milly said. Her face felt a little red. "Besides, I wouldn't tame *you*. I mean, I know you. I wouldn't want to . . ." She glanced over at Jasper.

"Exactly. So why on earth are you trying to tame my siblings?"

"Because . . ." Did she have a good answer for that? "I have to. I have to do this if I want to control magicks."

The broombranch shook itself and from its wood came a long, low whistle. *"I thought you were a smart child."*

Milly crossed her arms. "What do you mean?"

"Magicks aren't for controlling, and neither are broombranches. Do you really think the other witch tried to tame

us? That that's why my entire family has stayed here with her? I know what being laid under a curse feels like. Trust me, none of us are willing to undergo that whole thing again."

Jasper snorted. "That's a good point."

"Thank you, weird fuzzy bush."

"Still a cat. Hasn't changed since the last time we talked."

"If you say so."

"These flying twigs aren't much help, are they?" Jasper said, turning to Milly. "Maybe if we'd talked to them in the first place like I suggested, Rosas wouldn't be putting us through this trial. I don't feel like you have many options— unless, of course, you try to *really tame* one again." He gave her a very pointed stare.

Ash made a backward motion, as if he were physically flinching. But he didn't say anything. He was clearly waiting to hear what Milly would say.

Milly tried to avoid looking at the cat. "I can't do that. I *shouldn't.*" She looked up at the ceiling of interlocking broombranches. "I'm sorry, Rosas. I shouldn't make Ash, or any of them, do something they don't want to do." She glanced at Jasper again. Her palm burned; she still remembered the feeling of power that had come from taming a wind. She didn't like it anymore. "I guess I'll just have to tell Edaline I failed."

The cat crept up to the edge of the platform. "We still need to get down."

Milly scratched her head. "We could always jump?"

Jasper immediately backed away from the edge. "Let's *not* risk that. I can't just catch you every time you fall off something. Not in this form."

Ash swayed in the air. *"You could always ask, you know."*

Milly's eyes widened. "You wouldn't mind?"

"Of course not," the broombranch replied. *"I will never again be the steed of some wannabe master, but that doesn't mean I can't help a friend."*

"Yay. We're all buddies now." The cat climbed up onto Milly's shoulder. His tail was fluffed out and his teeth rattled in his mouth. "Boy, do I miss being a wind. Can we please get off this stupid platform?"

CHAPTER SEVENTEEN, PART TWO
be kind and do no harm

IT WAS ALREADY midafternoon when Milly walked into the kitchen. Alone. Ash had returned to his rooftop, and Jasper decided not to be a part of whatever else Edaline was planning.

Milly found Edaline leaning against the counter, eating an apple while she read a book.

With loud footsteps, Milly made her presence known as she stomped into the room.

To her annoyance, the older witch didn't turn. Edaline only pushed a plate with an uneaten sandwich in Milly's direction. A stool skidded past Milly and toward the counter.

Milly wanted to be annoyed, but the sight of food made her stomach betray her. She clambered onto the stool and ate her sandwich. She made sure to chew it aggressively.

When Edaline had bitten down to the apple's yellow core, she wiped a sleeve across her lips. "How'd it go?"

Milly wrinkled her nose.

Edaline cracked a grin. "Not well?"

Milly swallowed. "You tricked me," she said, then took another giant bite.

"How'd you get down?"

"Ash helped."

"That was nice of him." Edaline flipped to another page.

Milly put down her sandwich. A good third of it was still left. "You've never tamed a branch. You knew it was wrong and you still tried to make me do it! How is this supposed to help me become a witch?"

Edaline finally turned to face the girl. "Rosas said it went very well."

"I didn't learn anything!"

"Are you sure about that?" Edaline raised an eyebrow. "I heard you made a friend out of it."

"That's not a lesson, though. I still don't know how to control magicks. If I couldn't even tame a broombranch, how am I going to confront Hightop? I can't *friend* him into defeat."

"Not everything you chase is meant to be caught." Edaline shrugged. "Maybe there's more to magicks than trying to control them. And *maybe* you should think about other options than just fighting Hightop. Like not being found in the first place."

Milly buried her face in her hands. "I don't understand anything," she wailed through her fingers. Everything felt so needlessly complicated.

"Milly, why do you *want* to be a witch? To be powerful? To have control?"

She didn't answer. She didn't know how to say that those were things she wanted and hated at the same time.

"There's more to being a witch than power." Edaline put

a hand on Milly's shoulder. "It's okay. We can take a break if you want. But for what it's worth, you're doing pretty well so far."

Not well enough, she thought, and picked up her sandwich. When the moon in her hand came into view, she paused and stared hard. Why hadn't it turned red when she tried to cast the spell?

"Milly." Edaline must have caught her staring. "When you used magicks before, do you remember any common thread between them? Anything that triggered your powers?"

Milly thought back to the cliff and the fog and the flutter-wishes and the cloud. "I was, I don't know, desperate," she said. *And crying*, said a little voice in her head.[38]

"Anything else?"

Milly thought for a moment and shook her head.

Edaline pushed the book toward Milly. "Take a look at this. Cilla said you liked reading. Maybe you'll have some luck with it."

Milly looked down at the page, decorated with a cursive script and woodblock illustrations. There were no step-by-step instructions to this spell. No preparations. No ingredients. It had only the picture of a small flame next to three delicate words: *ask for me.*

---

[38] We treat this little voice like a dirty word. We don't ever like to say it out loud at parties, for fear that it will ruin the mood or upset our guests. But even this voice, in the most particular of circumstances, can be a noble thing. Not for the person who holds it, but for the one it is given to. Listen, do you hear it? It calls itself *Pity*.

Milly shook her head. "This doesn't look like a spell."

"What should a spell look like?"

"I don't know. It needs rules. Directions."

"Does it?"

"Isn't it easier to control magicks that way? I thought that was the point of having rules and regulations."

"Of course it's easier. That's why so many wizards don't ask. They demand. They don't care how things happen. All they care for is results. But magicks are delicate." Edaline turned her right palm upward and sang in a soft, gentle voice:

> *"Little light, if you please it,*
> *comfort those of us who need it."*

As she spoke, green tendrils of fire rose from her fingers, joining together into one gentle flame. "Yes, it is sometimes harder. But the point of being a witch isn't to do things the easy way. It's to do things *right*. Even if that means things don't always listen to you." She placed her hand next to a nearby candle, and the flame crawled onto the wick with its little fiery fingers. "Believe me, there are many things in this world that won't listen."

Milly thought about Jasper and wondered if he would have come along even if she hadn't forced him to. She looked at the moon on her hand, then turned it over and stared at her knuckles.

"Little light, if you—"

Edaline raised her hand. "Sorry, I don't mean to interrupt. Try to do it in your own words."

Milly crinkled her eyebrows and tried again. "Fire, appear in my hand."

Nothing.

She stretched her fingers, hardened the words. Tried to rhyme it. Even shout it. But not a single spot nor sniff of a spark appeared. Why was working with magicks so much harder when she was actually trying?

Edaline picked up the book and ruffled backward through the pages. She sighed, closed it, and set it back down.

"Keep trying," she said. "I'm going to prepare dinner."

Milly didn't feel like trying anymore. She wished she had more time.

With Edaline's back turned, Milly glanced at the book. Its title read *Fundamental Magicks* by Dragons Master Jyllan Iffrydt Yyllsyf; translated by Jeddison Licks.

Milly flipped to the first chapter and read:

Historically speaking, magicks do not seem to be bound to any specific language. Words do not define the spell. Rather, they describe the magicker's relationship to the spell itself. This operates on the fundamental idea that the magicks of Arrett are intrinsically wild and alive. Because every spell is unique at its moment of creation, no two magickers will ever produce the exact same results. When a witch uses consensual magicks, the same might be accomplished by a disciplined wizard using domination magicks. The difference lies not in the goal of the spell, but in the steps taken to achieve that goal. Witches pose every spell as an appeal. As the oldest magickers in Arrett, witches are very reluctant to ask of magicks anything they wouldn't naturally want to already do. This results in the drawback of being incapable of performing certain powerful spells. Certainly not for lack of skill, but out of their own moral self-restriction. However, this also means that witches are capable of working with many magicks far beyond any other magicker's comprehension. All they must do is ask.

Milly stared over at Edaline, still confused but a little less frustrated. She remembered the words covered up by the High Council's words, the one engraved into the stonework. "In other words, 'be kind and do no harm'?"

Edaline's eyes widened in surprise. "Yes! Exactly. And always use the magick word."

Milly turned her attention to the nearby candle. She watched how it danced and turned, leaped and flickered from the tiniest breeze. There was an unlit candle next to it, and Milly lifted her fingers toward it.

"I'd like to give her a dance partner." She paused. "Please."

A tiny, excited blue spark jumped toward the wick.

CHAPTER SEVENTEEN, PART THREE
the magick word

EDALINE SPENT MUCH of the day showing simple spells to Milly. Some seemed useful (like how to ask a grunkworm to give you light in a dark room), and she did her best to pick them up. Others didn't seem all that relevant (like what manners to use with a dragon at a leaf-juice party), and she stuck them in the back pocket of her mind for later.

Edaline seemed to have a point to all these tiny lessons, like she would reveal some grand message connecting all these random spells at the end of the day, but dinner had come and gone and Milly still didn't know what the point of it all was.

Every so often, Jasper popped in and out to offer an unhelpful word or two, but he mostly lay about in patches of sunlight and only moved when the branches shifted their formations. Every time she saw Horace, Milly tried to draw him into a conversation, but Cilla would just grab his hand and pull him away.

Milly really wished Cilla would talk to her, but her little sister didn't seem to want to.

Milly ruminated on all these thoughts while she washed the dishes by hand. She'd tried to ask the water to do them for her—several times in fact—but it seemed to know she didn't actually need the help.

"Edaline?" Milly asked.

"Yes?"

"Do you know why Cilla's so mad at me?"

Edaline shook her head. "Why don't you ask her?"

Because I don't want to. "Maybe I should."

Milly stared at the inside of her palm for a while. It started to itch.

"It'll be a while before I'm done here. I think she and Horace were in the garden. You can take a break and talk to her if you like."

"Will you talk to her for me?"

Edaline shook her head. "This is something you need to do yourself. Would you like my company?"

Milly shook her head.

Edaline nodded. "You can tell Horace I need help in the kitchen if you want privacy."

Milly exhaled. This was going to end badly. But she got off her chair and left the house anyway.

When she stepped outside, she found two pairs of footsteps (one big, one little) and a small groove leading away from the garden toward a nearby patch in the clearing. At the end of the trail, she saw little clumps of dirt being tossed out of a hole in the ground.

Milly approached the hole to see Horace and Cilla inside, shoveling with intense concentration. Cilla had a small shovel and Horace had a normal-sized shovel, which almost looked small in his hands. Next to Cilla's foot was a lumpy bag.

"Hi," Milly said.

Horace looked up and grinned. "Hello, friend."

Cilla didn't look up.

"Um, Edaline said she needed your help in the kitchen."

Horace nodded and climbed out of the hole. "Be back."

"Come back quickly, please," Cilla said.

"Okay." Horace handed Milly the shovel he'd been using, then walked toward the house.

Milly looked down at the top of Cilla's head. "Can I help?"

Cilla shrugged.

Milly put the shovel on the ground, slid into the hole, then pulled the shovel in with her. "What are you doing in here?"

"Planting."

"Oh." Milly looked around, tempted to make a snide remark, but instead stuck the blade into the dirt and began to scoop up clumps of soil. Cilla continued next to her at the same pace she'd been moving.

After another couple rounds of dirt, Milly spoke again. "Can I ask you a question?"

Cilla shrugged. Again.

"Why . . ." Milly trailed off. "Why are you so mad at me?"

"I'm not mad."

"Are you sure? You've been kind of—"

"I'm not mad!" Cilla stabbed the dirt. She wiped her face

with a sleeve, then grunted as she flung dirt into the air. Some of it missed and fell back into the hole.

"Okay. I believe you." Milly breathed in to steady herself. "Can you tell me why you don't want to go back to St. George's?"

"I already told you."

"I know, but can you explain it to me again? I promise to listen."

"No one there takes me seriously." Cilla grew more forceful with each thrust. "Nishi always makes fun of me. Doris doesn't listen when I tell her when Ikki pulls my hair. Marikit takes Junebug without telling me. And!" She finally stopped for a minute to gasp. "I keep asking magicks for help, but they don't listen to me. Ever! They only listen to you. And you don't even *want* to be a witch. It's not fair."

Milly frowned. "I didn't realize you were so unhappy."

"You didn't ask."

"Cilla, I'm . . . " Milly paused and put down her shovel. She took a very deep breath. "I'm *sorry*."[39]

Cilla didn't respond.

Milly swallowed, knowing what else she wanted—maybe needed—to say. "It was wrong of me to ignore you. I'm sorry I tried to take the book from you without asking. I'm

---

[39] *Please* is often called the magick word, and for good reason. It was, after all, the *first* word. The word that people use to *get* things. To *ask* for things. To *want*. But there are many words in this world with power, and perhaps no word so powerful as the one people use to *let go*, to *give*, to *reconcile*.

sorry I didn't listen to you. I'm sorry I took out my anger on you. I'm sorry I hurt the tree. I'm sorry I believed so much about witches that I shouldn't have. I'm sorry for a lot of things." She took a moment to breathe. "I'm sorry I hurt you. I can't force you to come with me, but we also can't stay here forever. Please forgive me. Come home with me."

Cilla stopped digging and threw the shovel up onto the ground. She picked up the bag next to her foot and dumped whatever was inside it into the center of the hole.

It landed with a heavy thud. It was the blade Milly had used to pierce Rosas's heart.

Cilla didn't look up. "Can you help me?"

Milly nodded.

The two of them climbed out and shoveled the dirt back in over the blade. They continued late into the day, side by side, until the entire hole was filled.

At the end of it all, the two girls sat next to their finished work, leaning against each other as the sun traded spots with the moon.

"Milly?"

"Yeah?"

"Thanks for coming after me. I'm—I'm sorry, too."

"I know."

After another minute had passed, Cilla spoke again. "Can Horace and Edaline come with us?"

"I don't know. They probably won't want to leave their homes."

Cilla bit her lip.

Milly took a long breath. "Maybe we can ask them."

"Okay."

Milly looked up at the sky shifting into darker colors. Her palm, for the first time in days, had stopped itching. She wondered if Doris had known she was a witch. She wondered what any of the other girls would say if they knew. Maybe staying with Edaline wouldn't be such a bad idea.

"Milly?"

She let out the breath she'd been holding in. "Yeah?"

"Something's in the woods."

CHAPTER EIGHTEEN
the north wind is nothing without its master

A TERRIBLE BANG echoed all around them.

Milly leaped up into a small patch of moonlight. She looked up and saw broombranches scattering wildly into the surrounding woods. In their wake, the moon was a sliver of silver being swallowed by the clouds.

Ash drifted toward Milly with a bag tied around his front end. *"Are you two okay?"*

"What's going on?"

Another loud *bang* shook the ground, followed by a scream.

"Milly! Cilla!" Horace's head appeared from the backdoor. "Shadows here! Hunger! Must run!"

Milly looked at the shovel on the ground nearby, the thing she'd just used to bury that evil metal. Then at Cilla, whose eyes were wide. Then at Ash, hovering just above them.

"Do you need a ride?" Ash said.

"No," she said. "I'm going back inside."

"Edaline knew you'd say that." Ash looped around and shot beneath the two girls, lifting them into the air.

"What are you doing?!"

"I promised her we'd run."

"But we can't!"

But they did.

Ash shot up through the canopy with Milly and Cilla on his back, away from the woods and into the clouds.

Milly looked back the whole time, watching with horror as shadows devoured the house behind them.

The surrounding sky grew more tempestuous. Dashes of lightning pricked their way through the clouds like thin, crooked needles. A low rumble of thunder reverberated around them the higher they climbed. Soon they saw nothing but the dark of the storm, with light unable to reach them from above or below.

"We have to go back!" Milly shouted over the growing wind. "Edaline needs our help!"

"We made a promise!"

"No!" Milly grabbed the branch with both hands. "We need to go back now!"

Ash wrestled against her. *"Don't try to steer me!"*

A large flash of lightning erupted in the cloud just beside them, and Cilla fell from the branch.

"Milly!"

"Great!"

Ash whipped around and zipped toward the girl. The momentum forced Milly to give up trying to take control;

she hugged her entire body against the branch as they went straight down. Apples and loose pages fluttered past her head as they rocketed to the ground.

"Get ready to catch her."

Milly squinted her eyes open and reached her hand out toward her sister. She grabbed Cilla's hand and the broom-branch leveled out as they popped back out of the clouds.

They were headed straight for the ground.

"Hold on!"

The branch steered its way toward the house, barely missing entire shoots of bamboo and snappy gripe jaws as it whipped back and forth. Ash steadied out and started to climb back into the air over the house.

A fierce wind blew them back to its entrance.

Ash spun sideways and the two girls tumbled through the front door.

Milly looked up and saw a faint light pulse from the other end of the hallway, where the common room was. She pulled Cilla up and ushered her back onto Ash.

"Get her out of here, Ash."

"Milly, what are you—"

Milly let go of Cilla and ran. When she tripped into the room, the light was brighter than she imagined.

The floor had been ripped apart. Flattened holes spotted the floor and walls where gripes had been in the process of crawling out. But they, and everything else in the room, had been frozen. They were paused in time with their claws extended, their teeth bared, their eyes shut to the light.

The light itself, unmoving, plastered the room like white paint. It came from Edaline's fingertips, pointing up in the air like the torch of a lighthouse.

Edaline herself stood at the center of the scene.

She, too, was still. She looked like a figure cut out of a painting. Or more like . . .

"A tree," Milly whispered to herself.

She took slow steps to the witch and, with trembling fingers, touched the witch's arm. Edaline's skin had turned fully bark. Flowers grew from her hair and coarse lines ran down her face like rivulets set aside for tears. Her lips were the color of berries, her skin like leaves. Only the witch's eyes remained the same. Fixed, horrified, on something above.

The cackle of a loud wind echoed through the hollow tree.

Milly looked back and saw the old witch, Lilith, in the doorway. She tried to run toward Cilla's side, but she could already see the witch's lips moving.

"Privacy, *please.*"

All the doors of the house burst open and an angry wind rushed toward Milly, flattening her.

Milly tried to shout, but the wind stole away her words before they could make it past her lips.

"What are you doing here?" Cilla shouted over the wind.

Milly's eyes narrowed and then widened at the realization. She could hear them.

"I'm here to help," the old witch said. Her gray eyes

appeared almost black in the shadows that surrounded her. Motionless shadows with hands and feet. The witch didn't even seem to notice their frozen limbs eternally reaching across the ground toward her. She locked eyes with Milly. "I don't remember you."

Cilla held on to Ash as thunder rumbled overhead.

Milly glared.

"Ah, yes. *You*. Aren't you the one who slayed the heart? The one who let the shadows in?"

Milly's shoulders shivered. The shadows twitched just beside Lilith's feet and turned. Slowly, they crawled across the floor. Toward Milly.

"What do you want?" Cilla asked.

"You see those shadows approaching your sister?" the witch said. She illuminated the hallway with green light seeping from her fingers. "They plague the world with their presence. Haunting people with nightmares of the past. You"—she pointed at Cilla—"are the last remnant of East Ernost. The *last* witch. They won't leave Arrett until you have."

Milly felt the mark on her hand throb again.

"Is that true?" Cilla asked. She glanced back at Milly.

"I can *help* you," the witch said. "But you have to come with me."

Cilla stared into Milly's eyes.

Milly shook her head and tried to say *Don't do it* over

and over and over and over. *She doesn't want to help us!* she wanted to say. *She only wants to use you! This isn't what a true witch would do!*

The shadows inched closer. They covered almost the entire hall now.

"What will you do, witchling? Run forever? Go back home? They'll follow you wherever you go. *I'm* your only chance."

The wind howled overhead, shaking the timbers of the house.

Milly raised her hand, to show her mark in some desperate attempt to stop the witch.

A shadow grabbed her wrist.

"Quick now!" The witch hovered just out of reach of the shadows. She extended a hand toward Cilla. "You don't *really* have a choice."

The itch on Milly's palm gave way to a throbbing pain. The shadow tightened around her wrist and pulled her deeper into the floor.

"Leave her alone!" Cilla shouted.

The shadow paused.

Cilla took the witch's hand. "I'll do it."

Cilla, no. You're not the one she wants.

Cilla smiled at Milly. "It's okay."

The witch cackled and yanked Cilla up into the air with one of her wrinkled claws. She looked up at the winding funnel in the sky, then pointed at Milly. "Take care of her."

The wind howled in defiance.

Lilith glared and lowered her voice. "Do what I tell you."

The winds picked up around Milly, ripping their way across the walls and tugging her hair across her cheeks. But the winds didn't hurt. In fact, they barely brushed by her. At the roaring of the wind, the shadows let go and retreated into the ground.

The witch and Cilla rose up into the sky. Milly tried to shout after them, but the wind swallowed up her cries.

Milly watched as the shadows abandoned her and stacked themselves on top of each other, stretching from the ground, reaching and reaching and reaching. Trying to grab hold of the witch.

Lilith shrieked. "You stupid wind! You take orders from *me!*" Green light spilled from her fingers like slow poison working its way through the dark clouds above, and the winds grew more frenzied. The witch flew away with Cilla as the wind turned its attention back on Milly. Its howls sounded mournful.

She closed her eyes.

"Make her stop!" Jasper howled. "It hurts!"

Milly's eyes snapped open, and she saw Jasper, not the little wind but a cat, standing in front of her. Shielding her from the wind's rage. His ears flat against his head, his claws gripping the floor.

Jasper's cries made something inside Milly snap. It was

a snap so loud it broke through all the noise rushing around her head. Milly raised her hand, and a white light consumed her vision. *"Please, just leave us alone!"*

The wind stopped howling.

Her hand stopped throbbing.

The whole world went very, very quiet.

When Milly opened her eyes again, she found herself kneeling on the ground. She looked up. Everything was dark, except for the shining eyes of Horace the half-giant. He grunted above her, and she realized that he'd put himself between her and countless piles of wood and debris. She felt Jasper shift somewhere next to her in the dark.

"Please, little light," she gasped. "Let us see. Anything at all."

A familiar spark of flame wiggled its way out of a crack in the dirt, crawled across her knuckles, and jumped onto her hair. It was warm, but it did not burn.

The half-giant let out a very loud groan and pushed upward until the wood fell from his shoulders. When he did so, a faint circle of light appeared above them. Milly picked up the cat and climbed out with the half-giant, the flame still nestled in her hair. When they escaped the unstable remains of the house, the storm was quiet, the shadows were gone, and neither Cilla nor Lilith were anywhere to be found.

Tears formed in Milly's eyes.

Without thinking, she ran back through the shattered

remains of the tree and found Edaline at the center of the wreckage, still standing. Still frozen.

Milly ran into the witch's arms and hugged her. She knew it didn't matter, that it was too late, but she didn't want to let go. It was the most she could do to thank her. To say how sorry she was.

Unseen by Milly, the witch's eyes finally closed. Elsewhere in the forest, a single bamboo bud sprouted from the earth. The forest mourned their mother and the witch who had once guarded her heart.[40]

---

[40] It has often been thought that when a bamboo forest is about to pass away, green shoots give way to the blooming of pink blossoms as the foundation of a new forest. Death and rebirth are a natural part of a forest's lifespan, and a time of both mourning and celebration for the children of the trees.

THE THIRD HIATUS
an orphan is nothing without her dreams

FOR HER ENTIRE life, Cilla had hoped she was different. She couldn't explain why and she didn't know how, but she knew she was. Somehow. She knew because she remembered things the others didn't. She remembered names of people she never knew, faces of people she'd never met. Sometimes she remembered words from a different language, words that sounded like things a witch might say. She used to think Milly remembered too, like when Milly talked to the house, or when Milly saw the ghosts, or when Milly looked at Junebug.

Eventually she realized Milly was lying.

She didn't know why Milly insisted on lying. She always knew Milly was a witch. Things listened to Milly. They never did when Cilla talked, no matter how hard she tried.

Cilla was always told she shouldn't *want* to be a witch, but what else could she be? What else would she want to be? Milly was a witch, and she was Cilla's favorite person. Most of the time, anyway.

When she found the book, Cilla thought it was her moment. And she thought that again when she ran away. And again when she met Edaline.

But magicks just wouldn't listen to Cilla. No matter what she said or how hard she tried.

So Cilla started lying too.

She met a cat and pretended she understood him. She looked out the window and pretended she saw ghosts. She lied so much that she even started to convince herself. Maybe that's why she'd been able to convince Lilith.

It was just enough of a lie to get what she wanted. What she *thought* she wanted.

Unfortunately, even dreams, no matter how good, can get twisted if they are built on a lie. Cilla didn't know how else to dream.

But she was determined to learn.

When the witch came for her the second time, she knew the witch really meant to take Milly. That somehow, for some reason, the witch meant to use Milly. Maybe even hurt her.

So she lied again.

This time, though, she didn't lie for herself. She had lied for Milly. And in a funny way, that was the most witch-like thing she had ever done.

CHAPTER NINETEEN
the making of a witch

MILLY, JASPER, HORACE, and Ash stood at the edge of the forest. This time on the side of the trees. This time looking into the city-state of Nignip, not out. This time not with fear of the unknown in their eyes, but fear of the known.

Hightop.

She knew now not to trust him. When she'd heard Edaline talk about him, she had told herself he would never be their best chance. But right now, he was the only one.

Their most immediate problem was Milly's hand. It hadn't stopped glowing all day. At first it didn't seem intrusive; it had been nothing more than a faint dim light outlining the mark of a moon. But as time went on, it grew brighter and brighter. Now it was about as bright as a star on a cloudless night.

Milly tried everything she could do to hide it. She balled her hand as tight as she could, but light seeped out the cracks. She found a rag to tie around the mark, but the light broke through the fabric. Nothing she did made it go away. There was no helping or hiding it. She had the markings of a witch.

Horace told her it looked fine. Ash pretended not to notice. Jasper said it'd get them all killed.

But here they were now, moments away from Nignip, and it hadn't stopped. Why hadn't it been glowing when she needed it to—and now that she wanted to hide it, why was it glowing as bright as a new fire? Why did her own body betray her?

Milly breathed in and looked at her friends. "You don't have to come with me," she said for the dozenth time.

"But we are," Horace said, speaking for the whole of them.

Jasper looked determined, and Ash rustled with something that sounded like anger.

"Okay, but you don't *have* to."

"We want to."

"But—"

"Milly," Jasper said, "if you really don't want us to come, just say it."

Milly didn't say anything. In truth, she was relieved to not have to face Nignip alone.

The party shuffled into the city looking very odd. At the front, a lanky half-giant with a shovel and a black cat upon his shoulder.[41] Just behind, a little girl with light bursting

---

[41] *All Strange Things Live in the Dark, Chapter 4*: Cats are one of the top five companions for aspiring witches. They are, by nature, hard to tame and, thus, hard to love. It is not known whether it is the witch that picks the cat or the cat that picks the witch. Either way, the general consensus is that the appearance of them together can mean nothing but bad luck.

out of her hand and a wild broombranch without any discernible rider to keep it on track.

As they passed through the city streets, Milly became more aware of people staring. Until those stares became whispers, and those whispers became loud enough to hear.

"Is that a . . . ?"

"Can't be. They's dead, aren't they?"

"Is she from the woods?"

"But she's so young!"

"Who cares how young it is. It's a—you know."

It didn't take long until many of them made no attempts to hide what they were saying. The more they talked, the louder they got. The bolder they grew.

And the more annoyed Milly became.

"I thought their 'kind' were outlawed."

"Someone should alert the High Council."

"Or Hightop."

"Is she the reason the shadows ate my radishes?"

"Is that an untamed broomstick?"

Milly had just about had it. She wanted to talk back at them. She wanted to say, Yeah? So what? I talk to magicks and have a mark on my palm. I'm friends with a talking cat, and I decided not to tame a broombranch. Why does any of that make me dangerous to you? Why are you so scared? Why won't you just say it already? Say it! Call me a—

"WITCH!"

A familiar round face screamed from a side street. "I knows a witch when I sees one, or my name ain't Ned Culligan!" The gnob stomped his foot down with a thwack.

Horace grabbed her hand and tugged her forward. "Come. Hurry."

"Why?"

"Just hurry."

The half-giant pulled her past the distracted onlookers as Ned continued to scream.

"Witch!" the gnob shouted again. "They's the reason our cities been plagued by shadow! They's the reason the winds have abandoned us. And *she's* one of them!"

One of the passersby immediately turned on him and spat. "*Shut it, Ned.* You know we don't use that word around here."

"But that's what she is! A no-good *witch*!"

"What'd I say?!"

Several of the other onlookers turned on Ned with rotten vegetables and pummeled him, forcing him to backpedal into his alleyway.

"You know I'm right!" he sneered. "You're all just too scared to call her what she is. A wicked, no-good, cheating w—"

A large tomato splattered against his teeth.

"Serves him right," Jasper said with his nose perked up in the air, staring back.

"I kind of feel bad for him," Milly said.

Jasper snorted. "Why?"

"He's scared. They all are. And they're not even taking it out on the right person."

Horace came to an abrupt halt. "Uh-oh."

"What's wrong?"

"Stay back."

"Let me see!"

The half-giant refused to move, so Milly pushed one of his big arms out of the way and peeked around him.

A parade of gnomes marched toward them, led by the one she'd previously seen talking to Hightop. Finnegan. His garb matched the rippling blue cloaks and gold emblems of the others except for a single red string tied around his pointed hat.

He whipped a wand out of his sleeve and pointed it directly at the half-giant. "Who are you and where are you headed?"

"Uh."

Enough hiding. Milly stepped out from behind Horace and opened her fist toward the gnome. "I'm a witch," she said. The light flickered as her voice trembled. "I'm here to see Hightop."

"Oh. Ah. I see. Do you mind—um, putting that away?" The gnome immediately lowered his voice and waved his hand furiously. "We can't have you upsetting everyone.

They're not entirely ready to welcome witches back into the world just yet."

As one unit, Milly and her friends said, "What?"

"Perhaps it's best if you follow us." Finnegan put his wand away and pulled out a pair of blue gloves. He handed them to Milly, his brow creased with concern. "And please, for the love of Arrett, do cover that up."

Milly looked at the others. Horace shrugged at her, and Jasper scrunched up his nose. Ash bristled again but didn't say anything.

She fumbled to put the gloves on and found that the light didn't break through whatsoever. "How does it . . . ?"

"Come along, come along."

The gnomes formed a circle around them and ushered them through the streets (which honestly drew more attention than it staved off). In fact, though the people around them had grown quieter with the gnomes' presence, Milly felt the weight of their stares all the more. For so long, she'd been used to being invisible. To that feeling of people glazing over her as if she didn't exist. Being a witch meant people noticed her.

She wasn't sure she liked how it felt.

Jasper jumped down from Horace's shoulder and walked next to her. "You all right?" he whispered.

"I'm not sure I like this. It makes me feel trapped."

"I understand how you feel."

Milly felt her cheeks burn. "I—I never really apologized to you, did I?"

Jasper shrugged.

"Do you miss being a wind?"

Jasper's whiskers twitched. "Don't think it really matters what either of us wants, does it? We're the same. Stuck. Tamed."

"I'm really sorry."

"Yeah," Jasper paused. Purred. "You know, you're not that bad, as far as humans go."

Milly laughed. "Thanks."

"I do miss being a wind, but oddly, I think I'll miss being a cat, too. I never had this many . . . what do you call 'em?"

"Friends?"

"Huh. Yeah, I guess so. Weird." He shuddered. "Let's just get your sister home quickly, all right?"

The gnomes escorted the party all the way to the tower, and up it and past it, toward the castle no longer hidden in the clouds but now hovering loud and bright above all of Nignip. Finnegan stopped at the door of Hightop's domain and took a deep breath. Milly saw a tiny shadow flick out of the way of his boot and disappear into the ground.

When she looked back up, she saw Finnegan pull on what must have been an invisible rope. A long, threaded ladder unfurled from the castle and landed without a sound at their feet. Horace poked it. The material looked like clouds braided into thick cords. When Milly touched it, the ladder felt dry. Soft. Solid.

Finnegan climbed up the first couple rungs. "Come along, come along."

"Why are we going up there?" Milly asked.

"All will be revealed when we're away from prying ears." He turned and glared at a young boy peeking out from one of the nearby houses.

The boy squeaked and ran off.

"Please, we must hurry."

Milly followed after him and looked down at Horace, who seemed apprehensive of the strange magicks.

"It's okay," she said. "It's much sturdier than it looks."

Horace frowned. "Ground good. Sky bad."

"That's rude," Jasper said.

One of the gnomes shoved past Horace and muttered, "Why do we even have to take this stupid giant?"

Milly scowled at the gnome until he took his foot off the ladder, then climbed back down and offered a hand toward the half-giant. "Come on, friend."

Horace let out a very pointed grunt, closed his eyes, and grabbed her arms with one large hand.

Milly held on with every fiber of her body.

"Too heavy?" he asked.

"No, it's fine," she said through gritted teeth.

Jasper clambered onto the half-giant's back, and together

they all climbed up the twisted ladder. Ash hovered just ahead of the train of gnomes following Horace, complaining the entire time about how long it was taking them.

As they climbed, Finnegan talked to Milly between short breaths.

"So first things first, your lot are legally permitted now. Or about to be. Probably. I'm pretty sure you'll be, anyway. So congratulations and all that. Don't fall from excitement."

Legally permitted?! Milly wanted to exclaim. But didn't.

"Anyways, we haven't told the general public yet. Mostly because the vote hasn't been officially counted. BUT it's pretty much guaranteed. Or so I hear. Or so it was. (This last thing with the North Wind might delay proceedings a bit.) We've been waiting on Hightop, who keeps stalling, but we finally passed a resolution that would let us employ a loophole to get around a clause that would let us—"

Milly shook her head at all the big words. She didn't understand what a single one of those meant.

Horace grunted. "They vote without him."

"Oh," she said. "Thanks."

Finnegan stopped to look down. "Well, *yes*, I was just about to get around to that part, if you would have let me finish."

A bead of sweat was forming on Horace's forehead. "Please don't stop."

"Fine fine." The gnome resumed climbing and talking

at the same time. "As I was saying, your kind's about to be legally permitted again. Not that you were ever *outlawed*, per se. Just, um, highly discouraged."

"How can you discourage someone from *being themself*?" Milly asked.

Finnegan ignored the question. "But now the High Council is officially welcoming all living witches back. As a formal courtesy."

"What he's saying is they made a mistake and feel bad but can't say that out loud so they're backtracking instead," Jasper *mrrow*ed.

"So why am I here?" Milly asked. "I needed to see Hightop."

"Well, we originally set out to find the Witch of the Wasted Woods and offer—ahem—our *congratulations*—"

"You mean apologies."

"—but when we arrived it appeared the entire place had been ripped apart by shadows. Which put *quite* the wrench in our plans. But now that you're here, I'm sure everything will still go smoothly."

Milly couldn't believe the words coming out of this short man's mouth. "You don't care about *witches*. You thought Edaline could help you get rid of the shadows!"

"That's quite the accusation."

"Well?"

"Know what?" Finnegan coughed loudly. "We're almost

there. Why don't we save our collective breath and continue this conversation at the top?"

Milly stared at the gnome's back as she climbed. She may have been a new witch, but she wasn't about to let herself be some pawn in whatever game these gnomes were playing. She was here to get her sister back. Nothing less. Nothing more.

AN INTRODUCTION TO CHAPTER TWENTY
a tale of two witches

MILLY AND HORACE shared a bench that wasn't at all big enough for the two of them. Jasper lay curled at their feet with his head buried underneath his paws, too bothered to listen to the dry bickering of politicks. Ash had been asked to wait outside with the other, albeit tamed, broombranches. Or, according to these gnomes, broom*sticks*. A civilized name for a civilized people.

The High Council of Pointy Hats and Flying Broomsticks wasn't completely made of gnomes. Statistically, only eighty to ninety percent of them were gnomes, which they argued made them a democracy. Similarly, not *all* of them were wizards. Some of them, for instance, were sorcerers. Some double-majored as summoners like Hightop, or moonlighted as a seer. And they had even hired an enchantress to be their secretary.

It hadn't always been this way. In fact, once upon a very recent time a witch used to head their order. A witch named Lilith.

Yes, *that* Lilith.

Let's start before the beginning, shall we?

Once upon a time, every magicker in Arrett was a witch. It didn't matter if they were a boy or a girl, a giant or a gnob. If magicks talked with them and they talked back, they were called a witch. Of course, this was back when all forms of magicks operated under PPAP, the *Prime Premise of Asking Permission*. Wizards were not yet around to simply take things. Enchantresses had not yet learned how to bestow magicks onto things that didn't want magicks. Summoners did not try to control beings of magicks that weren't meant to be controlled.

There were only witches and there were magicks, and the two got along quite well. Many years later, as people grew more comfortable with *taking* and magicks got more accustomed to being *taken from*, witches became a rarer thing to want to be. But there was still one powerful and respected witch. Her name was Lilith. Unlike Milly, Lilith always knew she was a witch and always wanted to be one. You see, she'd had the pleasure of being born into a world where being a witch was something you were still allowed to want to be. She'd never had to question if being a witch was wrong or wicked or even weird.

All that came much later.

One day there was a small disagreement over Arrett's trees. The wizards and gnomes didn't understand why only broombranches were allowed to fly, so they wanted to harvest broombranches from the forests that used to cover the coastlines of Arrett and use them as their own personal steeds.

Lilith and the witches said no.

So then they asked if it'd be okay to move a coven of witches out of East Ernost in order to gain access to just one single, very small grove of broombranch trees.

Lilith and the witches said no.

Then they said they'd ask the trees directly if they'd be okay with it.

The trees, obviously, said no.

So the wizards removed Lilith from the High Council and passed a bunch of laws that let them do all of that anyway.

There are some outside of the High Council who might have called what they did a "declaration of war."

Unbeknownst to Milly, she now sat across the room from the seat Lilith used to sit in. Unlike Lilith, however, Milly was no experienced witch. She had no understanding of legalese. She didn't have the trees on her side. She didn't even know most rudimentary magicks.

She did, however, have a ferocious desire to get her sister back and hoped that would be enough to carry her through this.

(Spoiler alert: It wouldn't.)

CHAPTER TWENTY
how many gnomes does it take to run an effective government?

THE ANSWER IS six hundred forty-two and three-quarters. Some may say that's too many. I argue that that's far too few. Either way, this council had about seventeen. Which, I hope you agree, is undoubtedly inadequate.

Milly sat and listened as the gnomes interrupted each other's interruptions. Finnegan sat in a chair next to Milly and translated events as they unfolded.

"The ones on the left are the pro-witch party," Finnegan said.

"We have a party?"

"This week you do. I'm sure the parties will change once they find a new issue to argue over."

Five gnomes and two humans argued for a complete reinstatement of the witches. They argued that the shadows had technically come *after* the witches vanished, and that the witches had been wrongly outlawed after the war, and that even if they had been the problem, they had by now surely learned their lesson. Besides, one of them said, what did they have to be scared of? It's not like any witch would be brave enough to defy them again. The last person seated on their side of the room, a strange antler-headed creature with very long limbs, remained silent.

"That's Venykk. Apparently, he used to be friends with Lilith. There have been many attempts to take him off the council."

The seven gnomes on the right side argued for continued banishment—or, in the case of the oldest one, total eradication. ("That there's Piddippin. Most of the gnomes on the right side consider his views too harsh, but no one will admit it if it means losing his vote.") They also complained about the proposition of a vote when they were missing a member of their council.

"It's kind of funny. As soon as Hightop went missing, council members who'd been dragging their feet all of a sudden wanted a vote."

All the meanwhile, an incredibly short gnome with an incredibly long beard sat at the very end of the room listening to each side.

"Grandmaster Mulligan. He may not get to vote, but in the end, whatever he says goes."

As they listened, Milly heard the arguments on the left begin to break apart and warp. They went from arguing for complete reinstatement of witches to a partial, really heartfelt apology to "maybe sending a gift basket." Who would they send the gift basket to? Who knows! At one point, one of the humans even recommended not calling them witches at all. "Why not let them practice their magicks and have them call it something else?"

"What's the point? They'd still be witches!"

"It was just a thought . . ."

Another from the right side squared his shoulders. "I think we all need to take into account this North Wind situation! He's gone missing. How do we know it's not the fault of a *witch*?!"

One of the pro-witch gnomes pointed at Milly. "Maybe we should ask her!"

"Ask her?" Piddippin scoffed. "What could a *little girl* possibly have to say about politicks? She couldn't even tame her own broombranch."

Milly imagined a furious Ash rustling his leaves furiously. The idea made her grin.

"What are you smiling at?!"

Milly opened her mouth as if to answer, but then pointed at her own mouth and shook her head.

That only seemed to make the gnome madder.

"Friends." The chamber quieted when Venykk spoke. His voice sounded like the arrival of an autumn wind creaking the door open. "I believe it is in our best collective interest to at least ask the girl her name. At this point, she is not a witch. She is a *person*, and we are discussing her *future*. So long as the child abides by our chamber's rules, I offer her permission. Let her speak." He turned his gaze all around the room, but none of the others dared look him in the eye.

Finally, he turned to Mulligan, who nodded.

Venykk turned toward Milly and dipped his mighty head. "The floor is yours, child."

Milly gulped, but her mouth was dry. She hadn't been ready for this.

Finnegan whispered. "Stand up and present yourself. And don't show any emotion. They won't take anything you say seriously if you show emotion."

No emotion? What had this entire meeting been but a boiling pot of emotions?

"You got this," Jasper said. "You're a witch. They won't say so, but deep down they're afraid of you. They're afraid of your truth. Say what you need to say."

"Well, get on with it, then!" The voice of the gnome was very familiar.

Milly locked eyes with the gnome who spoke and realized why. It was the gnome who'd once berated Horace's mother. She narrowed her eyes.

"High Council." Her voice was swallowed up by the room.

"Speak louder!" Piddippin said.

"High Council!" Milly said, too loudly this time, and paused as her voice bounced around the room. One of the gnomes snickered but stopped when Venykk stared at him.[42]

---

[42] As you've seen, a lot can be revealed in a voice. Voices are clothes that we wear for our insides. Some wear their voices discreetly, dressing only in muted

"My name is Milly. And I am a witch."

"Don't look like much, does she?"

"*Let her speak,*" Venykk said, silencing their chatter. He then turned toward Milly. "Tree-friend, why are you here?"

Milly took a deep breath and took off her glove. The white mark flooded the room with its light. "I am a witch from West Ernost, and I'm hunting down the person who stole my sister. Lilith."

The room didn't react at first with anything but shock, then one of the gnomes started to cackle. It set off a chain reaction of laughter bouncing in the halls. One of Mulligan's stern eyes widened.

"She thinks a dead woman stole her sister!"

"Maybe it's Lilith's *ghost.*"

"You scared of ghosts, little witch?"

Finnegan let out a long, deep sigh.

"*I'm telling the truth,*" Milly said amidst their noise. "I don't care what way this vote goes. All I know is I can't *stop* being a witch, no matter what your laws say or whatever you decide to call me. I was *born* with magicks. In fact, I *like* being a witch." She paused to feel the weight of her next

---

mumbles and sighs and murmurs and whispers. Others wear their voices boldly, displaying a colorful assortment of screams and shouts and whoopings and hollers. As for the wizards, they were used to dressing in colorful lies and deceitful slanders, which are clothes that only appear flattering to those who wear them. Milly did not have the desire to dress her voice in anything but honesty.

words. "But I would gladly give that all up if I could just have my sister back."

Mulligan stood from his chair, quieting the other gnomes. "*Little girl*, you do realize we are voting on whether or not to allow witches back into the world, yes? You realize that these statements, false though they be, indict your own kind?"

Milly felt her chin quiver but nodded anyway.

Mulligan chuckled and sat back down. "Well, I think we've heard enough. Shall we put it to a vote, then?"

The doors blew open, and a cold wind filled the halls. A ragged figure stood in the doorway and an angry voice bellowed out from the man.

"How dare this council vote without me?!"

It was Hightop.

Milly immediately sat back down. The wizard staggered into the center of the room, not even seeming to realize that Milly or Horace were there.

"I told you to wait until my witch *relocation* project had finished!"

Finnegan stood up and put his hands out placatingly. "Now, Hightop, we haven't voted just yet—"

"But you were ready to."

"I did what I could to stop them," the young toe-thwacking gnome said.

"Shut up, Chaddigan."

Mulligan sighed. "Take your seat, Hightop."

"No," Hightop snapped. "I have things to say. The old hag is *back*, and she's stolen a little girl! We can't vote on this until—"

"Take. Your. Seat."

Hightop's jaw snapped shut, and he stomped over to his seat. One of the other gnomes tried to whisper to him, but Hightop shook him off. When he did, he locked eyes with Milly.

Something like confused rage filled his gray eyes. But only for a second. He forced himself to smile before he pointedly looked away.

Milly whispered down to Jasper. "Do his eyes . . . remind you of someone?"

"A little bit, yeah. Kind of like . . ."

"Lilith."

"Finnegan," Mulligan said. "Please escort our guests outside while we finalize this vote."

CHAPTER TWENTY-ONE
the secrets of a fyin boomsick

MANY HOURS LATER, Finnegan paced back and forth while Milly, Horace, and Jasper sat watching.

"I wonder what's happening in there," he said to himself.

"Truly, a mystery to us all," Jasper said.

"They sure are taking their time." He glanced at the door. "Can't believe I'm stuck watching *children*."

Finnegan didn't seem to notice them, or care if he did. He continued walking back and forth.

"Hey!" Jasper skittered out of the way when the gnome turned around. "Watch the tail."

Milly looked from Horace to Jasper. "He does have a point. They're taking a long time."

Horace tilted his head.

"Maybe we could find something to do while waiting," Jasper said. "Look around or something."

"We might even find clues about Lilith's whereabouts."

"What?" Finnegan finally stopped in his tracks. "No no no, we have to wait here."

"*You* have to wait here," Jasper said. "I used to be free to go anywhere I wanted. Waitaminute!" Jasper laughed. "I'm a cat. I'm *still* free to go anywhere I want." He winked at Milly. "As soon as I run, you run."

"Wait, what?"

"Bye!" Jasper bit the gnome's ankle and ran down a hallway.

"*Yowch!*" Finnegan jumped in the air and rubbed his ankle. "What on—hey! Come back!"

Jasper jumped over a bookcase and knocked some of its material onto the floor. "Oops," he said, and kneaded the pages.

Finnegan pulled his hat off his head and wrinkled it in his hands. "Don't—no! Those are very valuable!"

Jasper turned the corner, and they heard a loud crash, followed by someone shouting.

Finnegan ran after the cat, turned back halfway, and said, "Please don't go anywhere!" then turned back round again and followed Jasper round the corner.

Milly and Horace heard more screaming and crashing bookcases. They locked eyes with each other, then hopped out of their seats and discreetly headed the opposite direction.

They ducked around a corner on the opposite side and found themselves at the bottom of a vast circular courtyard. Above them, the sky was churning with the beginnings of a storm.

Milly hadn't been able to see much of the castle on her way in, since the gnomes ushered her to the High Council's chamber as soon as they could, but now that she could see the castle, she gasped at how much bigger it was than she'd thought it could be.

A large winding staircase wrapped around the entire courtyard, each stone step almost the size of Milly. A second, smaller set of steps had been carved into the middle of the first. They were a different color than the first, polished and white.

Horace pointed at the big steps. "Stone people." He pointed at the smaller steps. "Grass people."

Round half rooms lined the winding staircase, protruding from the building. Glass walls contained the people inside the rooms, like flies trapped in giant dewdrops. Most of the rooms closest to the ground floor held clusters of gnome wizards in them. Banners atop the rooms said *Pointy Hats* in embroidered gold all the way up till the top floor of the cloud castle. There was nothing to read on the last floor.

"What are those?" Milly said, squinting.

"Witch rooms," Horace replied.

"What do you mean, 'which' rooms? Those ones right there."

The half-giant shook his head. "No. *Witch* rooms."

Milly looked back and forth, but none of the dozens of wizards scurrying around seemed to care that she and Horace were walking about. So she just . . . walked to the stairs.

"Come on," she said. "Let's see what's up there."

The two of them worked their way up the stairs. Some

of the rooms they passed were crammed full of gnomes surrounded by paperwork, arguing as feathers and ink danced in the air above them, recording every word they said. Another room held a woman surrounded by bottles as she tried to brew something in the pot beside her. The next showcased two wizards in riding stocks, training broomsticks to do tricks. Milly flinched and looked away until they got to the top.

Up here, the bubble rooms had been shattered, and the banners—written not in gold, but etched directly into the stonework—had been clawed off.

The last room, at the very end of the staircase, still had some of its letters left. Just enough for Milly to figure out what it used to say.

F yin B ooms icks

"You were right. These used to be witch rooms." Milly tiptoed over the shattered walls and looked around. The room had been mostly cleaned out, but not very well. Debris still cluttered the floors and a large table sat in the middle. "See anything?"

Horace followed her in, crouching down to avoid whatever was left of the ceiling. "Lilith?" he asked, pointing at a picture frame left on the floor.

Milly gently picked it up and wiped off the dust with her sleeve. It *was* Lilith. The picture had faded, but it was still richer in color than she expected. The older witch sat in a simple chair with a young boy on her lap. She didn't look quite as scary in this photograph. In fact, she was even smiling. The boy's face, however, was missing. Someone had burned a rough hole through it. Whoever it was must have not wanted him to be recognized.

"Who is boy?" Horace said, peeking over her shoulder.

"I don't know," she said. She flipped the picture over and saw scribbles on the corner.

It read *Lilith and Carlos, East Ernost.*

"Carlos?"

"Always snooping, I see."

Milly and Horace spun around at the sound of the voice. They saw Hightop standing at the top of the stairs.

He smiled at them disarmingly. "No matter. Finnegan thought he'd lost you two, but I knew you couldn't have possibly left the building. Too many things to poke for that curious bug in your head! Did you find anything *interesting?*"

Milly held the picture behind her back and shrugged her shoulders. "Not really."

"That's too bad." Hightop shook his head. "We're ready to finalize the vote. Told them I'd come get you two in case you wanted to see how it went."

Milly narrowed her eyes. She didn't see anyone else with the wizard. This was the time to ask questions.

"Where's Lilith?" she said.

Hightop's eyebrow quirked. "Why should I know anything about—"

"Earlier. In the room. You said that an old witch had stolen a little girl. Who else could it be except Lilith?"

One of Hightop's fingers quivered, but he quickly regained composure and sighed. "Look. I know I said I'd help you find your sister, but I have other important things to do right now. If you don't mind stepping along, we can—"

"No." Milly said.

"*Little girl*. There is important—"

"No!" The word was starting to taste good on her tongue. Milly felt her hand burn beneath the glove, like her anger wanted to burst the seams. It was a more powerful feeling than any magicks she'd ever felt. "You tricked me into killing the forest. You're the reason Edaline's . . ." She took a breath. "Lilith stole my sister again, and it's your fault. What do you know?"

Hightop eyed her with a mysterious look. "Do you really think you can stop the old hag? Your own *kind*?"

"I—I have to try," Milly stuttered. She knew she couldn't.

Hightop laughed. Hard. "Spoken like a *true* witchling." He cleared his throat and lowered his voice. "Very well, I'll tell you what I know. She's planning on taking your sister to the Rift. Their home, I suppose. Some ritual involving these gripes and gobblers. Maybe if you catch up to her, you can tell her the *truth*. Make her realize she's about to sacrifice the wrong little girl."

Milly couldn't believe her ears. "Why would she do

that? Does she really think the shadows and witches are connected?"

"Maybe she's gone mad. Or maybe—" He paused to narrow his eyes. "Maybe she feels shame. Maybe she knows witches don't belong in this world anymore."

Milly felt a cold lump fill her stomach, but she didn't show it. "That doesn't make any sense." She didn't really trust the witch, but what Hightop was saying didn't sound quite like the truth either.

"Why council not do anything?" Horace asked.

"About the witches?" He scoffed. "You've seen them. Gotten too scared to make the right decisions. Besides, it seems your little display made quite the impression. I don't think any of them realize quite how *dangerous* you are, little one. But I do."

"Where is the Rift?" Milly asked.

The wizard stared at her. "You really don't know?"

Milly looked back at Horace, whose face was ashen.

"It was practically in your own backyard. It's over the edge of the cliffs, past West Ernost. Where the war ended. It's—"

"Home."

Hightop rolled his eyes. "Anything else you'd like to know, or can we head back now? I'm itching to get this awful business over with."

Milly shook her head.

"Let's get to it then." Hightop turned toward the steps,

then stopped. "You know, you never told me you were a witch. Can't say I'm not a little hurt. I thought we were *friends*." He laughed and continued down. "Oh well. I suppose now that you can be a witch in *public*, there won't be any more reason to hide, will there?"

Milly and Horace shared a worried glance, then followed the wizard back down the stairs.

CHAPTER TWENTY-TWO
everything has a price

THE COUNCIL ROOM was crammed full of noise and people when they returned. Milly couldn't help but glance down at her hand a third time. She felt it burning beneath the glove. What was happening to her? It felt like her own body didn't know if she was a witch or not. Like there were two Millys inside of her, wrestling for control. The one that wanted to be a witch, that wanted to be kind and powerful at once, that wanted to befriend and defend magicks to her last breath.

And the *other*. The one who would do anything to save her sister, even if it meant taming a wind. Even if it meant hurting someone. The side that wanted to be powerful without consequence.

The only thing that the two had in common was this: they were tired of asking for permission.

So when Milly walked back into the room, she was already ready to leave. Regardless of what the council's decision was.

As before, all members of the council sat to the left and right of Mulligan. Hightop calmly walked over to his seat and winked at Milly from where he was. While the gnomes and humans around him argued violently with the others across the aisle, he appeared to be calm. Frighteningly so.

Milly stood next to Horace, pressed against the back wall by the crowd of people. There was nowhere to sit with how many bodies now filled the chamber. They were mostly gnomes and humans from other parts of the castle, but Milly also recognized citizens of Nignip pushing in from the outside of the room. A familiar giant stood just outside the door poking her head in. Her loud voice boomed through the room. "Wurches gooooood!"

Horace's face cracked into a wide smile, and he echoed his mother.

For a brief moment, Milly felt the pain in her hand subside. She looked around the room to see if she could also spot Jasper when she felt a fuzzy head bump into the back of her knee.

She looked down. "Oh, good; you're here!"

"Yeah, I had to sneak back in after they chased me out of one of their libraries."

"I'm glad to see you," she admitted.

Jasper blinked. "Yeah, you too. Did you find anything useful?"

"We found this."

"A picture? Anything else?"

"We need to go back to St. George's. Hightop said the witch was bringing Cilla back there."

"What? Why?"

"She thinks she can use Cilla to get rid of the shadows. She wants to . . . sacrifice her."

After several more moments of the crowd shouting and arguing, Mulligan finally stood up and looked out over the room without a word. Little by little, the chamber quieted until there was a strange, deathly quiet.

Mulligan sat back down and nodded his head at Venykk. "Starting with the oldest member, announce your vote. *Yea* to reinstate witches in this hallowed chamber. *Nay* to exile them from the traditions *officially*."

Venykk stood up and, with a very still voice, spoke. "Yea."

"Nay!" Piddippin said quickly after.

"Nay," said the next.

"Nay," said yet another.

"Yea."

They went on like this until there were eight yeas and eight nays, with only Hightop's vote left.

Everyone held their collective breath.

Hightop stood from his chair and smiled at the room. "For many years, I have strived to be on the right side of history, and I hope to continue that tradition today." He looked directly at Milly. "If they ever screw up, I'll be the *first* to admit my mistakes. But for now, celebrate, little witch. Return home. I vote *yea!*"

It must have been quite shocking, for it wasn't until one person broke the silence with a cheer that the chamber erupted into noise again.

Piddippin cursed at Hightop. "You traitor! You've handed the vote to them!"

A couple gnomes tried to shout their objections over the growing crescendo, and Mulligan shouted from his chair, "WITCHES LEGAL NINE YEAS TO EIGHT NAYS," but it didn't matter. The chamber erupted in pandemonium. Several angry gnomes reached for Hightop, but a large crowd had already stampeded to him, some cheering, others cursing.

"We need to get out of here," Milly said to her friends.

"Agreed," Jasper said.

"Okay," Horace said. He picked up Milly and Jasper and tried to wade toward the door.

"SHE'S ONE OF THEM! A WITCH!" Someone shouted, and several eyes turned from Hightop onto Milly.

The already crowded room got more packed as people pushed in from the outside. Mulligan attempted to silence the chambers, but no amount of sternness could quiet the pressing mob. Horace tried to push through to the door, but not even the half-giant could force his way through the crowd.

"Let her down!"

"Give us the witch!"

Milly tried to glance back to see what was happening in the room. It looked like Hightop had somehow managed to slip away while the rest of the High Council did their best to keep people from stomping on their desks.

Suddenly, Milly felt Horace's body jolt away, and she realized that the half-giant was being lifted up and over the crowd. Into the arms of Horace's mother.

She squeezed him tight and said something to him in a language that sounded like thirty-two rocks tossed in a giant hamster ball.

Horace responded in the same language, using a much longer string of words than Milly had ever heard him say before. Then he pointed down at something, toward the stables where the broomsticks were kept.

His mother nodded, locked eyes with Milly, and smiled. Then the giant turned and, with Horace on her shoulders, and Milly and Jasper on his, they stepped over the people scurrying up the stairs. They had no competition whatsoever for the giant steps, which made their getaway all the quicker. Milly laughed at the faces below her. Though she'd never noticed it, an invisible weight seemed to have lifted from her chest.

A *witch*. She could actually *choose* to be a witch now! Of course it made sense. Of course this was the thing she'd once wanted to be, the dream hiding deep inside her that she'd ignored and forced out for so long.

But . . . the weight wasn't completely gone. Being a witch didn't mean people would stop treating her differently. It didn't mean her sister wasn't still in trouble because Milly had kept being too scared to tell the truth.

She needed to go home. She needed to find Lilith and stop whatever she was planning to do. She had to make sure Cilla was . . .

Horace's mother stopped next to the broom stable and

lifted Horace off her shoulders, who then lifted Milly off his shoulders, who held Jasper in her arms. When her feet hit the ground, Milly turned toward Horace's mother.

"Thank you," she said. "I remember you from before. When the gnomes . . ." Milly gulped. "Anyway, thank you."

The giant nodded her head, then looked expectantly at Horace. She said something in rock tongue.

Horace looked taken aback and said something harsh back.

His mother shook her head firmly.

Horace rubbed the back of his head. "You run," he said. "We stay. Mother say not safe."

Milly looked back and saw that the crowd was finally working their way down the stairs. They'd only made it half-way. "But I don't want to leave you here."

"We leave Nignip. After you run."

"Milly," Jasper said. "We shouldn't argue with a giant."

Milly's chin quivered. "Thank you, Horace, for every-thing."

"When find, tell Cilla hello?"

"Of course. You two stay safe, okay?"

"Okay."

Milly turned toward the stable, where she saw Ash pull-ing against a silver thread. The broomsticks around Ash just sat against the ground. They'd all learned to stop trying to escape a long time ago.

Milly ran to Ash and tried to undo the rope, but when she

undid the knot, it just twisted itself back into shape. Horace's mother saw it, too, and Milly saw the giant's neck tense.

"I've been trying to get out ever since they took you," Ash said. *"But these blasted gnomish magicks just won't. Let. Go."*

Jasper sniffed the rope and hissed. "Domination magicks," he said. "Not unlike the magicks you used on . . ."

"You?" Milly finished the cat's sentence so he wouldn't have to.

"Yeah," he said.

"How can we undo it?"

"Can't," he said. "Not unless you're willing to pay its price. Gnomes don't look very kindly on promise-breakers."[43]

Milly ripped the gloves off her hands. The light from her palm flickered with her own uncertainty but dimmed into a calm silver as she put her hands on the rope. A bitter scent hit her nostrils. She remembered the flutterwishes. She knew she could break this. "Do you think they'll try to make witches illegal again if we start breaking rules?"

Jasper laughed. "Probably."

She narrowed her eyes.

And snapped the rope.

The knot instantly fell limp to the ground as Milly felt her arms burn with the sensation of an invisible cord wrapping itself around her wrists. The feeling didn't last long,

---

[43] Winds and witches agree: the only thing better than keeping a promise is breaking a cruel one.

however, since it was meant to tame broomsticks and not little girls.

Just as before with the flutterwishes, the rope faded away into the white fire of her hands and Ash flew free.

The other broomsticks appeared to notice. Some of them cowered back while others poked up their trimmed yellow-leafed ends.

Milly looked over at them. "Do you want to be free, too?"

They didn't answer for a moment. Not until the nearest poked out and bristled its yellow leaves. *"Free us, witch."*

Milly lifted her hands and closed her eyes. "I don't know what I'm doing," she said, "but I can try."

A loud, violent crack erupted, and she snapped her eyes open to see the entire roof of the stables torn out from its roots. *But that doesn't make sense! I didn't . . .*

No, it wasn't her at all. She watched in awe as Horace's mother tore the stable apart beam by beam, stone by stone. Dozens of invisible ropes lashed against her forearms and legs, making her grimace each time, but she didn't stop. Every time a rope remade itself, she bit its fibers and spat them out. Every time a beam tried to reconstruct itself, she kicked it over and ground it to dust.

Soon, no amount of the gnomes' clever magicks could reconstruct what wasn't there to build

Milly looked at the giant, whose arms were now red and whose chest was heaving. "Why did you . . ."

The giant took a deep breath and spoke in a ragged voice.

Horace interpreted it for Milly: "Mother say she hurt now. You must run. Must save sister. Must . . . hurt later."

Milly lowered her hands and looked down at her wrist. A thin, crooked red line coiled around it, and she shivered, wondering what price she'd have to pay to break her sister's promise.

"Uh-oh," Jasper said.

Milly heard angry shouting and snapped her gaze back up to see the crowd running across the ground now.

One of the gnomes raised his wand at them. "That's mine!" A vine pulled itself out of the ground and reached for one of the brooms.

Horace's mother stepped in front of the broom and caught the vine. It tried to wrap around her fingers, but she snapped it apart with ease. It is much harder to tame a giant than it is to tame a broombranch.[44]

Milly turned to Horace, horribly aware of how much she'd miss her friend. "I wish we'd had more time. We barely got to know each other."

---

[44] So hard, in fact, that no known magicker has ever successfully done so. Giants are born of the mountains. The strongest giant was so strong that he once held down all four winds when they attempted to abandon Arrett. (That giant's name was Ovid the Small.) As such, the city of Nignip used sneakier methodology to keep the giants quiet. They used different magicks. Things like politicks and knowledge and isolation. Horace's mother knew how to get around these, in her own way. She knew that if all the city's laws were written in grass tongue, she'd have to teach her son grass tongue. And that if she couldn't be tamed, she could stand in for those who could be.

"See you soon." The half-giant smiled, then lifted Milly and Jasper and deposited them on top of Ash. "Take care of witch friend."

"I'll do my best," Ash said, and shot off into the sky, surrounded by the other freed broombranches. They chittered and bristled and laughed among themselves as they made their escape.

But Milly couldn't laugh. She kept her eyes on the giants the entire time, wishing she could help them, too.

CHAPTER TWENTY-THREE
an east wind, who is nobody but themself

MILLY, ASH, AND Jasper struggled against the winds as they raced through the sky. A storm brewed above them, tossing its wild curls in their face. The other broombranches had abandoned them long ago. Wind whistled through the tangles in Milly's hair, as if trying to pull her off. The tips of her ears burned from the cold.

"Couldn't we have gone around?!" Jasper wailed. He was wrapped in a blanket tied to Milly's back.

"There isn't time!"

"This is more fun!" Ash said.

A booming echo reverberated, and Milly clutched tighter, shivering and hugging her body as close to the broom as she could.

"Just tell me when it's over!" Jasper said.

"Aren't you a wind?"

"A *little* wind! This is . . . this is *not* little."

She heard a *poof* and felt a soft wave of dampness hit her.

The world slowed down and the broom righted itself. With her eyes squeezed shut, she felt a warmth on the side of her cheek.

Milly squinted one eye open, then both. She sat up and gasped.

Beside them was the sun, rising in the east.

It was bigger, truer than the sun she knew. Somehow, if the sun she'd known from below was the size of a copper piece, up here it filled the whole sky. This sun could not bear to share the sky with any spot of blue even if it wanted to. Despite being so close to it, she felt warm without burning. Here was the sun, unclothed in all its glory, vulnerable and unashamed.

She laughed and lifted her hands.

Loud thunder rolled through the clouds beneath them, and Milly grabbed the broom again. "What was that?" she whispered.

From the clouds emerged a large pale figure, blocking out part of the sun. Steam blew from a hole in its center, and the thunder rumbled once more. The creature disappeared back into the clouds.

Milly stretched her neck to see if she could spot another sign of the mysterious being.

A large gust of wind blew up from beside them, and the hill rose again, higher this time, a large white wall in front of Milly's face. Before her was a large, unblinking eye the size of St. George's. It stared at her with an intensity that made her shiver. A pillar of smoke jetted from the top of the creature's back. Another rumbling filled the sky before the creature fell back down into the curling wisps of cloud.

Milly felt her chest tighten. "It's a whale. A giant whale. In the sky."

"Yes, witch." The voice that came from beneath the white surface was very deep and terrible. "To some, I am nothing more than overcast. A cloud that brings rain to their fields. To others, I am the storm that whips across the coast. To you, little one, I am a whale."

She gulped. The sound of their voice left her equally in awe and in fear. The whale could have swept them out of the sky with one swish of their tail if they wanted to, but they hadn't. Yet.

"You seem to be more than just that," she said.

"And what do you think I am? Maybe you should ask that shivering friend on your back." Now they turned their eye on Jasper. "Surely you remember me."

Jasper poked his head out, shivering even more despite the warmth of the sun. "Y-you're the . . . you're the E-E-East—"

"Wind," they finished, rolling up once more and blinking their heavy eye. "I, caller of *little winds* who have abandoned their duties catching rain from the cliffs. I, finger painter of waves and shorelines. I, who swallow anchors and spit out ships." Their voice grew louder and darker with every word, thunder rippling through the clouds and lightning sparkling in between the cracks.

Even Ash shivered at the sound.

"But," the whale continued, "it does not matter what I am. The real mystery is, what are you?"

"I'm a girl," Milly said, warily.

"No." The wind grew loud, then soft. "I mean *what* are you? Some call themselves kings, others call themselves knights. A few,"—they paused—"even like pretending to be gods."

Jasper shrunk deeper into his blanket.

"I suppose," Milly started, "I might be a witch."

"Suppose? *Might?*"

"Maybe I'm a mother. Or a sister. Or a thief or a trouble-maker or—"

"No," the wind said. Their voice thundered. "I did not ask what others call you! I did not ask what others have decided you are. What do you call yourself? Tell me. *What are you?*"

"I don't know!" Milly shouted. Then, quietly, she swallowed. "I . . . I don't know."

The wind slowed until it was no more than a slow breeze against her knuckles. "Good. An honest answer."

Milly shivered. The rain against her skin felt ice cold.

"And you, little wind. I see you have taken quickly to your name."

Jasper stayed silent.

The giant whale laughed, their voice causing lightning to flash beneath them. "A reluctant witch and a tamed wind who thinks he's a cat. Not to mention a broombranch! You have tamed many things for someone who calls herself a *witch.*"

"I'm not tamed!" the broombranch squeaked.

"Aren't you?" The wind blinked, then turned their attention back to Milly. "So then, witch, what is it you desire of me?"

The whale rolled, causing a giant wave of wind to send Milly and the broom soaring upward.

Drifting back down, Milly flattened her wild hair and straightened her clothes. She thought long and hard about her next words, weighing out the consequences of what they'd cost her.

"Can you help us get my sister back?" she asked.

The East Wind quieted, and the air grew still. "The last time a wind trusted a human, that human betrayed us with a domination spell. He brought no small amount of suffering. He shook the very bones of this world, and left Arrett's heart broken and hurt and afraid."

"Do you mean Hightop? I thought he ended the war."

"The war, yes. But the hate? Hate doesn't end, child. It can only hide, buried in its own shame until some foolhardy witch decides to dig it up again."

"That's why I need your help."

Pools of angry winds circled beneath. Milly tried not to look at them. "What is the difference between you and Hightop? If I help you, what will you do with the magicks I have gifted you?" The rolling of winds increased, some threatening to snatch at Milly's dangling feet.

Milly hugged her arms to herself. "I just want to save my sister," she whispered.

The winds ceased. The sky grew silent, and the whale's mighty head did not reappear.

"You will not need my magicks. Not when you already have this little wind at your side. I will not be able to help you fight Hightop or my brother whom he has tamed. But—" They took a mighty leap from the clouds, higher than hey'd soared before, rising until all of the whale but the tail was visible. "There is one thing I can give you."

"What do you want in return?" Milly choked.

They stared at Milly for a brief moment, blinked their wild eye, and then crashed down, causing a massive wave of fierce and violent winds to rise.

"I just want to save my brother."

The winds blew around and through Milly. They sent her spiraling down the storm, past the Needsy Woods, and straight on her way to the terraced cliffs of West Ernost.

CHAPTER TWENTY-FOUR, PART ONE
a good witch is nothing without her home

DROPS OF WATER rolled across Milly's face. There he was, St. George's, hidden in the fog atop its hill by the edge of the cliff. Just the same as he had always been.

The sun hung low in the sky. It peeked out from between the clouds, brushing one last yellow stain across the rice fields.

But Milly also saw the gripes.

They cut deep into the hills, shadows so dark they filled the valleys like rivers. They reached upward, over people's houses and toward St. George's. From this height, they had the appearance of one massive creature, hungry and devouring and never satisfied.

How long had they lain hidden, shrunken, beneath the ground?

How long had she been oblivious to their presence?

"Where to, little witch?"

Wordless, she pointed to the foster home, and the broombranch changed direction.

Jasper peeked his head out over her shoulder and shivered. "Lilith is here."

"How do you know that?"

"The stench. It's strong."

"What does she smell like?"

The cat hesitated. "Death."

Milly's breath quickened, but she adjusted her grip and thought of Cilla.

The three descended to St. George's. Milly dismounted the broombranch and untied the blanket around her back to let Jasper out.

The cat shook himself with intense vigor, then sat down and groomed the knots out of his anxious fur.

"Can you guys wait here? I . . . I need to do something first."

"Sure."

"Don't take too long."

Milly left them there and walked up to the door. She put her muddy hand on the frame and whispered, "Hello, Georgie."

The door swung open.

It didn't even surprise her.

Milly slipped her shoes off and walked in. She wasn't sure what to expect. It felt like such a long time since the last time she'd been in these halls. The wood beneath her feet was so familiar, comforting even though it was cold. Up ahead, she heard rapid footsteps thud against the floor, followed by Nishi and Ikki shouting at the top of their lungs.

She passed by one of Abby's socks lying in the hallway. Mostly, she noticed the smell of Doris's rice buns drifting in from the kitchen and followed her nose to the source.[45]

When she entered, she found Doris's back facing her. The old woman's shoulders were bent over a chopping board, the knife in her hand a metronome.

Thwick. Thwick. Thwick. Thwick.

Milly knocked on the doorframe.

"Dinner's not ready yet." Doris put down the knife and slid the ginger she'd been cutting into a giant pot of boiling water. "If you want a snack, grab something from the cupboard. I don't want anyone out in the garden tonight. Not with those shadows out there. The whole cliffside's gone—"

The chopping board fell from the woman's hand as she turned and caught sight of Milly, her face pale like she was looking at a ghost.

"Hi." Milly felt her cheeks flush.

"Milly!" Doris practically leaped forward and lifted Milly up into her arms. Her tears smeared against Milly's cheeks. "My dear, dear child. I thought you were lost forever."

It didn't take long for Milly to cry, too. She grasped the back of Doris's clothes and held tightly. "I missed you," she said. "I'm so, so sorry."

"There's nothing to be sorry about."

---

[45] The scent of a home-cooked meal is one of the most powerful, yet overlooked magicks of all. It is a comfort to the hungry. A guide to the lost. A home for the prodigal.

"I'm a wi-witch," she tried to say, sobbing through the words tumbling out of her. "I understand if you don't want me anymore, but I thought you should know."

"It's okay." Doris put Milly down and wiped the corners of her eyes.

Milly swallowed. A question burned inside of her. She thought she knew the answer, hoped it was the answer she needed to hear, but she was too scared to ask out loud. Instead she said, "I'm sorry I left."

Doris shook her head. "No, no. It's okay. Are you hungry? Do you want food?"

Milly shook her head and looked around the house. "I'm sorry you got stuck with me. I'm sorry you got stuck being a mother."

"I'm not stuck." Doris stared at her with wet eyes. "I chose to be a mother. Just like I also chose to be a carpenter." She took Milly's hand in hers and traced the mark on Milly's palm. "And if I had to do it all again, I'd do it all exactly the same."

Milly stared at her feet.

"Milly, are you sure you're a witch?"

"I'm sorry," Milly said again, even though she wasn't sure what she was sorry for.

"Do you want to be one?"

Milly nodded.

Doris smiled. "You're a good witch," she said, and squeezed Milly once more. "I have leftovers if you want them."

Milly shook her head. "I—I have to do one last thing. And then I'll be back. Promise."

"You're not going to tell me what it is, are you?"

Milly shook her head. "I can't."

"Is it about Cilla?"

Milly didn't answer. She didn't have to. She knew her face must have given it away.

Doris sniffed and straightened her lips. "I trust you. Do what you must. And when you come back, you'll have a warm meal and a clean bed waiting for you."

"What about the others?" Milly asked. "They don't know what I am yet. What if they don't want me to stay here?"

"You're their sister, Milly. Witch or not, this is your home."

"Doriiiiiiiis." It sounded like Nishi. "I can't find Junebug anywhere!"

Milly felt her heart leap.

"You're not ready to see them, are you?"

Milly shook her head.

Doris struggled to open the wall's wooden slat, a sneaky exit through the kitchen. The outside storm was gathering its strength. She nodded at Milly. "Go ahead. We'll be here waiting."

Milly nodded and jumped out of the house. Like before, she fell to her knees, catching herself with her hands on the grass.

"And, Milly?"

She turned around.

"Please, be safe." Doris closed the slat.

Milly looked at her hand and saw that it no longer glowed. All that was left was the familiar outline of a silver moon. She snuck back round to the front of the house, where she saw Jasper and Ash hovering in the air, trying to get away from the stubby fingers of the gripes reaching for them. The shadows surrounded the front door, just inches away from the thin crack of light leaking out from St. George's.

"Get away from my house!" she shouted. As soon as she did, the shadows turned toward her.

"*Look out!*" Ash exclaimed.

Milly glanced down and saw a hand reach out of the ground for her ankle. She jumped back and held out her hand. "Please, little light, I need your help again."

Nothing happened.

"Milly! Look up!"

The broombranch came flying toward her, and she jumped off the ground, away from the gripe. Ash caught her backward in the air.

"I don't understand. Why didn't anything happen?"

"Some magicks are scared of the dark," Jasper said.

"Are you scared?"

"Sometimes."

"*Where are we going?*"

Milly scrambled around on the broombranch until she was facing the right direction. "We need to find Lilith."

"Can you smell her?"

Jasper poked his nose up into the air, then shook his head. "This storm is making things difficult."

Milly looked down at the landscape. With the sun gone, the gripes and gobblers were bolder. They stampeded through the gardens and devoured whole rows of vegetables. They sloshed through the rice farms, stuck their dirty hands in, and tore up the earth. It was almost like they were looking for something.

"Hightop said the witch was looking for the Rift . . . somewhere East Ernost used to be . . . Oh! I know where they are."

"Where to, little witch?"

Milly pointed toward the sea. "Follow the cliff until you find a white tree."

CHAPTER TWENTY-FOUR, PART TWO
a good witch is nothing without her temper

ELMA'S OUTLINE GLOWED against a moonless canvas. Though the winds howled and the little lights in her branches had hidden away, though all the stars had abandoned the sky to the curling wind above, though her white bark could only barely be made out, Elma didn't bend an inch.

Milly studied her palm, searching for the mark that had been part torment and part comfort, but the darkness overwhelmed the moon on her hand.

A total eclipse.

Milly squinted against the black to see a figure across the clearing. Lilith. The old witch stood just past the tree, watching the waves in the distance, oblivious to the gripes and gobblers reaching their claws up the cliffside.

Ash drifted down to the tree and Milly dismounted. She put a hand on Elma and muttered a short prayer under her breath. (It was so quiet that not even I could hear it.) Then she stepped forward.

"It's about time you showed up," the witch said without turning her head. "How was the weather on your way here? Bad, I hope?"

Milly squared her shoulders, determined to not let Lilith get to her. "Where is she?"

Lilith ignored the question. "Cilla doesn't belong here, and neither do you." The old witch let out a long, haggard breath. "This is the only way to send the gripes back. I was too afraid to do it once. I'm not afraid anymore."

Milly was close to her now, close enough she could see the glint in the witch's eyes.

"We talked, your sister and I, and Cilla understood this is what a hero has to do. Sometimes . . . we get our hands dirty. Sometimes sacrifices need to be made."

Lilith finally turned toward Milly.

"I almost tried to stop her at the last second. I wanted to tell her she wasn't what they wanted, that they wanted *you*. But . . ."

Milly stared at the witch's crooked nose, at her tired frown, into her gray eyes. She remembered the photograph she'd found. The soft smile on the young Lilith's lips. The gentle way she put her hand on the child's shoulders. This Lilith seemed miles away from the witch she'd seen in the picture.

Something, she wasn't yet sure what, was starting to click into place.

"A real witch wouldn't do the things you have done," Milly said.

"Oh?" The witch looked taken aback but smiled. "And you think *you're* a real witch? I'm not the only here who's tamed a *wind*, am I? I thought you would understand better than anyone, witchling. Desperation drives you, and yet"—the witch shook her head—"guilt keeps you back. You don't even *fathom* the power at your fingertips, what that wind you keep dressed as a *cat* can do with just the right *encouragement*."

Above them, the curls of winds stretched and collided. Clouds shifted and formed. The North Wind howled amid the thunder rolling above.

Milly looked over at Jasper, who was crouched next to Elma with his ears flattened against his head.

She shook her head. "I don't want to use him."

"Not even to save your sister?"

Milly felt her hand burn. Could she? She had tamed the wind. That meant she could demand Jasper's help without asking, didn't it? The more she thought about it, the more the mark on her hand flickered.

Jasper's fur started to glow, ripples whipping through it like wind currents. Then she looked into his eyes and saw terror.

"*No.*" Milly clenched her fist and looked straight into the witch's eyes. "I can't. I won't."

"Then you won't fight back." The witch closed her eyes. "You know what must be done, don't you?"

"Yes."

The witch looked upward. "Makisuyo, make sure the witch's little friends don't come any closer."

"She can't tell me what to do!"

"Milly, what are you doing?!"

The North Wind roared and a cold wind blew past Lilith and Milly, pinning Ash and Jasper to the ground.

Milly gulped. "You want me to sacrifice myself to the Rift because you think this is how to make the shadows leave Arrett."

"Yes."

"How do I know you're telling the truth?"

"You don't."

"What will I find there?" She looked out over the cliff.

"No one knows. No one except Cilla."

Milly looked over at the others, being pressed to the ground by the anger of the North Wind. "Promise you won't hurt them."

"Of course."

"No. *Promise.*" Milly locked eyes with the witch. "Swear it on something you can't back down from."[46]

"I swear it on the North Wind."

Milly didn't stop staring. She knew this witch was not who she claimed to be. She didn't know how, or why, but the witch, too, was only a disguise. Inside was someone too scared, too unwilling to show their true face. "Swear it on

---

[46] *Rules and Regulations of Being a Witch, Chapter 14*: Swearing is a form of magicks in which a witch decides to *tame themself.* They become bound, by magicks, to their word. It requires humility on the part of the one with power and acceptance from the one without. For this reason, swearing can be potent but dangerous.

something that matters to you"—Milly lowered her voice, sure of the witch's true identity now—"*Hightop.*"

The witch's gray eyes widened, and for a moment Milly could see Hightop's own gray eyes staring back at her.

"O-okay," the fake Lilith said, "I . . . I swear it on my own mother."

Milly turned toward the sea, toward the gripes and the winds, toward the Rift, toward the heart of Arrett, toward East Ernost, her old home.

She felt the wizard's eyes staring at her. For a brief second, his composure fell away and he ran a hand over his face. "Can it even work?" he whispered. Then he pulled his hand away, and his eyes were hard and emotionless. The mask had been put back on. "You know what has to happen, don't you? You could be lost forever."

"I'm not going in there to help you," Milly said. "I'm not going to fix your shadow problem. I'm not going to be a hero or save your neck or please the High Council or prove that witches are good."

Milly let her hand burn bright. She stared into the waves below her.

"I'm only going in there to get my sister back."

She jumped off the cliff.

Briefly, she wondered what it must have been like when Cilla fell off the cliff. If her little sister thought she was going to die. Milly wasn't sure if she wanted to keep her eyes open or closed. There was no wind whistling past her ears. No light from the moon showing where the ocean's surface lay. No Ash whipping past her head to catch her.

The fall began slow and ended fierce.

Milly barely had time to make out the white caps of the waves before she crashed into them, her mouth still open in a half scream. The waters hit the back of her throat hard. Wicked, icy fingers cracked against her teeth and stung against her skin; it felt as if her lungs had collapsed inward from the impact.

And then, the entire world disappeared.

AN INTRODUCTION TO CHAPTER TWENTY-FIVE
a west wind, who quit her job

A WET NOSE nuzzled its way through Milly's hair until it found her forehead. Whatever the creature was licked her face until she blinked her eyes open. Milly sputtered and turned to the side to avoid the barrage. She squinted her eyes open and saw a fuzzy face come into view. It had a pink nose and blue fur and round ears.

"Junebug?!"

Milly sat up and the little borkoink jumped off her onto a wood floor. "But you—and I—and this—" Milly rubbed her eyes with the backs of her hands.

When she reopened her eyes, she found that she had been dressed in new clothes and placed in a bed. But the bed felt familiar, as did the rest of the room.

Junebug ran around on the floor, trying to catch its own coil of a tail.

Milly slid off the bed, trying to avoid stepping on the borkoink as it ran circles around her legs.

"Where am I?"

"That is a very poor question. I'm surprised you don't

recognize your own house," said another familiar thing. She looked at one of the other beds and saw Jasper sitting there. "Hello again. Welcome to St. George's."

Milly studied the cat the same way she studied a math problem. With both wonder and confusion. He didn't look different. He didn't sound different.

"Are we . . . dead?" she said.

The cat chuckled. "We are in the Rift, dressed in the clothes of East Ernost. This is home to all the in-betweens. Whatever you call a ghost or a prayer or anything else you throw into the thick of a wind, that all ends up here."

"But how did . . . how'd we get *here*?"

"You jumped. I followed. Your little stunt broke the spell you had on me. I could've let you come in here alone, but— well, I thought you'd like the company." The cat jumped down from the bed—when he landed, Milly realized that he didn't quite touch the floor, but hovered just above it—and headed for the door. "Come on. I'll show you around—no! Not you." He swatted at Junebug, who had bitten through the cat's transparent tail.

Milly clambered after him. "Is Cilla okay?"

"She's here, if that's what you mean."

It wasn't.

"If you want her back, you'll have to ask the person in charge of this place."

"Who's that?"

"The West Wind." The cat's tail twitched. "Hurry up, we

haven't all day." The cat led her through a distantly familiar home. She had no reason to believe it wasn't St. George's, but everything felt a little off. The bathroom was on the wrong side. The beds were odd instead of even. The floor was worn in different spots.

As they neared the kitchen, she heard their voices (faintly, like her ears were still underwater).

They entered the room and Milly saw . . . everyone! Not just the girls she grew up with, but former residents of St. George's who had been lost, memories of sisters and parents and brothers and pets. The ones whose names Doris remembered only in her sleep, the ones whom Milly had long forgotten.

She'd chosen to forget. Forgetting was the easy thing to do.

Sitting on the counter behind all the flickering memories sat Cilla. Getting her hair braided.

Milly opened her mouth to say something, but Jasper shook his head. "Don't bother. She won't notice you."

"Why not?" she whispered, as if that would change anything. Salt stung her eyes.

"You're something of a trespasser. Ooh, I like the sound of that word. You can see them, but they can't see you. None of them *chose* to be here—"

"But Hightop said—"

"He lied. Cilla didn't choose this. But you did, and that makes you a trespasser."

Milly bit her lip. Of course Hightop had lied. Just like he lied about everything.

Sitting on the counter behind Cilla's hair was another little girl. This girl's skin was painted entirely blue. She paused braiding Cilla's hair and stared directly at Milly.

Junebug exploded from between Milly's legs and jumped into Cilla's lap. Cilla laughed and hugged the borkoink, then jumped off the counter with her braids half done. She and the rest of the memories darted out of the room.

The blue girl sighed and stood up, then floated down to the floor.

"Who is that?"

"You'll figure it out," Jasper said, then started to sink through the floor. "Assuming all goes well, I'll see you again on the other side. If not"—he paused, his body halfway between worlds—"well, I suppose this might be goodbye."

"Thank you, Jasper."

"For what? I was supposed to take care of your sister. Feels like I did nothing but botch things for you."

"Thank you for being my friend."

The wind blinked once. Twice. Then nodded. "I'll be waiting for you, witch." With that, he sank the rest of the way through the floor.

Milly gave him a stunned wave, then looked back at the girl in blue.

The girl's skin was a whole myriad of mismatching shades, as if a thousand different pieces of origami had been folded over and underneath each other. Her hair was draped in red-orange and yellow leaves and her nails painted to look like beetles and dewdrops.

Milly hesitated before taking a step forward. "I'm here to bring my sister back."

"Yes, I know." The blue girl tilted her head. "But what makes you think she'll want to go back?"

Give me Cilla! is what she wanted to demand. Instead, Milly said nothing.

"Out there, all you people do is argue and shout and fight all the time. You destroy things that don't belong to you, try to take things that should be left alone. In here, I can take care of the children and other odds and ends that you continue to throw away."

"Out there?" She looked at the girl's dress, and now saw the intricate spiderweb laces lining its creases. "You're the West Wind."

"I'm a lot tougher than I look." The wind laughed at Milly's shocked expression, then tilted her head the other way. "I'll let you leave if you want, but you can't take any of them away. They're already safe here. Much safer than where you want them to be."

"Where exactly . . . is here, anyway?"

The wind walked to the side of the house and looked out over the hill. "A place where magickers can't ever hurt anyone again."

Milly looked at the other girls. "Are they dead?"

"Oh, no. Their fate is much worse." The wind's lip twitched. "They're forgotten. Your people, you keep memories of your loved ones alive with prayers. At least, you used to."

"I didn't forget," Milly said.

The wind tilted her head at Milly. "Take my hand."

As soon as Milly touched her hand, a mighty gust blew through them. Milly grabbed tighter. The winds tore away at the walls and pulled the floor panels into the sky, transforming the room around them until they stood on a cliff. Milly looked down and saw that they were standing next to a small sapling on a hill which overlooked a valley.

"Hello, Elma." The wind bent down to kiss the sapling, then slid down the hill.

Milly looked at the sapling, now recognizing the tree in its infancy, then followed the wind down the hill in similar fashion. She laughed when her feet met the wet grass, slick from the dew, as she sped down the slope. A soft, cool wind whipped her hair back.

She tripped over a rock and screamed, the ground right before her nose, when suddenly her entire body halted in midair.

The West Wind appeared in front of her, tut-tutting. "Be careful. I can't always catch you."

Milly felt herself uprighted by the wind's currents, then deposited back on the ground. She ran to catch up with the wind, who was now strolling through the trees with her hands behind her back.

"This is East Ernost. Or at least, what it used to be." The wind led Milly past a line of trees and into a bustling village. "They used to have festivals here. There's Teddison Licks, Jeddison's grandkid, playing his mandolin. There's Lola's Bakery, best place to find a pan de ube. And here"—she stopped, pointing at a little house—"is where Lilith lived with her little one, Carlitos."

The door opened and out walked the old witch—except not quite as old, wrinkled, or hunched as Milly had last seen her—holding the hand of a very young Hightop.

Milly's eyes widened. "Lilith was his *mother*?"

The West Wind nodded. "Almost everyone in East Ernost was a witch. Or related to one. It was here that the winds first discovered that Arrett had a heart. Or, as you call it, magicks."

Milly and the West Wind followed the vision of Lilith and Hightop through the village as they stopped by a local farmer to pick up strawberries, walked to a bookstore to pick up *The Misshapen Misadventures of Tom Fool*, waited in line at Lola's Bakery for something sweet. Hightop shuffled his feet just from the smell of the rising bread.

"He seemed so . . . innocent back then. Happy." Milly shook her head. "Why did he disguise himself as his own mother?"

The West Wind sighed, and with her sigh a soft wind blew through the scenery. Bigger walls popped up from the earth. The very ground under Milly's feet shifted as stones rumbled up to make roads. Lilith's back began to hunch over, and the child Hightop vanished.

"Lilith moved them out of East Ernost when he was a young boy. He entered Nignip determined to forge his own way in the world, apart from his mother's reputation. He was ashamed of being related to a witch. Knew other communities looked down upon them for being kind. For being 'weak.' So he changed his name to Charles. Became a world-renowned wizard and . . . well, he felt guilty, I think. After the war, he banished all the memories of his own mother from his mind." The wind opened her hand, revealing a small vial. "Almost all of them."

The West Wind lifted her other hand and blew. Another soft wind brushed over her fingers. Grass withered and regrew crooked. Houses were torn down and trenches filled the ground in their place. The child Hightop had been replaced by a young man, now a wizard dressed in battle robes with a hard look in his eye.

"Even during the war, the gnomes couldn't live with what they'd done. But they would never admit that." The West Wind walked Milly through the scenery until they were back at the foot of St. George's. Sitting on the hill was a young Edaline showing a magick trick to Cilla and . . . a past version of herself! Milly ran up to take a closer look. Edaline was talking to a smaller, pudgier Milly, who was laughing as a tiny flame darted between Edaline's fingertips. Edaline showed Milly the marks along her wrists, branches on either side.

The West Wind came shoulder to shoulder with present-day Milly. "Turn around," she whispered.

Milly could hear screams coming from behind her, and the mighty howling of an angry wind.

She shivered. "I don't want to."

"Child, you must," the wind said firmly, but not cruelly. "You need to know what happened to those who were forgotten."

Milly shivered against the wind blowing around her, then she felt a small hand enter hers and looked up to see the West Wind's eyes piercing into her own.

"It's okay."

Clutching on to the wind's hand, Milly slowly turned and watched as the entirety of East Ernost was ripped into the sea. The North Wind grew in size overhead, a mighty hurricane dragging the world apart. And, at its eye, Hightop with an outstretched arm, casting the spell.

The world grew louder, the shaking more violent. Water fell from the sky in torrents, filling the gaps between the divorced halves of East and West Ernost.

Milly gripped the West Wind's hand tighter.

Then—

Everything stopped, and they were back in St. George's.

The entire back half of the building had been ripped away, and there was Doris, busy building a new wall for what Milly knew would become the library.

"After my brother was tamed and East Ernost had been devoured, the witches had no choice but to hide and the shadows had no choice but to reveal themselves."

"What do they want? Are they going to destroy Arrett?"

"Destroy Arrett?" The wind seemed genuinely confused. "Of course not. These shadows, they are not Arrett's. They belong to you. They are your every shame, guilt, and unsaid prayer. They are *shadows*. They only want to be remembered. But Hightop, that wizard, is the worst offender. He thinks he can keep them away by erasing memories. Thought he could keep them away by erasing Cilla. By erasing *you*, the last witch. The shadows are nothing to be afraid of."

The wind walked Milly back through the different time-lines until they were standing in front of the house again. "Arrett hid their heart for good, but it never left you. Part of it is here, in the Rift." The West Wind pointed at St. George's. "Part of it is in your home, in all the children who are lost, all the sisters whom you love."

Now the wind turned over Milly's hand, and she touched the mark. The white peeled away to black, which peeled away to red. "Part of Arrett's heart is in you."

"Because I'm a witch?"

"Because you listened to the suffering of this world."

Unbidden memories came to Milly, of her half-giant friend and his mother, of the flutterwishes, Edaline and Emm, the thinning broombranches, her sisters living in St. George's Home for Wayward Girls. Milly felt tears in the corners of her eyes. "What must I do to get my sister back? Please, I'll give you anything."

The wind smiled. "Milly, all you ever had to do was ask."

As she spoke, a soft wind blew once more. It took with it the grass, the hills, and the house, too.

When Milly turned, she saw not the wind, but Cilla. Sitting all alone in the grass with her eyes closed. Milly ran to her, gathering her sister in her arms.

Cilla slumped down into her embrace, and Milly lifted her. The wind continued to pick up all around them.

"*Take your sister and return home,*" the wind said. "*Arrett needs their witch.*"

"Wait," Milly said. "I don't know what I'm supposed to do!"

"*Remember us . . .*"

The Rift disappeared.

And Milly awoke in the middle of the sea, clutching Cilla.

CHAPTER TWENTY-FIVE
a good witch is nothing without her kindness

LIGHTNING CRACKED ACROSS the sky. In that brief flash of light, Milly saw a silhouette of Ash above her head.

She tried to shout Ash's name, but water snapped against the back of her throat and she sank beneath the waves.

"I'm coming!"

Milly kicked upward until she could reach up and out of the waters. She felt the broombranch at her fingertips and grabbed tight.

"You're still alive? Weird."

The broombranch hovered next to her, trying his best to not get his straw-like leaves wet, and she pulled herself onto the branch. She propped Cilla in front of her. "Cilla? Cilla! Wake up!" She hit Cilla's back with a flat palm.

Cilla coughed several times until she blinked her eyes open. "Milly?"

Milly laughed as tears dripped down her face. "You're okay!"

"I knew you'd find me." She smiled.

Ash tipped to the side and briefly dipped into the sea. He

pulled away and shook himself off, forcing the two girls to let go of each other and hold on to the branch.

"I don't mean to interrupt this fine meeting, but I am made of wood and this is a lot of water."

"Mind getting us out of here?"

"You do not have to ask me twice."

"What are you going to do?" Cilla asked, fear back in her voice.

Milly looked at the palm of her hand. The red outline was bright and fierce. "I'm not sure yet but . . ." She paused. "Ash, please take us back to the tree."

"Are you serious? The wizard's still there!"

"I know."

"Okay. It's your second funeral."

The three of them flew fast and high, parallel to the wall of the cliff, until they zoomed past the edge. Ash slowed, then looped around. From up above, Milly could see that almost the entire world had turned to shadow now. All except for a small flickering spot of light beneath the tree. Hightop.

"We need to help him," Cilla said.

"I'm not going to *help* him. I'm going to make him pay!" Milly retorted.

"No, Milly." Cilla grabbed her hand. "We need to help him."

Milly couldn't believe what she was hearing, after all that Hightop had done to them! "Why?"

"It's what a good witch would do."

Milly froze with her mouth wide open. She didn't want to admit it, but Cilla was right.

"Are you sure you want to go down there, little witches?"

Milly locked eyes with Cilla. They nodded at each other. "Yes."

The broombranch descended until they were hovering just above the ground. Milly jumped down and landed among the shadows. Strangely, none of the apparitions reached for her. In fact, it seemed that none of them even noticed her. One of them did grab for the branch, and Ash darted out of reach.

"Milly!"

"It's okay, Cilla. I'll be okay. You and Ash keep your distance. I'll be back soon."

"I don't want to leave your side. I don't want to be alone again."

"You won't be." Milly smiled to encourage Cilla to be brave. This time she believed it to be true. This time she wasn't lying.

Cilla opened her hand, revealing something. "You'll need this."

"What is it?"

"Just take it."

Milly quickly grabbed the item before turning around, carefully picking her way through the gripes and gobblers and toward the tree. It was a vial. The same one the West Wind had shown her.

Not a single shadow lay a finger upon her.

Huddled beneath the tree stood Hightop, still dressed in the rags of his Lilith disguise, desperately throwing flashes of light in every direction. But the spells only bounced off the thick, pebbled hides of the gobblers. They disappeared into the inky substance of the gripes. Hightop's magicks did nothing.

Hightop cowered and screamed and gnashed his teeth. His clothes were torn, his eyes mad, but the gripes and gobblers only made their circle around him smaller and smaller.

"Stop!" Milly ran toward the wizard. The shadows fled away from every patch of grass her feet touched.

Hightop turned his mad gaze and wand upon her. "You! This is all your fault!" He raised his wand. "I call upon all the powers of the North Wind to smite you!"

But nothing happened.

Not a breeze stirred the air. No crack of thunder replied.

Milly's anger returned. It burned white hot inside her, so much so that tears formed at the corners of her eyes. She heard Jasper's voice whisper against her ear.

"The winds are offering you their strength."

"What do they want me to do?"

"Destroy him," she heard something from the ground say.

"Avenge us," said another.

Now the three winds stirred above her, and she heard their howling tempests echo from within her own heart.

Milly's insides felt like they might burst.

"Stop trying to control everything!"

She took one step forward.

"Stop trying to tame the winds!"

The inside of her hand burned like an iron.

"Stop trying to *use us!*"

"It's all up to you now, witchling," she heard Jasper say.

"Milly, stop!" Cilla's voice cut through all the noise.

The vial in her tightening grip cracked open. It exploded in a flash of white light, causing the gripes and gobblers to flinch away. In that moment, all of Hightop's memories knocked against Milly's mind. They were begging to be let in, she realized, to show their true selves.

And she had the power to choose whether they would be heard or not.

Most of her didn't want to hear them. Most of her wanted to shut them out, to banish them from the world, to let Hightop be blown into the sea along with the world he had created.

But then another voice, a quieter one, spoke. And she realized it sounded very much like herself.

"Be kind," it whispered, *"and do no harm."*

She opened her hand and allowed the memories in.

Hightop's memories scurried around every corner of Milly's mind. In one of them, Hightop stood among the council, turning his eyes away when the gnomes banished his own mother from the room and tore the banners from the walls. In another, he snuck into Edaline's room while she was sleeping and stole away the *Summoning Book*, which he had coveted ever since he arrived at St. George's. He rode high into the eye of a storm, his whole body shaking, as he attempted to chain the North Wind.

Most of them felt loud and abrasive, but only a few of them were truly angry. In most of them he seemed . . . lost. Sad. Afraid.

Finally, only one memory remained. This one was quiet and small. So small that Milly could only find it after all the others had gone, so quiet that Milly had to coax it out.

It needed her permission to speak.

CHAPTER TWENTY-SIX
the lost boy

A YOUNG BOY sat on the floor of his house reading *The Marvelous Adventures of Tom Fool*. In the other room, his mother conversed with a customer who was dealing with some sort of sickness called "giant's foot." Suddenly, someone's entire hand covered his face.

"Gurrs who!"

"Corrine," he laughed. "Knock it off!"

The hand vanished from the boy's eyes, and he looked up to see his giant friend smiling down at him.

"Wurna play?"

"Sure," he said, and scrambled up. The two of them ran out the back of the house and headed toward their secret hideout, a grove hidden in the nearby trees.

For most of the afternoon, they built a well together. The giant hauled large stones to the center, and Hightop plastered mud against the sides. All the while they shared tall tales and dreams and aspirations.

They did this until the sun had dipped below the tree line and their arms had grown weary. Looking at their work in progress, they nodded at each other in approval and began walking back toward the city.

They were just in front of the house when Hightop heard the voice.

"Hey there, *big toes!*"

Corrine immediately grabbed Hightop's hand, and she tried to pull the boy along. But Hightop stopped. He couldn't help it.

"*Big toes!* Turn around when we're talking to you!"

Hightop turned and saw the source of the shrill voice cutting through his ears. It came from another boy, Trevor, standing among a group of other kids from the city.

Hightop tore his hand from the giant and formed his hands around his mouth so he could shout louder. "Go away!"

Trevor's eyes shone with recognition, and his smile turned into a sneer. "Guys, it's our lucky day. Looks like *witchboy* is hanging out with the *big toes* again."

Hightop gritted his teeth. He hated that name. Hated it so much. "Go away!" he said again. "Go find something better to do!"

"Why? It's true, isn't it? Your mom's a witch." The kids now circled around them, and Trevor poked a finger into Hightop's chest. "That makes you one, too."

Corrine tried to pull at Hightop's arm, but Hightop just ground his teeth harder. "I told you to go away." He put his hands up.

"Oh no." Trevor laughed. "Are you going to hex me?"

One of the other kids smirked. "I heard witches like to *tear your skin off and eat your fingers.*"

"Yeah," said another kid. "They *grind your bones into dust and turn you into soup.*"

"Sometimes at night, they'll *turn into bats and haunt the village.*"

"That's not true," Hightop protested. "None of that is true!"

"How would you know?" Trevor grabbed one of Hightop's hands and twisted it, revealing a black mark on his forearm. "You could only know this because you're a scrawny little *witchboy.*"

"Stuhppit!" Corrine cried.

Tears filled Hightop's eyes, and he felt the back of his hand burn with a power he'd never felt before. He tore his hand away, and the mark burned with a bright light.

Suddenly, the kids around him were scared. They backed up as the light burned harsher.

Hightop knew he could summon magicks to do his bidding. Maybe he'd ask fire to come and light up Trevor's stupid hair. Maybe he'd get the earth to swallow him up. Maybe he'd control Trevor's own fist and use it against him. Instead, Hightop closed his fist and punched Trevor, knocking him into the dirt.

"*I'm not a witch,*" Hightop growled. "*I'm nothing like my mom.*"

"Okay, okay," the bully mumbled from the dirt. "I believe you."

The kids scattered and Hightop let out a long exhale. That

power. That control. It felt kind of good. When he turned, he saw that Corrine had withdrawn from him, fear in her eyes. And, just past her, both of their mothers were watching from the open door of the house.

The giant's mother ran up, worried and then flustered when she saw the dust on Corrine's fingers and the mud on Hightop's hands. She told Corrine off about running away without a word and getting back so late.

Hightop's mother approached slowly, and Hightop could tell that even though her voice was kind, her eyes shone with a deep sadness.

Hightop stared into his mother's gray eyes. He knew he should feel bad, that he should apologize for what he'd done. But he didn't want to. He didn't feel bad for hurting Trevor.

He wished he had hurt him *more*.

He just wished his mother hadn't seen it. He wished he could make his mother forget what happened.

Hightop blinked, and the memory was over.

Suddenly, Milly understood the wizard's deep shame. The guilt which lay at the core of his being. His desire to choose who he could be. She saw not a man, but a little boy watching the wizards drive his mother from her home. She saw him regret doing the same.

When the light from the vial vanished, Milly found Hightop curled against the tree. Clutching his body. Wand broken on the ground.

Hightop was crying.

"Mother," he choked between tears. "What have I done?"

Milly lowered her still-throbbing hand. The red moon cut through the blackness like a hot knife. Seeing the wizard at her feet, she no longer felt anger. No need for vengeance.

The storm inside of her quieted, and she unclenched her fist. How could she destroy the boy whose mind she'd been inside?

All Milly could feel was pity. She cried with him.

AN OUTRODUCTION
a south wind, who wants for everything

WHEN I SAW her cry, I was surprised.

No, not surprised. That's not nearly strong enough.

I was confused. Flabbergasted. Shocked. Upset. Stupefied.

I was angry.

This is where I wanted to step out of the story and grab our hero by her shoulders. I wanted to scream at her, demand to know why she wasn't being a hero.

This is not what the heroes do. Heroes fight, dominate, overpower. They beat back cruelty with a hammer. This is how they win.

But she hadn't done any of that.

Instead, she decided to be human. Only you humans are capable of showing this kind of mercy. I wish I understood, but I don't. I can't.

I don't understand Milly. She continues to be a problem I cannot solve. I wrote this story to figure her out, and I am afraid to say I leave all the more confused.

Up until now, most of these little asides and footnotes and unnecessary commentaries have been written by my secretary. I had no problem with them doing so as long as it kept them amused and away from the rest of my work. I am, after all, prone to hyperbole, and I do enjoy the crisp snap of a half-truth or two.

For this, however, I make an exception.

Have you figured it out, dear reader mine?

Do you know who I am?

I didn't want to do this.

I didn't want to say.

But we can't all have what we want; you deserve to know.

Sit down, child. Calm your beating heart. I have one last story to tell.

There once was a little disc on the edge of the stars, spinning their way through stories without a worry or want in the universe. Their name was Arrett.

Arrett was a happy world. They kept their heart on their sleeve and sang without shame and cried without guilt. They hungrily ate up the words of their older siblings and pocketed them inside mountains and buried them along streams.

One day, they met and fell in love with the South Wind.

But both were young and did not know what love meant. The South Wind thought to love was to wreck, and so wreck he did. He blew through gardens and uprooted flowers. He carved scars through hills and yanked fish out of the sea for fun. He upturned all pages of narration and left third acts in half-written chapters. He wanted to belong to Arrett, but he didn't want to be tamed.

So he stole Arrett's heart and scattered its magicks all across the world.

The South Wind enjoyed it when the inhabitants caused trouble, but he underestimated how much trouble they'd cause. This wind spread rumors on his currents of how witches were ugly and giants were cruel. For all words are made of magicks—even something as petty as a rumor. Soon, these new magicks ran rampant, causing even more damage and terror than the South Wind ever dreamed of.

He could have done something. He probably should have. But instead, he stayed back and silent, and let Arrett deal with it all on their own.

You know some of the rest already. Of the small giant Ovid who chained down the Wind, but he did not do this with a rope at the end of the world. He forced this wily wind into a much more secure prison. He fashioned this wind a body, he gave this wind a name, and then he handed this wind a pen and told him to tell a story.

So here I sit, watching as my siblings and a little witch girl heal the hurt I have caused. Here I sit, pen in hand, watching this girl fix the mess I made.

Hightop is a product of the world he was born into. The gripes and gobblers are the circumstance of what happens when we shove our feelings down our own throats, refuse to see things as they truly are. My situation was created from my own selfish desires to control. To wreck.

In many ways, you might call me the villain of this story.

Perhaps you're right. I obviously can't tell the difference anymore.

I used to think Milly was the true troublemaker. She's broken my story into pieces now, all in some misguided need to feel compassion for a wizard and save her sister.

I don't know. Maybe I had it all backward.

I don't think I understand, but I dreadfully want to.

Is that too much to ask?

CHAPTER TWENTY-SEVEN
sometimes all you need is a very good cry

MILLY LOOKED UP to the sky as the winds descended to the cliff and manifested themselves into three shapes.

The North Wind shaped himself into a bull, muscles rippling in constant movement as currents of cold drafts and streams of dark clouds. The East Wind took upon their form as a whale with a mighty sail for a tail and steam blowing out the top of their head. Lastly, the West Wind unfolded her paper self. The more layers she unfolded, the larger she grew, until she was a full-sized sapphire-eyed dragon with a red tongue and yellow claws.

Lastly, a fourth wind joined them: Jasper, who billowed his winds out and shrunk them back in, curled them into sleek, black fur and stretched out his currents until they were paws. Here he was, the new South Wind, her friend.

The four of them stood before Milly in the dark, and she stared back at them, the moon on her hand now their only source of light.

Cilla and Ash joined her by the tree, opposite from where Hightop lay. They were terrified. They begged Milly to run.

She raised her hand toward the winds. "If . . . if it's okay, I'd like to ask for your help with one last thing."

The North Wind billowed. "I've just found my freedom. I'm not going to give it up for you."

"Easy, brother," the East Wind said. "You haven't even heard what the little witch girl wants."

The West Wind stared at Milly with unblinking eyes.

Jasper drifted down from the others and hovered in front of Milly. "You freed us, witch, but I don't recommend attempting to tame *four winds*. Are you sure you want to go around asking for more favors?" Jasper's voice sounded grave, but he laughed and winked.

"I want everyone to remember. I want us all to know the names of our ghosts. Our in-betweens. Our shadows." She looked down at the earth and saw a gripe looking back at her with a curious head tilt. She breathed. "But I don't have the power to do that alone."

Milly looked up at the three of them, all now sitting in silence. "I need your help," she said, and bowed her head. "Please."[47]

Both the North and the East Wind looked toward the West Wind. She nodded toward the newest member. "I think we should let our little brother decide what we must do."

[47] I mentioned before that history is like a snake shedding its skin, growing out of inconvenient half-truths and convenient untruths. However, now I will tell you another secret. Although history changes, pieces of the whole truth always stick around. No matter how hard people try, they can't cover every single light with a shadow. Soon enough, someone special comes along, someone who is a little bit curious and a little bit courageous. It is very hard to find someone who can fix something instead of wreck it, but they exist. It is these people who truly understand magicks.

"You mean it's up to me?!" Jasper gasped, then snorted. He turned to Milly. "Of course we'll help you!"

The West Wind laughed and folded herself back into a tiny blue girl. She pulled Milly to herself in a tight embrace.

"See? You needed only to ask."

Without another word, she turned to the other winds and the three of them shot up into the sky. Milly looked down at her hand. It glowed with a loud, warm light. The eye of a giant hurricane formed above the children, and the three winds hooted and roared with excitement.

Jasper winked once more, then turned into a wild gust and joined his siblings.

Cilla grabbed Milly. Ash quivered in place. Poor Hightop shook violently beneath the tree.

But Milly looked up, face to the wind, and laughed.

The storm stretched across the cliffside and the skies opened. Rain splattered across the terrain, striking the gripes and gobblers on their faces. Forcing them to pull away.

While Arrett cried their heart out, the memories of those lost pulled themselves out of the earth. Across West Ernost and Nignip, gnomes and giants and wizards and witches alike stepped out into the rain. Soon their tears rolled down and kissed the ground. The gripes and gobblers softly came out, revealing themselves. Memories all across West Ernost and Nignip and Delfin and more seeped back into people's minds, as if the holes in their brains were being filled and made whole again.

When it was over, Milly looked to the tree. The wizard had disappeared, but he'd left his broken wand behind. From Elma's branches, a tiny flame flew toward it.

A little green bud sprouted from the wand's splintered ends.

Milly hoped that meant something.

Suddenly, her eyes widened. She grabbed Cilla's hand and bolted away from the tree, a singular thought echoing through her brain.

They needed to tell Doris!

Milly found Doris in the doorway of St. George's. Doris stared up at the sky with worry, her hair matted against the sides of her head.

"Doris!" Milly and Cilla shouted. "Doris!"

The old woman turned toward the girls, and her eyes lit up.

"We're back!" Milly crashed into Doris with a hug. "We're home now!"

Doris smiled, truly smiled, for the first time in years. She bent down and squeezed back and didn't let go. When she spoke, there was no pause, no moment of uncertainty.

"Girls! I'm so glad you're home."

CHAPTER TWENTY-EIGHT
good stories end with troublesome girls

THERE ONCE LIVED a house on the top of a hill by the edge of a cliff. His name was St. George's Home for Wayward Girls. Living with him were the kindly carpenter-mother Doris Barterby, one lazy moss-bull, fourteen little girls, the ghost of a cat, and a blue borkoink named Junebug.

Tonight St. George's stood beneath the light of a milky full moon. Accompanied by playful wisps of clouds and the whisperings of a late wind.

Sitting in the open windows of his library were Milly and Cilla, swinging their legs out and watching the stars slow-dance overhead. Next to them sat Jasper, visiting again, curled with his head beneath his two front paws. Outside, Junebug snapped at wildflowers on the moss-bull's toes.

Come autumn, it would be one year since Milly had first left St. George's.

St. George's knew his girls were all content and safe, and that was enough for him.

Milly, however, didn't know what to do with herself.

When Milly had first returned, Doris refused to let her do anything but rest and read and teach magicks to whoever was curious. Including Cilla. Since the whole affair, Doris's mind seemed to have gotten sharper, now full of the memories she'd lost. She listened with rapt attention and worked every day with the renewed energy of a much younger woman. Milly could have sworn she even had fewer wrinkles on her face.

Over the past few months, Doris had gradually allowed Milly more responsibilities, but Milly still felt rather unhelpful. In fact, the longer she'd been home, the surer Milly was that Doris no longer needed her.

It made her happy, but now her problem was figuring out what to do. And so, for the first time in her life, Milly stopped thinking about being a mother all the time and thought of her own childlike dreams and childish affairs.

She was almost thirteen, after all. There wasn't that much time left to be a girl. She didn't tell any of this to Cilla, but I'll bet Cilla knew anyway. Neither of them seemed bothered enough to talk about it.

While they sat there, and Doris readied Ikki for bed, and Nishi chased Marikit around the room, and Lissy and Abby began a too-late pillow fight, and Mei chased the tiny bat fluttering around in the rafters, St. George's felt the presence of a stranger approaching the foster home. This person was dressed in long, tattered robes and a pointed hat.

The stranger smelled of magicks, just as pungent as that last witch that had come.

St. George's tensed his timbers, unsure of this intrusive presence, unwilling to let anyone take one of his girls away again. But then, the stranger placed the palm of their hand on his front door, and he recognized something strange beneath the magicks, the smell of something familiar.

St. George's relaxed, and the stranger knocked on his door. Their knuckles rapped softly against the wood, and St. George's knew from the gentle touch that they must be a friend.

When Milly opened the door, she couldn't speak. And then, when she did open her mouth, she began to cry. At first, St. George's was afraid Milly might be scared, but the stranger threw off her robes and took off her hat.

She had locks of bright green hair studded with flowers. She knelt down and hugged Milly, and Milly hugged the woman back. The stranger asked her a question.

Milly nodded her head, even as she was burying her face into the woman's shoulder.

A strong wind blew through St. George's, warming him from the inside out. The wind made the scent of flowers rise throughout St. George's, and he absorbed their sweet scent.

Bamboo blossoms.

If the house could smile, he would have.

Milly didn't need him anymore.

For her, at least, he had done his job.

ACKNOWLEDGMENTS

First to my editor, Maggie. This book's best ideas came from you.

To Ms. Peggy, who used to lend me a puzzle every week. You are the reason I love searching for solutions instead of problems.

To Hillary, for the Spotify writing sessions and falling asleep during video calls.

To Liz, for growing up with me and this talking cat.

To Gabrielle, for your love and your patience.

To my sister, Ysabel, for inspiring me to always do more and be better. To my tatay, for teaching me to be honest. To my nanay, for showing me how to be brave.

To my kids.

To M, who once told me they were going to be the first female president of the United States after they came back from leading a team to the moon. To R, who showed me how to perfectly balance temper with kindness. To J, who always offered me their extra animal crackers and taught me how to use TikTok. To S, A, and A, who helped me understand what it means to be a good sibling. Milly's best qualities belong to you.

And last of all, to my cat, for teaching me the importance of a well-timed nap.